Burning Roads

By William Joseph Roberts

Dead Man's Run: Book 1

Three Ravens Publishing
Chickamauga, GA USA

Welcome to the world of the Car Warriors: Autoduel Chronicles — Tales from the freeways of the future, where the right of way goes to the biggest guns and death sports rule the airwaves. From clandestine highway battles to prime-time arena combat, jump behind the wheel, follow the fast-paced action, and never forget to Drive Offensively!

Car Warriors Autoduel Fiction is licensed by Steve Jackson Games Incorporated and set in the *Car Wars* universe.

BURNING ROADS By William Joseph Roberts
Published by Three Ravens Publishing
threeravenspublishing@gmail.com
P O Box 851, Chickamauga, Ga 30707
https://www.threeravenspublishing.com
Copyright © 2023 by Steve Jackson Games

Publisher's Note: This is a work of fiction. Names, characters, places, and incidents are a product of the author's imagination. Locales and public names are sometimes used for atmospheric purposes. Any resemblance to actual people, living or dead, or to businesses, companies, events, institutions, or locales is completely coincidental.

Credits:
Burning Roads was written by William Joseph Roberts
Cover art by: oldmanlogan

Ebook ISBN: 978-1-951768-84-3
Paperback ISBN: 978-1-951768-85-0
Audiobook ISBN: 978-1-951768-86-7

Thank you, to all of our backers of the Car Warriors Kickstarter project!

Jessie D. Foster
Kevin A Davis
David Hankins
Alyssa Casto
Jeffrey Riggs
Jorge Markin
Randal Dilday
Julian W. Thompson
Jeff Dodge
Rich Neves
Cursed Dragon Ship Publishing
Stace Johnson
Val Cassotta
Jef Farnsworth
Jeffery Sergent
Jason Walters
Mark Wagner
Keith Unger
Jonathan Hurley
Jim Tullis
Mark Strahm
Karl J. Smith
John Pieper
Dustin "TinyMonster" Rhoades
Jedikiah Springfield
Larry Southard
Jeff Johnson
James Emil Conason
Aaron Spriggs
Scott Long
Reed Snyder
K.C. L'Roy

Tee Stoney
Todd DeWolfe
Brian Thacker
Caleb Pittman
David A. Jepson
Tad K
David Glover
Ramón Terrell
Eric Stuyvesant
Gavin Inglis
Mark Stallings
Brooks Moses
Brian Healy
KB Carlisle
Andrew Franklin
Stephen Dedman
Rolf Laun
Wild Card
Marc Alan Edelheit
Rob Kamm
Peter J. Jansen
Nicholas D Miller
Danny White
Jordan C
Kenta Washington
Robert Gilson
Marcus Evenstar
Sammy
Kim the Troublemaker
Jonathan Bowen

Brian John Skillen
Jim Davenport
Monty Rasmussen
Alex Rath
Ch. N. Heinzl
Bart Kemper
Jim Tetrick
Jason Lankford
Glitz & Blam
Eric Moorefield
Jerry 'Archer' Schaefer
Milton Fernandez
Jim McLaughlin

Table of Contents

Dedication:

It should go without saying, that this book and the Car Warriors series couldn't have happened if it weren't for the creative genius of Steve Jackson and his amazing team at Steve Jackson Games. Without them, this opportunity would have never happened.

Author's Note

My original plan for DragonCon 2022, was to do a day trip down to Atlanta, hang out with Steve Jackson, play games, have fun, and relax.

Never in my wildest dreams would I have thought that I'd end up landing a licensing deal to write fiction in any of his universes, let alone the **Car Wars** universe. But in the end, that's what managed to happen.

It's a wonderfully expansive world already with forty years of game modules and content to pull from while creating new universe canon in the current "present" of 2072.

Once I started to dive into the library of data, I found so much more that I never realized existed. Cars, guns, characters, scenarios ready to be written about and brought to life. I hope that the research has paid off and I'm doing justice for the old school fans of the game while appealing to readers new and old.

I'm grateful for the opportunity to play in Steve's universe, and honored that he's confident in myself and the Car Warriors team to let us play in his sandbox.

Shake the ground!

William Joseph Roberts

A word from Steve

The **Car Wars** game has been around for a while now. It's practically a tradition. We've been driving offensively since 1980 . . . six editions now. Design your car, set up a few ground rules (but not very many!), load 'em up, and go. The right of way belongs to the biggest guns.

When Scott Tackett told me he'd like to do some **Car Wars** fiction, I listened. Scott's Three Ravens Publishing has a great stable of new authors plus some friends who have been writing for a long time now. Good combo. And he's got big plans. If the Dead Man's Run series goes as planned, there will be more than a dozen novels and at least one volume of short stories. So, if you like it . . . we'll be back.

If you'd like to see the game that spawned all this, check the back of the book. Just like the old paperback days, there's an ad. Tradition is important!

And I hope you enjoy this story. I sure did.

— Steve Jackson

Chapter 1

"**M**issile lock!"

"I can see that, Ricky," Luise yelled back at me from the gunner's seat.

I disabled the warning lights that flashed across the dash to the tune of the targeting lock alarm.

A fiery jet of oil shot out from beneath the lead car, coating the track and the two cars ahead of us. Cutting the wheel hard to the left, I tapped the emergency brake, throwing us into a sideward slide, then floored it. My hands numbed from the vibrations of the maneuver resonating through the steering column into my palms. The car's four 2,000-horsepower drive motors spun up to their maximum revolutions per minute. Attempting to gain traction, the race-slick tires billowed heavy white smoke, squealing as we slid sideways across the track.

Three missiles soared past us, one of them grazing the nose of our modified racer, ripping away metal and carbon fiber before deviating from its original course and slamming into the track's infield. The acrid smell of burning rocket fuel seeped through the cracks of our vehicle and assaulted my nostrils.

"Get around these *estúpidos* before we get toasted," Luise said.

Correcting our skid, I brought our nose to bear on the lead car. I pressed both steering yoke-mounted triggers. Our forward-firing heavy machine guns roared to life with the rat-a-tat-tat that was both soothing and fear-inducing.

Something dropped to the roadway from beneath the car in front of us.

"Mines!" Luise shouted.

"I see them," I said, then adjusted our angle of attack, swerving to miss the micro mines. Our tracer rounds carved a line of destruction across the pavement, just missing the lead vehicle.

"I can't get a clear shot around these two slushboxes. Clear me a path, Luise!"

"You got it, Ricky," she said, then leaned forward, flipping up two protective switch covers mounted to the passenger side dashboard. "Fire in the hole!" She shouted, activating both switches at once.

Two rockets streaked away from their roof-mounted launchers. Heavy black smoke trailed behind them, marking their flight path, and hindering our line of sight. One flew wide, missing the intended target entirely. The second rocket impacted low on the rear of the third-place vehicle, sending it flying off the course. It soared, tumbling end over end in mid-air before slamming down roof first onto the protective concrete barrier along the trackside. The car crumpled across the barrier, the impact of the landing distorting the car's uni-frame body beyond the point of repair.

Rounds struck at our rear armor. New damage warnings flashed across the heads-up display. The car's power packs flashed red on the damage control screen, and our main power readout flashed a warning, registering less than thirty percent power remaining.

"Get that guy off our tail!"

"With what?" Luise responded. "The flame thrower is out of fuel, and we used up our micro mines on the first lap."

"I don't know. You're the gunner. You could at least throw rocks at them or something."

More rounds impacted our rear, absorbed by what was left of our rear armor. I cut the wheel hard right, popping the brake to toss us into another slide, drifting the next turn right on the tail of the first and second-place teams.

I tapped at the triggers, barking the machine guns while the two lead vehicles' sides were exposed as they came out of the turn. The .50 caliber rounds chewed up the sides of both lead vehicles as we came out of the corner. Bits of carbon fiber, glass, and metal from the vehicles confettied the roadway. I popped the brake once more, over-steering to the left to steer clear of the debris field.

No sooner had I straightened our course and fired at the rear of the second-place vehicle that our tail slid out from under us. We skidded sideways, impacting hard into the barrier.

"Lean back," Luise ordered, her gloved hand holding her semiautomatic hand cannon appeared right in my line of sight and she fired.

The car that had been firing on our rear had moved up alongside us and had started to pass by the time I realized what she'd been firing at. The opponent's Fuzion supercar suddenly launched forward with a burst of speed.

The hand cannon locked back with an empty mag. "Frack!" Luise fumbled with the magazine release, letting the empty mag drop to the floorboard. Before she could slam a full magazine home, their Fuzion pulled directly ahead of us and fired, engulfing the front end of our Fuzion in white hot flames that streaked with blues and greens as it flowed across our front end.

Flames scorched their way through the center of the windscreen, melting the polycarbonate glass like it was warm butter. The white-hot torch shot through the cab, scorching the rear wall of the compartment. Melted globs of windscreen oozed into the space, falling across the dash and center console, igniting the interior of our car.

"Ricky! Hit the fire extinguisher!"

Sometimes Luise was the absolutely brilliant mind of our team and I was the knuckle-dragging Neanderthal that she took pity on. I was a little pissed that I hadn't thought of that. I slammed my fist down on the emergency fire extinguisher release, but nothing happened.

"Ricky! Hurry, my legs are on fire!"

"I did, and nothing happened! The system is dead!"

Something hit us hard from the front, spinning us to the left. The lower side of the dash collapsed in on itself, pressing down against my legs. I could feel the chittering of tires skidding across the pavement as we continued to slide sideways. The steering was shot. No matter which way I turned the wheel, nothing caused a response.

Brakes, nothing

Throttle, dead.

Our slide came to an immediate and abrupt stop, collapsing the passenger door inward, crushing Luise and her seat against the rear of the compartment. Flames roiled from the console and rear of the cabin, igniting everything that would burn. Hot acrid smoke seeped through my helmet to burn my throat and fill my lungs. I struggled to get the slightest breath. Static-filled as it was, the headset in my helmet popped and transmitted a gurgled sigh over the team channel. The sound of mortal release first filled and then echoed sharply in my ears.

"Luise!"

She was gone. I knew she was gone, but I tried to reach her through the flames. "Luise!"

Fire boiled out from beneath the driver's side dashboard. The acrid chemical smoke and super-heated air filled my lungs, choking me in short quick breaths. I screamed out, but could only hear the roar of the blaze around me. Sharp spikes of pain shot through me. Flames and extreme heat penetrated their way through the protective layers of my fireproof suit. Pain raced further and further up my legs, faster than the flames climbing them.

I squeezed the release latch for the safety harness, but it refused to budge. I drew back my hand to find the plastic within the mechanism had oozed out of the latch, coating my glove and suit. The molten plastic ignited in the extreme heat of the fire. All around flames surround me, basking me in their deadly glow.

I pushed out against the door with my elbow. Pain shot through my arm into the shoulder.

"Luise!"

"This may be it, Chuck," the announcer shouted excitedly, "this may be the last we see of Ricky Turner." The sound of his voice sounded tinny and distant.

The roar of the flames subsided, replaced with the silent calm of darkness that surrounded me, engulfing my mind, body, and soul.

I opened my eyes at the sound of my name to a small, dimly lit room.

"Luise?"

The smell of antiseptic cleaners hung so heavy in the air that I could taste it in the back of my throat. A small vid display mounted high on the wall flashed from one race to another while the talking heads continued. Text of the day's results scrolled across the bottom of the screen between ads along with the not-so-subliminal messaging of the latest products out on the market. My image flashed up on the screen, and I fumbled for the remote to turn up the volume.

"You can say that again, Alex," Chuck replied. "I sure hope he had a Gold Cross membership because that's the only way he's coming back from a crash like that."

"You aren't kidding, Chuck. Wait, what's this? This just in folks. The American Autoduel Association has declared that a full investigation into team Vixens and the use of illegal equipment will be conducted."

"That's extremely bad news for team Vixen."

"No doubt, Chuck. We haven't seen a full investigation like this launched by the AADA since the spring of 2062 when Banzai Ranson illegally tipped his rockets with nano-nuclear warheads."

"If this investigation looks anything like that, the Vixens are in for a world of hurt. Everything attached to the Vixens racing team will be locked down for judicial scrutiny by the inquisitors of the AADA, including *all* of their personal accounts."

"That won't be an easy thing to come back from, Chuck."

"No, it won't, Alex. I doubt we'll ever see the Vixens on the race circuit again, even if they are acquitted of the charges."

"In other news, The Blackskulls came out on top in today's North Atlanta Division five competition with The Guilded Girls in second place and Team Harbinger in a close third."

"The Blackskulls have been an interesting front-runner this season, climbing the leaderboard from dead last as this season's last-minute rookie add-in."

"If I didn't know any better, Chuck, I'd swear someone's been fixing the matches for them."

Chuck let out a nervous laugh. "You never know what might be happening behind the scenes of the Autoduel circuit, Alex. You might have hit the nail on the head, but I'm sure that we'll never know." The view flashed again to the burning remains of what might have been a car. The pavement all around the few unrecognizable bits of melted metal had sunken in and melted to produce a shiny, glass-like surface. Three emergency fire trucks sprayed the area, containing the still-burning lithium core of what was once a car's primary power pack.

I pushed myself up and got a better look at the room. It was small. Barely large enough for the bed I was lying in, and at first, I hadn't noticed the writing below the vid screen. On the wall under the video display was a large golden cross inside of a golden circle, and beneath it written in a bold but soothing font was the slogan,

Out of darkness, we bring light.

Thank you for trusting Gold Cross with all of your rebirth needs.

Don't forget to ask an associate about our monthly premium renewal specials.

"Well that doesn't make me feel any better," I tried to mumble but the words hung in my throat, coming out as a hoarse whisper. My mouth felt like I'd been sucking on cotton balls for a week. I pushed myself up, adjusting my position, and looked around to see if a nurse had maybe left some water on the side table. My hands came away from the bed wet. The sheets and my gown were soaked through with sweat. No wonder my mouth felt like a strip of dehydrated algae.

I rubbed my face, wiping it with the dry edge of the sheet. "I must have had a nightmare," I mumbled to myself, my voice sounding as dry and raspy as it felt.

"Luise…"

God, I missed her. Smart, funny, curves in all the right places, and one hell of a gunner. I hadn't thought about the crash in almost two years. I'd pushed it to the darkest recesses of my mind and tried my best to forget about it. If the fire teams hadn't pulled me out when they did, I'd have been toast too. My legs were pinned by the crumpled front end and broken in six places. Luckily all they had to cut away was part of the dash to pull me out of what was left of the car after we crashed. After the fire really took off, all the crews could do was to keep the surrounding area cool. The only thing the recovery team could find of Luise was her teeth and her Identity Chip.

The car was a total loss. The fire had been so intense that the only thing left of the car was melted slag. Once the lithium in the high-density power packs ignited there wasn't much anyone could do but contain the conflagration and protect the surrounding area.

"Crashing is one thing, but burning alive is something I never want to get that close to doing ever again."

The display strobed through a myriad of colors and intricate geometric patterns that formed into a blueprint-style sketch of a new weapons system, drawing my attention.

"Uncle Albert's sure to have your every desire," a perky little blonde in a tiny bikini top and urban camouflage pants said as she stepped into view on screen. She toted a light machine gun, holding it in both hands with two belts of ammo that she wore criss crossed over her chest like bandoleers.

"Don't settle for those imitation brand names. Uncle Al's guarantees the largest selection from coast to coast!"

Dozens of weapons systems flashed across the screen. Autocannons, flame throwers, machine guns, mines, lasers, and rocket launchers faded in and out of view. "If it's in stock, we got it!" she shouted, then bounced in place. "Uncle Albert gives you the weapons, gadgets, and accessories you need! But don't take my word for it!"

The screen suddenly flashed to a pair of Autoduellists standing in front of a battered and bruised Fnord Motors Smokin' Joe. "Uncle Albert has saved our tailpipes more times than I can count. Without his overnight delivery and dirt cheap prices, there's no way we could ever keep up with the corporate teams no matter how much of socket-brained slushboxes they are."

"Thanks, Uncle Albert," the Gunner said, then fired off a round into the sky.

The perky little blond reappeared, this time stroking the tail fin of a mini rocket that rested across her lap.

"Guaranteed, you won't find prices lower than ours for your Autoduelling needs."

The scene shifted again, and she appeared suddenly in mid-bounce over the backdrop of the original Uncle Albert's shop. "And don't forget to ask about our fast-fast-*fast* delivery! Don't wait! Come on down now, and find exactly what you never knew you needed before at Uncle Albert's Auto Stop and Gunner Shop in all of these fine locations."

The perky announcer vanished from the screen, replaced by a fast-scrolling list of addresses for all of Uncle Al's locations in North America to the twangy tune of Uncle Albert's theme song. No sooner had the commercial ended and the latest death game took over the screen than my agent and lawyer, Johnny B. burst into the room.

"Ricky, baby… I'm glad to see you're finally awake. You don't look any worse for wear. It's amazing what these cats at Gold Cross can pull off these days. How you are still you, even though you aren't even you anymore. It just blows my mind, you know."

The man was nothing if he wasn't attention-grabbing. Being memorable wasn't a bad thing to be in his line of work. Johnny B. was the kind of guy who could talk a mechanic into buying a metric screwdriver set or a nun into believing his time trolling Ponce De Leon Avenue was spent helping the poor and less fortunate of the streets.

His bright fuchsia pink three-piece suit and fedora, offset by an expensive designer teal blue shirt and his teal dyed goatee, accented by a bright pink feather in the teal blue band around the hat could have competed with any pimp on the street. And honestly, I'm not sure that line of work was beneath him. He closed the door and straightened his suit jacket before taking a seat at the end of the bed.

"If those sons of bitches from the Vixens team really did have thermite-laced napalm jets illegally installed on their vehicle, we are going to crucify them. That kind of modification might fly in the national circuit, but not in the amateur leagues. I'm going to sue them, their sponsors, and their sponsors' sponsors so hard that their long-dead great-grandmothers will feel my wrath!"

"What in the world are you going on about, and why am I in a Gold Cross hospital?"

"Oh…," Johnny went wide-eyed and he just stared at me for a long minute. "You don't know yet, do you?"

"Know what, Johnny?"

"Your name is on the lips of the world, Ricky."

"What?"

"Yeah! Exactly," he shouted, jumping to his feet, "and it's beautiful and glorious, even if it is a bit tragic. But tragedy sells!" The look on Johnny's face was more confused than hurt as he searched for the right words.

"You're all over the news, Ricky. I couldn't have set this up better. It's great! Everyone knows your name, baby! You've become an overnight household name. You're a sensation!"

My head really started to pound at that moment. I heard every word coming out of his mouth and understood each and every one of them, but it still didn't make any sense.

"I still don't get it, Johnny. What the hell is going on?" Johnny gave me his most pitiful and solemn look as he retook his previous seat at the end of the bed. He placed a gentle hand on my shin and patted it.

"You died, Ricky." The words came out of his mouth as soft and soothing as a mother speaking to a sick child. "And by now, the entire world knows about it. It's a major news headline, Ricky!"

"How?"

"How what?"

"How did I die, Johnny," I asked.

He looked slightly taken aback. "Oh, that. You crashed into a wall then those two hoopties from the Vixens doubled back setting you, Parker, and the car on fire with their thermite-laced napalm jets. There was nothing left of the car to salvage but ash once the power packs ignited."

"Don't I know that from experience," I mumbled.

Johnny made a popping sound from sucking on a tooth. "I know you know, Ricky. I know, you know." He patted my shin again.

"Parker! Where's Parker?"

Johnny shook his head. "He didn't make it, buddy."

"Oh, frack me…" I said when the realization hit me. "You said I died?"

Johnny nodded. "Yeah."

"How?"

Johnny stood and paced for a moment, taking a second to collect his thoughts before responding. "You got sideswiped and shoved into the path of a burned-out truck which you collided with, tumbled a few times, then impacted the support pillar for an overpass."

"So, it was just the crash itself that killed me?"

Johnny shrugged, quietly thinking. "Either that or the inferno afterward when those *criminals,* the Vixens, set you, Parker, and your car on fire. Illegally, I might add!"

I rubbed my face out of frustration and took a deep breath. "That is probably the last thing I ever wanted to hear, Johnny." I took a moment to calm myself, which was hard to focus on with the grinding teeth ringing in my ears. "If I died in that crash, then please explain how I'm here."

Johnny smiled wide and stepped over to the end of the bed, motioning to the large golden cross on the wall. "Gold Cross, of course."

"But, *how?* I didn't have an account with them."

"Well, remember all those *medical scans,*" he asked, accenting his words with air quotes, "that you had to go through the morning of the race?"

"Yeah."

"And remember all of that paperwork I had you go through for insurance purposes after we signed our contract agreement?"

"Yeah," I said, getting more frustrated by the moment.

"Well, let's just say a tiny part of all those scans was a download of your gray matter on the off chance that something happened to you in the arena."

"Wait? What? I don't understand. How could you do that without my permission? That's unethical and probably illegal."

Johnny shrugged again. "What's it matter? I paid for the reboot out of my own pocket, Ricky. And if I hadn't, you wouldn't be sitting here right now with me, about to be one dirty stinking rich mofo once we put the Vixens in…the…ground!"

"But I never signed up for that."

"For what?"

"The reboot."

"Listen, Ricky. You didn't have to, my man. It's a standard boilerplate section down in the fine print of all of my contracts. It's simple. I paid for the service upfront, and you reimburse me for the expenses. And should something happen between now and then, I have the contractual right to reboot you as I see fit with whatever brain tape is on hand to ensure that I can recoup the costs of the initial service, which will then be added to the total accrued gross debt." He smiled.

"That's immoral."

Johnny shrugged. "That's just business, baby. I have to protect my investments. But…, you do need to remember that that was your *one* freebie, sort of. If you want to be reuploaded for another reboot, then you'll have to fork out the coin for that on your own."

You'd think there would be some sort of law against anyone doing anything like that, but he's probably right in the long run, and I don't know what good arguing about it would do at this point. I'll just have to be a little more patient and read all of the fine print on any future contracts, I guess.

Johnny adjusted his glasses, tapping the side of his Ataakin focals to scroll through some new notifications he'd just gotten. "Alright, so listen, Ricky. I've gotta go take care of this other thing I've got going. They're about to release you. Just finish up the paperwork, and they'll call a cab for you when you're done."

He turned and opened the door to a small closet and removed a plastic bag. "Here's everything that was in your locker at the arena. Clothes, shoes, wallet, gun, etc. Go home and get some rest for now. Once I have the Vixen's ovaries in a vice, I'll let you know so you can watch when I destroy them."

Chapter 2

Even though Johnny B. was fired up over the crash and destroying the Vixens, I thought that was just Johnny B. being Johnny B. Never in my wildest dreams would I have imagined that just another crash on the amateur circuit would turn into such a sensational news story.

When the taxi pulled into the front drive of my apartment building, the Druid Hills multiplex, the last thing I expected to see was a crowd of people surrounding the entrance.

"Is there some sort of event going on here tonight?" the cabbie asked.

"Not that I know about…" I looked out the window at the few dozen people and hovering drones that waited around the entrance. Once they realized the cab was pulling in, the crowd rushed forward, pushing their way to the front to look into the rear passenger window.

"Mister Turner, Mister Turner. Do you plan to press charges against Quirk and Charm?" one of the people asked.

"Did you know that you were racing against an Autoduel championship team?" another shouted over the roar of questions.

"You sure you want to get dropped off here?" the cabbie asked.

"Yeah…" I said, reluctantly. "I really don't have any other choice. I live here."

"Scan in to confirm this is where you want to go then."

I placed my hand under the scanner so it could read my Ident chip. It beeped and responded with a line of digital gibberish.

"Fifty-six bucks, pal."

"What? That's highway robbery."

"That's just business. *And,* that's the discounted fare for being a fellow cabbie, even though I'm in another cab company's territory." He pointed down at the Ident screen on his dash that showed some of my personal details, including my occupation.

He wasn't wrong about that part. It was just part of the gig when you drive a taxi. You have to know your territory like the back of your hand. Any time a fare takes you into another cab company's territory, you can either drop the fare at the border or charge them extra for the trouble. By law, it was fair game to protect your territory and any potential fares. Any other cab company that encroached on your territory becomes fair game for elimination. It wasn't the greatest of policies, mainly because you could easily get a fare killed if you weren't careful, but there were several unofficial locations where challenges could be carried out.

"Mister Turner," several of the people shouted.

"This isn't going to be fun…"

"Good luck, buddy," The cabbie said, chuckling. I looked down at his driver's card inserted in a specialized holder mounted on the back of the seat.

Raphael Barze
City Center Riderz

"Try not to work too hard, Raph," I said, then forced the door of the cab open. As soon as the door started to open, it was like the world was engulfed in light brighter than daylight. There were so many camera flashes when I stepped out of the car I could have just as easily been at a rave party.

Drones fought for space among the crowd of people shouting questions at me about the crash and what my next steps were going to be... Was I going to go back to the Autoduel circuit after being brought back by Gold Cross... What was it like being brought back...

So many questions.

I just wanted to get through the door and into my apartment. The more I ignored them, the more irritable and demanding they became. When I had finally pushed my way up to the door, I scanned in, the door unlatched, and I slipped quickly through into the foyer.

Luckily none of the reporters wanted the story bad enough to follow me into the building. To help moderate the number of break-ins and general criminal activity, if someone wasn't on the *welcome* list for a residence, law enforcement would be automatically called by the system if their Ident chips were picked up on the building's internal sensors. And not being a tenant or guest was one of the fastest ways to get the law called down on you.

I let out a long breath once the elevator doors closed and tapped the button for the eighty-second floor, then leaned against the back wall. "That was fracking intense…"

What did they mean about national championship team? Johnny B. never said anything about Quirk and Charm. Maybe he just didn't know? Or he did know and that's why he was so fired up because he could smell a major payday. Either way, I'd have to call Johnny in the morning.

The elevator dinged as it slowed and came to a stop, announcing my arrival at the eighty-second floor. The smell of dusty urine struck me as soon as the doors opened.

"Home sweet home," I said, then stepped out of the elevator, making my way around the circular hallway to my door on the opposite side of the building. The place wasn't bad. Just old and well-worn. The twenty-year-old carpet was so worn it was threadbare or nonexistent in some of the higher traffic areas and the once pristine white walls were now a dull beige at best.

I opened the door to my apartment and was met with an all too familiar smell of mildew. Roaches scattered in all directions.

"Yeah… Home sweet home."

I laid down the paperwork from the Gold Cross hospital on the small entryway table then dropped my keys, lighter, and other odds and ends out of my pockets into a bowl that my mom had received as a housewarming gift when she and dad first moved into this apartment.

That's when I noticed something different in the mirror hanging on the wall above the table.

My hair looked like a matted-down afro. But that's when I noticed a real difference. The scar above my right eye that I'd had since I'd gotten into a fight with Donald Lazarus down the street on the basketball court was missing. Other small and barely noticeable scars that I knew were there were missing too.

I stood straight and looked myself over good in the mirror. Everything looked right. I looked as healthy as ever even though I did look somewhat…younger.

"Maybe there's a bright side to being cloned and reborn?" I said to the picture of my parents and me hanging on the wall a few steps further into the apartment. "Would have never happened if I didn't have to pay off your medical debts, Dad. Don't get me wrong. I wouldn't give up the extra time we had for anything. And I've found that I love being behind the wheel. But, now I'm stuck between a rock and a hard place."

I shook my head and sucked in a clearing breath. "Sorry, Dad… Love ya. I just wish you were here. You'd know what to do."

I continued into the apartment. Removing my pistol and holster, I dropped them on the kitchen counter and went for the fridge. Before leaving the hospital I had to have drunk over a gallon of water. No matter how much I drank, I couldn't shake that dry cotton mouth feeling.

I grabbed the half gallon of algae milk from the fridge door and started to chug, at least I did until I gagged on the chunky, viscous mess. I gagged, fighting to hold my lips together I rushed to the sink and spewed the rancid mess into the basin. I turned on the faucet to wash out my mouth, but nothing came out. Both hot and cold taps were drier than my mouth had been. I gagged over the rancid milk again, returning to the fridge and grabbing a bottle of beer. Aligning the bottle cap along the edge of the countertop, I smacked the top of the bottle, removing the cap. The cold beer foamed, filling my mouth as I swished it around, washing the rancid taste out of my mouth. It took the entire bottle of beer to even make a dent in that rotten flavor.

"Ada." I said to activate my Automated Daily Assistant.

"Yes Ricky," Ada responded from a multitude of speakers around the small living space.

I took another whiff from the open milk jug. There was no question. It had already gone bad. "What day is it?"

"Tuesday."

"Okay, so I was in the hospital for three days." I returned the lid to the jug and looked at the expiration date. October 2nd, 2072. "I don't get it. I just bought this milk on Friday." I dropped the jug into the trash and grabbed another beer from the fridge.

"Ada, what's the date?"

"October 25th, 2072, Ricky."

"Wait, that can't be right. The Autoduel was on September 10th. Ada. Confirm today's date."

"Today's date is October 25th, 2072."

"How is that possible?" I took a long pull from my beer "Ada, how long does a Gold Cross reboot normally take?"

"That's a great question, Ricky," Ada said in her perfectly chipper voice. "An upload into a blank clone only takes a few hours if there is a blank clone available to install the individual's mind into. If a new body must be cloned, the process can take up to six weeks in some cases depending on what stock is on hand."

"Stock on hand?" I took another swig from the bottle then retrieved the packet of paperwork they'd given me at the hospital and flopped on the couch. When I opened the packet, the first thing to grab my attention was *We're sorry*, in big bold red letters on the opening page. The rest of the letter was an apology for the slowness of the procedure. It continued to say that with today's modern medical and technological advances, a full procedure can take as little as two weeks with the proper preparation and availability of materials when growing a new cloned body. Due to the lack of base-type material in stock to work from, it had taken the full six weeks to grow my new body and install my consciousness.

"Go figure. It really isn't a surprise that they didn't have my *base type* in stock. I'm sure Johnny B. would say it's *just business*, Ricky." I tossed the packet onto the coffee table and leaned back into the couch, taking another long swallow.

"Ada, turn on something slow and soothing." A light synth beat with a harmonic undertone played throughout the apartment. I took in a long, relaxing breath then exhaled slowly. "It's just good to be out of that hospital and back home. This is good. Cold beer, chill music, a whole new life. No other worries in the world other than finishing this beer before it gets warm." I took another sip, enjoying the hoppy brew. No sooner had the bottle touched my lips than the doorbell chimed.

I looked over and glared at the closed door. "That had better not be Johnny B. I'm glad to be alive, but I'm not exactly happy with him at the moment." *It could be one of those reporters too*, I thought. They could have snuck in through a service entrance or something.

Taking another slow pull from the beer, I retrieved my pistol—hammer back and the safety off—and headed for the door. "Who is it?"

"Delivery," a male voice replied.

I activated the peephole display mounted to the wall beside the door. A small, wiry-looking guy in a light-colored windbreaker stood in the hallway holding a box. I opened the door a crack and peered out, making sure the guy could see the gun in my hand. He nervously gulped, taking an unconscious step back.

"Are—re you Mister Ricky Turner?"

"I didn't order anything," I said, nodding.

Something on the floor beside the guy moved. I shifted, opening the door just enough to find one of the ugliest, bug-eyed dogs I'd ever seen at the other end of a leash wrapped in the guy's right hand. Fumbling with the box and leash, the guy pulled a holosheet from inside his jacket and held it out to me, letting it unfurl over the top of the box.

"Sign here, please."

I tapped my finger against the sheet and started to sign. "What is this?"

"Congratulations and condolences, Mister Turner," he said, shoving the box into my arms. "You have been named as the primary beneficiary for the estate of one, Parker Hensley."

"Parker's estate? What are you talking about?"

"You are now the sole owner of all of Mister Hensley's worldly possessions." He turned the holosheet around and tapped at its surface, scrolling back up the display. He cleared his throat and began to read. "Federal, state, and local tax bills will be sent out no later than the end of the next fiscal quarter at which time mandatory compensation will be required within no less than three standard business days with the exact amount in payment or face prosecution to the fullest extent possible of all applicable tax laws."

"Wait. What?"

The guy smiled wide and tucked the holosheet away inside his jacket, then draped the end of the leash over my arm.

"We at Posthumous Estate Processors thank you for your business and would like to remind you that our end-of-summer specials are just around the corner for all of your estate processing needs. Call, click, or sign up today and receive 20% off any package purchases or services. We hope that you have a very nice day," he said, then turned and started walking away.

"Whoa, now. Hold on there, buddy. What about this thing?" I nodded down at the bug-eyed dog.

Without turning around, the guy said, "Oh, he's yours now. He was part of the estate."

"But I don't like dogs." I looked down at the thing. It was a short, squat chunk on tiny stick legs. Huge eyes bulged out of its head, reminding me of a gremlin. It looked up at me and grumbled. "It is a dog, isn't it?"

The guy stopped and pulled out the holosheet, scanning through the massive amount of text as he scrolled through. "It says here that he's a Genowares third-generation transgenic Boston Terrier."

"Does he have a name?"

The guy looked back at the sheet one more time. "Buster."

"Buster, huh?" He was doubled over, licking himself when I looked back down at him. When he noticed me looking, he hopped up and stared at me with those big bug eyes, tongue lolled out, drool dripping onto the hallway carpet. "You sure are an ugly little shit."

That's when he licked his own eyeball.

"I really need to start reading the fine print before signing anything," I said, pulling him along into the apartment before closing the door. "Me casa is su casa, I guess."

Chapter 3

After a few days of rest and catching up with what I'd missed over the last month and a half, I thought it might be a good idea to see if I still had a day job. That, *being able to afford to live* part just happened to be a bit more important than normal and was a major driving force for me at this particular moment. Luckily I didn't have to worry about rent. When my folks first moved in, the apartments in this building were sold as condo apartments instead of renting out, and they'd paid off the loan on this place years ago and then I inherited it after Dad died.

While the power to my apartment hadn't been cut off, the water had been. It took every last bit of savings that I could scrape together to be able to pay off the service charges, late fees, and catch my account up to current before they would turn the water on so I could at least take a hot shower. And then there was the issue of cleaning up after Buster. I couldn't go without water in that apartment for another day.

Luckily, I didn't have to call a cab or take the bus to get to work. Henry's garage was only around the corner and three blocks away. After sneaking out the back door of the apartment complex I could catch some fresh air and take Buster for a much-needed walk. Maybe I'd get really lucky and I could teach him that he was supposed to go outside, not inside.

Henry was probably the grumpiest curmudgeon I'd ever had the privilege of meeting, but he was fair and paid well. Years ago, he'd originally hung out his shingle and opened his doors as a mechanics shop for general repairs and bodywork. The man was nothing if not a miracle worker when it came to dents and dings. Henry was so good at what he did that once he'd finished working over a job, you'd never know it had ever been damaged.

After opening the garage, he slowly added other services to his stable of offerings. First came a twenty-four-seven towing service, *when* there was someone available to man the phone and to drive the truck. Then there was the roadside fleet service he offered to several local transport companies, then there were the junkyard and discount auto parts followed by the sometimes available taxi service. And that's where I came in.

Driving a cab in Atlanta wasn't a half-bad gig. You got to talk to a lot of people, both good and bad, the hours were flexible, and I got to be behind the wheel of a car. It never failed to amaze me. No matter what I was doing, I would normally screw things up. But being behind the wheel of a car just felt natural, like it was destiny or something.

And then of course there was the best part of driving a cab. It covered the regular bills so I could afford to live.

When I rounded the privacy fence into the yard, it didn't look like much had changed over the last month and a half. The stacks of junk cars looked exactly as they had when I last clocked out before heading to the Autoduel arena. I tied Buster off to one of the rims stacked outside the door then went inside.

Just as always, the sick-sounding door chime dinged when I opened the front door and stepped through into the shop's three-chair waiting room.

"Hold the frack on for one damned minute," Henry shouted from the maintenance bay. His voice sounded muffled through the heavy door that separated the waiting room and the maintenance bay.

A few moments later, Henry rushed through the shop door, wiping down a grease-covered part with an old shop rag. "Well frack me," he said, coming to a hurried stop just inside the door. "What the hell are you doing here, Ricky? You're supposed to be dead." He stepped into the small front office, setting the rag-wrapped part down on the counter he stooped down and began rummaging around underneath it.

"My agent had a Gold Cross account set up on me," I replied. "I only just got out of the hospital."

Henry grunted then placed two shot glasses on the countertop. He turned around and started to fumble with the large dial combination lock on the ancient safe at the back of the office. After a few more minutes of cussing and smacking the latching mechanism, he opened the safe and retrieved a purple velvet bag. "Well," he grunted, forcing himself back to his feet. "I'm glad you're back, kid. You're one hell of a hard worker. It hasn't been the same around here without you."

He opened the top of the bag, removed the lid from the bottle, and poured a shot of bright amber liquid into each of the glasses. I wasn't sure if it was a whiskey or a rum of some kind.

Henry picked up one of the glasses and held it up, waiting. I picked up the other glass, and he clinked the two together. "Welcome back, kid." Then he slammed his shot back. I did the same and the harsh vapors of the liquor overwhelmed me. I had barely swallowed the shot before the coughing fit started. Setting the glass back onto the counter I caught my breath and looked up at him.

"What the hell was that?"

"Whiskey." He chuckled.

"That isn't whiskey. That tastes more like parts cleaner.

"Oh, it's whiskey, alright. It's the real stuff from way back, not that fake fracking shit they make these days."

"Are you trying to kill me?" I coughed, trying to get a clear breath again.

"Why? Do you think I should?" He capped the bottle and returned it to the safe, then closed the door and spun the combination knob. "We could see if you've got nine lives like a cat."

"No thank you. Rebooting once was bad enough."

"Well, I'm glad you're back, Ricky. But you better damn well remember that the next time you leave me in a lurch like this, I'm just going to fire your ass outright and put Dave in a cab."

"Why the hell would you want to go and make me deal with people?" Dave asked as he entered through the shop door, then stopped in his tracks, eyes wide when he saw me.

"Ricky," he said with a nod.

"Dave…"

He started into the room, looking me up and down as he walked around, circling my position, then poked the side of the arm with the end of the crescent wrench he'd pulled from his pocket.

"Dave," Henry groused. "What the hell are you doing?"

"Just making sure I didn't take a bite of the wrong something by accident." He took a step back and leaned against the shop door. "You doin', alright?"

"About as well as I possibly can be, considering how it could have gone," I said.

"Are you going back?" Dave asked.

"Back to what?"

"Back to the nunnery, of course," Henry said sarcastically, cutting in. "Where the hell else do you think he'd be talking about? Back to the fracking arena, you socket head."

I shrugged. "What other choice do I have? I have to pay off my debt to Johnny B for the reboot."

Dave nodded. "Good thing they supply the vehicles for amateur night, considering your last set of wheels is a pile of ash and slag now."

"I'll still have to find a gunner. Apparently, Parker didn't make it."

Dave fiddled with the dirt under a fingernail before he chewed on the nail. Tearing it away with his teeth, he spit the piece into the floor then wiped his finger on his grungy coveralls. "I might know a guy."

"Like who?" Henry asked.

"Someone," Dave said with a defensive nod. "Don't you worry yourself about it, old man."

"Old man, my ass." Henry picked up a loose nut from the end of the counter and threw it in Dave's general direction.

"What the hell? You're going to get pissed just cause I happen to know a guy?"

"I don't want *your guy* to do anything stupid that's going to cause me to lose Ricky again. I can't afford to lose him. But you… you, I'd almost pay to get rid of, but I'll be damned if anyone would want you." Henry pushed his way past Dave and opened the shop door. "Don't get Ricky killed, and both of you get your asses back to work." I could still hear him grumbling after he'd slammed the door and wandered back into the bay.

"So, you know a guy?" I asked, turning back to Dave.

"Yeah," Dave said slowly. "I might happen to know a guy. Are you sure you want to trust someone you've never met before with your life?"

"I did it before."

"Yeah, and how well did that work out for you?"

"Well, actually, it was going pretty well up until that last match. And according to Johnny B, the only reason we lost was because Team Vixens cheated."

"Fair enough, fair enough," he said, nodding. "Let me make a few calls then."

Chapter 4

Luckily, Dave liked dogs. He liked dogs well enough that he agreed to keep an eye on Buster for me while I did my routes. And let me tell you, it felt *good* to be back in the seat. I don't know what it was about being behind the wheel of a car, it just felt natural. When I slid into the seat and grabbed hold of the wheel, it was like the car becomes an extension of myself. And to be behind the wheel of *my* cab, just felt like a little slice of heaven all unto itself.

Fergie, my thirty-year-old classic Fragmaster sedan wasn't the prettiest ride on the road, but she still turned lots of heads. When her previous owner sold her for scrap, Henry just couldn't bring himself to put her through the crusher. He patched up the grenade launcher ports then replaced the power pack and two of the worn-out drive motors—the reason the previous owner had gotten rid of her in the first place. After a fresh coat of the deepest darkest black cherry paint you could get and it still be reflective against lasers, he put her back on the road as the first of his planned fleet of taxis.

Granted, Henry did remove and sell the grenade launchers for a nice price, he didn't want to leave me completely defenseless in case someone out on the road got stupid. It didn't happen all that often, but it did still happen. So better safe than sorry, he equipped her with a forward ram plate, a pair of forward-firing light machine guns, as well as a rear-firing flaming oil jet and spike-dropper hidden away in the trunk.

My first fare of the day was a bit farther out than I expected, and not in the best parts of town. Instructions were to pick the fare up in the Wildwood apartment complex just off Jolly Avenue in Clarkston and deliver them to Chevelle Lane in College Heights. It was only about seven miles distance, and if traffic wasn't bad it shouldn't take me more than fifteen minutes to get them there. Without the night differential, it would probably come out to a $30 fare in the end. Just enough to cover recharging, my cut per hour, and a few bucks back into Henry's pocket.

When I pulled into the apartment complex on Jolly Avenue, a guy standing near the mailboxes at the entrance of the complex started waving frantically at me. I was a little surprised the guy hadn't been wearing his pants half off his ass or decked out in head-to-toe gang colors, which would be on par for this part of Atlanta. He just looked like any average joe blow. Brown slacks, black polo that he wore untucked, almost like a uniform you'd see someone wear at one of the stores in the mall.

Must be the fare, I thought.

He opened the rear passenger door and jumped in before I could come to a complete stop. The guy must have been in one hell of a hurry since he slammed my door.

"Where to?"

He rattled off the address in a hurry, and I punched it into the onboard Ada. He was a bit on the anxious side to the point of being twitchy, which worried me. Luckily he didn't carry the sores and tell-tell signs of a tweaker, but something had the guy worked up. The display showed that the destination was at the end of Chevelle Lane and it locked in the fastest route. I pulled a quick U-turn in the apartment complex's driveway, barking the tires slightly as I did, and turned left heading north on Jolly Avenue.

I kept a close eye on all of my fares through the rearview mirror. It was something that had just become a habit after a few less-than-desirable fares that turned out to be muggings in disguise. And this guy was starting to give me that bad gut feeling like he was about to do something stupid that I was going to regret.

He stared off into the distance, watching the scenery pass by out of his window. This in itself wasn't out of the normal. While there were those sorts of people who would chatter your ears off once they got into the cab, or unload their emotional baggage using me as some sort of counseling session, lots of people just climbed into a cab and quietly took in the sights and enjoyed the ride.

This guy though.

He was fidgety. His fingers kept moving, scratching at random itches, fiddling with bits of trim on the door panels, or tapping out a beat on his legs. His nervousness was starting to make me nervous. A fare is a fare, but I really wasn't in the mood to deal with someone else's bullshit. That's when he leaned forward, propping his elbows up on the back of my seat.

"Hey, bro. Aren't you that guy from the news?"

"Don't know what you're talking about."

He started snapping his fingers like he was trying to jump-start his brain. "Ronny, Robby…Um…" He leaned forward, trying to get a better look at my medallion, the permit that says I've been certified as an authorized taxi driver in the city of Atlanta.

"Ricky! You're Ricky Turner!" He slapped the back of the seat and chuckled. "I'll be damned. You're famous, brother."

"I don't know about all that, man."

"Yeah, you are. I've seen your mug plastered all over the news lately. They've been saying the other team cheated, installing illegal gear on their car and shit."

Maybe driving a taxi wasn't the best of ideas right after something as headline-worthy as a scandal in the AADA, but I still had to make a living. Hopefully, this wasn't going to be a regular occurrence for all fares I picked up. The American Autoduel Association was good at quelling stories they didn't want to blow up or get out, but somehow my situation had taken on a life of its own and flared up like a wildfire in a tornado.

"Me and my brother were down at Twin Cams for their wings and beer meal deal night when that race was on. You were kicking some serious ass out there, man. The way you drifted that car around the other crashes, even at full speed. Man, I haven't seen moves like that since before Abby Boehmke retired. And how the hell is it right for veteran drivers to think they can come into an amateur autoduel and cheat like that? The AADA needs to ban them for life, if you ask me."

"I don't know about all that. Abby Boehmke is a legend. I don't know that anyone could ever out-drive her," I said, then looked up in the rearview mirror. The guy got silent, like he was really thinking about something, then he suddenly swallowed hard. He shook his head and started again.

"So if you burned to a crisp in that crash and you're just a cabbie, how are you still here?"

Yeah, let's go ahead and bring up the part I hated the most about this situation…But I bet he was the type that wouldn't let it go.

"My Lawyer arranged and paid for a Gold Cross reboot without my knowledge. Kinda pissed about it, but at the same time, I'm glad he did."

He licked his lips nervously like he wasn't sure if he could ask the next question or not. Then he leaned forward again. "What's it like to be a reboot? That's got to be crazy, knowing you're a clone of the you that burned up in that car. I mean, what's it feel like?"

And there was that finger in the wound again. I know he didn't know how much it bothered me, but I really wish the guy would let that part go.

"It's… strange to say the least," I said. "Disorienting… You find odd little things that are different, like missing scars, but otherwise, I just feel like me."

"Did everything come out the same?" he asked.

"What do you mean?"

"Like…," he started then nervously bobbed his head. I could tell he was thinking of the best way to ask his question. "Like, did *all* your *parts* come back in their proper place and proportions? *Nothing's* missing?"

I realized exactly what he was getting at when he looked up in the mirror and then down at his own crotch.

"Ah, that…" I cleared my throat, awkwardly. "Uh, as far as I can tell, yeah. Unless they reprogramed me to believe a lie while I was still processing."

"Wait?" He sat back, frightened. "You telling me they can do that? I heard some crackpot conspiracy theorist rattling on about that before, but I thought he was just loony. You telling me that he was right?"

I shrugged again. "No idea, man. But in this day and age, it wouldn't surprise me one little bit."

He shook his head, "That's just some scary big brother nightmare if it is true."

"No doubt. If it is true, I think I'd rather be blissfully ignorant of the whole mess and keep on living without knowing the truth."

He stared out the window again for a long minute, silently watching the world go by.

"Wait," the guy started. "If you're an Autoduellist, why on earth are you driving a cab?"

I shrugged. "It pays the bills."

He shook his head again, trying to comprehend the words. "But you're an *Autoduellist*."

"I'm just an average Joe trying to make it to the next paycheck and hope I can afford more than the cheapest of the dirt cheap algae ramen. I haven't been an Autoduellist for very long, man. And amateur night doesn't always pay out to the runners-up. I've been in matches where we were so close to the win–losing by millimeters–but only the winner was awarded any of the prizes. That last race being one of them, the rest of us were just shit out of luck."

"That really sucks man," he said, then started to fiddle with the window trim.

"Yeah, well, it is what it is, man."

He let out a long sigh. "It really doesn't make what I'm supposed to do any easier."

When I looked up in the mirror, conflicted indecision painted his face.

He flashed into motion, drawing a pistol and pushing it across the top of the seat before I had the chance to even blink, and placed the gun against the back of my head. "If you're the praying type, you've got about two seconds to say your p–"

"What the hell do you think you're doing?" I shouted, cutting him off.

"Making bank and earning cred with the ONYX. Now hand over your cred chip," he said, snapping his fingers at me.

I let out a chuckle. "You seriously think you're going to *make bank*, by robbing a taxi? Exactly what makes you think I have anything worth stealing man? I'm a fracking taxi driver for frack's sake. And exactly what sort of street cred do you earn by robbing me? Do you get extra points if we run over a few hookers while we're at it?" I cut the wheel, aiming for the sidewalk.

"Hey man, what the hell are you trying to do? You trying to kill us or something?"

"Well, why not? I already died once. What's another time?"

I swerved again, this time in front of an oncoming bus, just barely squeezing between the bus and a parked car along the opposite side of the street. I buried the accelerator into the floorboard. "You still haven't answered me. What the hell makes you think I have anything worth stealing?"

"Hey, come on man, slow down already!"

We swerved again, dodging between two large box trucks, cutting one of them off to drift the intersection, scraping across the nose of some tiny compact car.

"Answer me!"

"Okay, Okay! You got a reboot, didn't you?"

"Only because my sleazy agent sprung for it as an insurance policy to make sure he could recoup any losses he *might* encounter during the course of our contract.

"What?" he asked.

I cut the wheel hard to the right, slamming him against the rear passenger door. "Yeah. Kinda fracked up, isn't it?" I shouted over the screeching of tires. I straightened the wheel and dodged another oncoming car. Smashing the accelerator to the floor again.

"He called the Gold Cross account an investment in both of our futures. That I should be thanking him for looking out for me when I couldn't."

"Man, that's seriously fracked up, and I'm sorry, but it doesn't change anything."

He slid forward, pulling himself up against the back of the seat. When I looked up into the rearview mirror, I saw the tip of his gun appear from behind the seat.

I slammed both feet down onto the brake pedal, sending him sliding forward, dangling awkwardly over the front seat as the cab came to rest.

Reaching across, I grabbed for the guy's gun with my left, drawing my pistol from my shoulder rig with my right. Before he could right himself and scramble back across the seat, I had the barrel of my pistol under his chin, hammer back.

He didn't hesitate to let go of his gun. He knew he was beaten. And before he could get any bright ideas, I tossed his gun into the air, flipping it around to catch it by the barrel. Bringing the butt of the grip down across the guy's temple, I pistol-whipped him into unconsciousness before I safed and holstered my own weapon.

With a shove, he fell into the back seat, slumped over, like a dead-drunk fare. I pulled the car over to the curb. It took a few minutes of digging through the junk Dave must have collected in the trunk while I was out being rebooted before I found the tie straps I had been looking for.

I dragged the guy from the back seat to the sidewalk and hog-tied him with the strap. I opened the passenger door and sat down on the front seat. "Ada."

"Yes, Ricky?"

"Call 911, please."

The automated assistant immediately dialed, reporting back in her semi-robotic voice that the call was going through.

"Once they answer, please give them my information, our location, and that there has been an attempted mugging."

I grabbed his pistol and tucked it away into the back of the glove box. Now, I just had to wait. And sitting there waiting wasn't necessarily the greatest of things. With nothing better to do, my mind began to wander. I started thinking about everything that had recently happened to me.

It almost felt like the universe had it out for me. Like I'd been slapped with some sort of karmic debt, and now I had to somehow pay it back.

First the crash and the reboot, and now this. I just wanted to get back to something resembling a regular life. Even if it was a menial job of some sort, as long as it was steady, paid the bills, and maybe didn't have the potential to get me killed.

But then, there was nothing like being behind the wheel of an armed vehicle in the arena. Driving around on the streets, even with armed and armored personnel vehicles just wasn't the same.

I probably would miss it? But then, it made me wonder if I'd freeze and lock up as soon as I stepped foot into an arena. There was no comparison in my opinion. Driving in the arena was so much different from driving around city streets. I could almost smell the acrid stink of spent gunpowder and burning tires.

I let out a long sigh.

"I guess we just take it one day at a time at this point."

Chapter 5

"Can you believe it, Chuck? After only seven weeks since his horrific crash and fiery demise, Ricky '*The Reboot*' Turner is climbing back into the saddle. We haven't seen a comeback like this since Zofia Moon ate the big one three years ago and before her clone had managed to grow hair she climbed back into the seat to seek retribution on the other team for breaking her winning streak."

"It is very much surprising and somewhat disconcerting, Alex. As most of you out there know, a Gold Cross clone is an exact replica, especially with their new patented Fast Vat technology. It is very possible to be up and functional in a much shorter amount of time. While most cloning technologies involve months of rehabilitation, a Fast Vat clone is all but ready to go. They will lack any edge they may have previously had because muscle memory doesn't transfer over with the individual's memories."

"No doubt, Chuck. You would think that Ricky would be a rehab nightmare at this point, but he's looking spry for a dead man. So, what can our teams expect to see out there in tonight's Autoduel challenge, Chuck?"

"Tonight's challenge, Alex, will be a match of Aces and Eights. With $5,000 on the line, none of tonight's competitors can afford to give less than their best."

"Well, I sure hope that Ricky can handle the challenge. What can they expect to see out there on the arena floor?"

"Even though the oval track itself here at the Atlanta Motor Speedway is rough and full of potholes, the amazing maintenance team has been working day and night to prepare the track for tonight's event, Alex.

"It looks like they have prepared the infield, creating a figure eight course that incorporates the turns of the original oval track."

"That they have, Alex."

"I just hope that no one accidentally finds that missing chunk of track on the high side of turn three. I'd hate to see what that would do to the undercarriage of one of these sponsor-supplied cars."

"I would too, Alex. That could be catastrophic for one of tonight's teams. The goal of tonight's challenge is to score as many points as possible by passing between the designated markers set up across the course while running a figure-eight loop that begins in the center of the infield, goes around turns one and two, then cuts across the infield again to go opposite around turns three and four before returning to the infield once again, completing the lap. The course has also been adjusted by our maintenance teams to include a number of jumps and obstacles to add an extra level of complexity to tonight's event."

"And as you know, Chuck, tonight's event has been designated as a non-lethal race. What sort of weaponry can we expect to see in use by our competent teams of Autoduellists?"

"Our vehicles for tonight's event, Alex, are hatchback variants of the Fnord Motor Company yellow jacket sub-compact chassis, supplied by Vinedustries, the leader in today's networking and information technology needs.

These vehicles have been lightened to the point of having almost no armor, except around the vital areas. While armed with a single .223 caliber turret-mounted machine gun set for three-round bursts, the weapons are intended for use to disable competitors' vehicles, not eliminate competing team members. If a team is found to be actively targeting another team member, they will be immediately disqualified, and their vehicle disabled by kill switch.

"That being said, accidents do happen, Chuck."

"That they do, Alex. That they do."

Bile started to creep up into my throat when we first pulled in at the arena. On the way here, I think I was more nervous about being nervous than anything else. The smell of freshly laid asphalt permeated the air. It looked like they had recently patched several of the deeper craters on the main course. Even though most races used electric vehicles these days, the thick viscous stink of old burnt oil and race fuel still hung heavy throughout the arena like it was the lifeblood of the complex. Once we'd made it to the locker room and I started to suit up, my nerves seemed to calm themselves.

Just another day in the arena.

Just another day behind the wheel.

The sponsors had supplied *one size fits all* fire-resistant suits to all team members. Corporate logos covered every square inch of the garments, with the simple Vinedustries logo taking up the most real estate diagonally across the front and back of the one-piece jumpsuit. The helmets left in our lockers were plain black and adjustable race helmets that could be easily fitted to a range of head sizes. I wasn't sure if I wanted to know who had previously worn my helmet. It had several scuffs across the left side, and what looked like a few dried droplets of blood that had settled on the front underside lip and stank like a locker room. Nothing I saw in the contract ever said that sponsor-supplied equipment was supposed to be new, only supplied.

It was a good thing Dave walked into the locker room at that moment because I could feel the bile starting to climb back up my throat.

"Alright, I know I told you Bert would be perfect," Dave started to say when he walked through the door, "but I just found out he's been in jail the last two weeks for petty theft."

Behind him I noticed someone else leaning up against the metal frame of the doorway. He wasn't a big guy, maybe five foot two, five foot three at most. He was balding on top but otherwise wore his greasy brown hair long and loose down to his shoulders.

"Who's that then," I asked, chin nodding in the direction of the guy.

"Ricky, Darius. Darius, Ricky," Dave said, pointing to each of us. We both nodded at each other before looking back to Dave to continue.

"Okay, and who is Darius, exactly?"

Dave put his hands in his pockets and shrugged then looked back to Darius. "He's Darius. A good guy who knows a thing or two and is good with a gun."

I looked at Darius and said, "What have you done before?"

Darius hooked his thumbs into the belt loops of his jeans. "Done a few matches out on the highways against the ONYX a time or two for shits and giggles."

"Yeah," I said with a half laugh. "How'd that turn out for you?"

Darius pulled up his shirt to show me a large scar on the front of his torso that was much larger on his back. "We made it out, but not before those assholes gave me this little parting gift. Ruptured my spleen and pancreas with that shot. It even nicked my left lung on the way through. But in the end, I *won*, they didn't."

I looked at Dave, and he gave me a questionable side nod about the story, then shrugged again. "Listen, he's up for the gig and doesn't want anything up front."

"Yeah, man," Daris said. "As long as I get half of whatever the pot is when we win, I'm in."

"You'll have a .223 light machine gun in the roof-mounted cupola turret. Think you can handle it?"

"Hell yeah, I can handle it. That ain't nothing but a pop gun."

"Deal," I said then started to walk toward the door.

Darius cleared his throat. "I do have one question."

I stopped in my tracks and turned back to the two of them.

"Okay, shoot."

"What's with him?" Darius asked, pointing down at Buster who had sat on the ground next to Dave. Buster looked at me, then at Darius, and let out what sounded like a grumbling growl. "Is he alright and all? He looks like his eyes are about to pop out of his head."

"Yeah, I guess," I said and continued toward the door.

"Is he yours?"

"Sorta…" I said.

"How is a dog, sorta yours?"

"He belonged to Ricky's last gunner," Dave answered.

"Okay, and?"

"I inherited him."

"Wait, did you just say his last gunner," Darius asked, pointing his thumb in my direction.

"Yup," I said, zipping up the collar of my suit. I continued out of the locker room toward the pits.

The cars they'd supplied us for the event looked like nothing more than Baja-style tube frame rail buggies. The cockpit area had what amounted to a little bit of sheet metal surrounding it for what they were considering *armor-plating*. Thin plastic sheets covered other sections of the frame, giving it a somewhat finished look from a distance, but it didn't amount to anything more than surface space for sponsor stickers.

I climbed into the seat, strapped into the harness, and slid my helmet over my head. Darius must have speed changed because before I realized it he was standing there smiling at me. He climbed through the passenger door into the gunner's position mounted in the back passenger's seat. He started to fiddle with the controls, arming the turret and checking the action.

I checked over my controls and activated the power plant. Readouts on the rudimentary dashboard flashed to life, running through a diagnostic sequence before giving me a full status readout.

Dave leaned on the driver's side door. "Have you ever been in one of these before?"

I looked up at him and shook my head. "No."

"I've seen them often enough on the broadcasts," Darius said, then chuckled as he spun the turret left, then right.

"These things are set up for multiple styles of events." Dave leaned into the window. "Hit that button right there," he said, pointing up at a red button overhead where a rearview mirror would normally be, "if for some reason you lose numb nuts, and it'll recenter the turret and lock it in the forward firing position. All you have to do to fire it at that point is to pull this cable right here." He tapped at a thin cable strung along the center of the roof panel.

"Gotcha," I said just as the five-minute warning siren warbled to life.

Buster let out a grumple when Dave slapped the top of the car and stepped back. "Alright, man. Get up to the rally line and kick some ass."

Buster barked and bounced against the side of the car like he was trying to jump in.

"What?" I picked him up, all snarls and grumbles, and placed him on my lap. "You're a mean little shit, aren't you?" I scratched at the top of his head. "Sorry, little dude. You can't go along with me for this ride." I handed him off to Dave. "Keep him with you."

"What am I supposed to do with him?"

"I don't know. Buy him a hotdog or something?" I closed the door and looked back at Darius, tapping on the roof to get his attention. "You ready?"

He shook his head, pulling himself out of the gunner's screen mounted behind my seat. "Hell yeah, I'm ready." He let out a shout and smacked the roof of the car.

We were the last to pull up to the rally line. Seven other cars were ready to go, their pit crews doing final checks. I glanced back over my shoulder the best that I could and saw Dave at the pit wall still holding Buster. The ugly little shit nipped at Dave when he grabbed his paw to wave at me.

The pit crews scattered like cockroaches when the thirty-second warning buzzer sounded.

This was it. Do or die, there was no backing out now.

The bark of the starting gunshot sounded, and I floored it. The small hatchback lurched forward at a surprising rate of speed. Normally I wouldn't expect a car this size to launch off the line as fast as it did, but they did say that they were modified for arena use.

The first two laps weren't horribly exciting. I avoided the ramps just to get a good feel for the little hatchback. It wasn't unpleasant to drive. Nimble, and responsive for sure. I just wished it had a little more between me and the other teams.

Being bunched together from the starting line, fighting for that number one slot wasn't the time to be firing at each other. That sort of racing only caused a situation of mutually assured destruction at this range. I was glad that Darius hadn't started firing at the other teams right off the line. Having the concentrated fire of seven other teams all aimed at you is a surefire way to lose a match or to get dead in a hurry.

Just as we cleared the first turn on lap three, the chaos began.

Two of the other cars just ahead to our right decided it was time to mix it up. I could hear the teams shit-talking each other on the pit comms over the roar of the crowds and the hum of electric motors.

One of the cars dropped back suddenly and then slammed into the rear quarter of the other, spinning them both out in an attempted PIT maneuver. This caused two more of the pack to swerve, cascading into the rest of us.

I cut the wheel hard left, popped the parking brake, and floored it, breaking away from the rest of the pack. Our front wheels popped across the edge of the next ramp as we drifted sideways around the obstacle.

Darius let out a loud whoop and opened fire at one of the cars behind us.

I overcorrected, slaloming the car across the hard-packed soil of the infield before straightening it out and aiming for the next set of markers.

We cleared the points, and I shifted our course, heading toward the high side of the track out of the next turn.

The rat-a-tat-tat of our light machine gun and Darius's shit-talking was quickly answered by the plinking of return fire. They had to be targeting our tires or drive motors. Rounds mostly peppered the rear of our car, but a number of rounds struck at the undercarriage. I guessed they were most likely ricochets off of the pavement.

One even managed to penetrate the floorboard and impact the dash console in front of me. It seemed to be nothing more than cosmetic damage for the moment. The readouts still functioned. Power supply capacity, the status of all four drive motors, tire pressures, and power pack temps, all seemed fine.

I glanced back as we rounded the turn after taking the next two sets of points and saw the rest of the pack bunched together, except for one car.

Considering there wasn't any difference in the cars, all I had to do is not screw up, and we could outpace the rest of the pack.

"Can you hit them at this range with that thing?" I shouted back at Darrius.

"I don't know what kind of range it has, but I can sure as hell try."

Three round bursts sounded off from overhead, the report of each round vibrated through the car's chassis.

Darius punched the roof and let out a victorious shout. "Hell fracking yeah, baby!"

"What?"

"I nailed those bastards!"

Finishing the turn and heading back into the infield I glanced back and spotted smoke rolling out from under the front of the car trailing behind us.

"I didn't think it would do it, but damn! I don't care what else Dave says about you, you're a great shot!"

"What?" Darius shouted. "What does he say?"

I glanced back and saw a red-faced look of rage building to a head.

"I don't know. Stuff?"

Darius punched the back of my seat with all his force. I jerked the wheel on accident, skidding us slightly. It was pure luck that I did at that specific moment.

We dashed past the first ramp at the intersection of the figure eight in the infield, barely missing one of the damaged stragglers from the pack's first collision that seemed to appear in our path from out of nowhere on the opposite side of the ramp.

Correcting the skid, we cleared the other car, straightened, and blew past the opposite landing ramp.

Darius shoved my shoulder from behind. "What the hell did Dave say, man?"

I was really starting to question my judgment at that point. First Johnny B and now this. Maybe trusting some random guy that Dave knew with my life wasn't such a great idea after all.

Keeping the pedal to the floor, I adjusted our course, going wide to get just the right angle to pull in tight along the inside of the next turn, and scoring a few extra points in the process.

That's when I saw the flash of movement out of the corner of my eye. Some deep-seated nugget of self-preservation must have triggered, because I was now holding Darius's fist in my right hand while my left had a white-knuckled grip on the wheel, holding us at the bottom of the corner at full throttle.

Rounds peppered the rear driver's quarter panel of our car.

"How about you do your fracking job and shoot back at them?" I shouted, shoving Darius's fist away. Coming out of the corner we hit the straightaway into the infield once again.

Rounds strafed the same side as before. I jinked us right, shifting our course to pass to the right of the ramp. Tiny geysers of dried Georgia red clay sprung up ahead of us, cutting a line across our path. I cut back to the left, then swerved right, trying to keep them guessing which way we were going.

"A little help would be nice right about now!"

Darius crossed his arms, slumping in his seat like a spoiled-ass brat. "Give me one good reason why I should!"

"Because if I die, you die!"

That's when the barriers went up. Steel cage-like structures rose up from the arena floor, flanking either side of the ramp.

There was nowhere else to go.

"Shit!"

I cut the wheel hard, aiming our nose for the ramp, trying to keep control and not end up in a skid.

Never taking my foot off the accelerator, we slammed into the ramp at top speed and were shoved into our seats by the sudden and overwhelming G-forces as we climbed the ramp.

The bile bubbled up, burning the back of my throat, threatening to escape when we hit the apex of our arc and weightlessness overtook us for that brief moment in our flight.

Before we hit the landing ramp, more rounds impacted the undercarriage of our car. Red warning lights flashed across the dash panels, marking the rear left drive motor as having taken damage.

We slammed into the hard-packed surface of the landing ramp, landing nose down. The front bumper dug into the dirt, kicking up a thick cloud of red clay dust. More rounds plinked off of our rear before I could straighten us out. There was a pull to the left in the steering that I had to actively fight against.

"Can you do something about that annoyance behind us?"

"If you'd keep us steady, I might be able to do something," Darius shouted.

More rounds pummeled our rear, sounding like a seriously bad summer hail storm on a tin roof.

Starting into the next turn, I looked back to check our six. Darius cursed and swore with every three-round burst from our gun.

Three of the pack were gaining on us and gaining quick. I glanced down at the dash. The same drive motor flashed red, reminding me of the damage we'd sustained earlier. Our speed read all of sixty-nine miles an hour as I fought to hold us on the inside lane of the turn. It wasn't much of a difference from the eighty-eight miles an hour I'd been able to maintain on the previous turn, but it was enough to allow the other teams to start catching up to us.

"Fracking stupid ass worthless gun!" Darius released his harness and rolled down the passenger window.

"What the hell are you doing?" I shouted at him.

"Taking care of the problem, that's what! This fracking gun is a worthless fracking pea shooter! I can't do anything with it." Hooking his feet around the roll cage frame he slid himself out of the window and sat on the door. He leaned down and grinned wide. "Just hold it steady, and I'll take out these socket heads." He drew a polished chrome hand cannon from the cargo pocket of his race suit and leaned back out of the window.

"Are you trying to get us disqualified? This is a nonlethal race!"

Darius's entire body tensed and jerked with each booming crack of the high-caliber revolver. He let out a triumphant whoop, slid back into the cab, and returned to his seat.

I turned but couldn't see any of the other vehicles behind us on the track.

"Did you get them?"

"Hell yeah, I did! I think I might have hit one of the forward power packs. The thing started smoking after that last shot."

He wasn't lying about getting the hit. When we came out of the last turn onto the straight stretch heading to the infield I glanced back, and a cold chill ran down my spine. Flames and smoke billowed from the car Darius had hit. From that brief glance, it looked like they had swerved off the track and collided with one of the barriers along the service apron at the bottom of the track.

Darius let out a whoop and laughed. "That's right you sons of bitches! That's what you get for fracking with us!" He slapped the back of my seat again.

Pain raced through my legs at the thought of being trapped in a burning vehicle.

I never want to go through that again.

"That's enough," I shouted.

"What? Those slushboxes got what was coming to them. They should have known better than to mess with us."

I turned and glared at him. "I said that was fracking enough! Do your fracking job and keep your mouth shut!"

The track shifted again. New barriers, lined with what looked like spikes sprung up from beneath the infield on the straightaway. I slammed the brakes, cutting the wheel hard to the left then mashed the accelerator and steered into the skid, drifting us around the first obstacle. Darius flew forward. A loud ding resounded throughout the cab when his head impacted the metal tube frame of the dash. The track shifted again. New barriers sprung up, replacing the previous barriers that dropped back into hiding below the track's surface.

I popped the brake, cutting the wheel hard right then steering into an opposite slide. The nose of our car clipped the end of the new barrier, sending us spinning out of control. Darrius flew into my lap, colliding with the driver's door as we impacted another barrier, crumpling the driver's side of the car inward.

We got fracking lucky.

Rounds pummeled the passenger side of the car, penetrating the nearly non-existent armor of the cab. Darius jerked in time to the sound of three dull thuds from rounds penetrating the cab and impacted in his torso.

"Hey!" I tapped at the side of his helmet. "Darius! Get off!"

I checked for a pulse like I'd seen people do on the vids, but had no clue if I was doing it right. I hoped he was still alive, but if we sat too long we were both sure as dead. After a quick check and not finding anything, I struggled to shove his limp form over the center console and back into the passenger side of the cab.

The dash readouts flickered and skewed to the left side of the screen. One of the rounds had struck the lower corner, spiderwebbing the screen.

Available power was down to thirty-five percent, and both of the driver's side drive motors read as non-operational and disengaged. Three of the four power packs flashed red, registering damage to the circuitry and a main bus failure on the auxiliary power supply circuit.

We were seriously fracked.

I didn't know if the damage was from the crash or the gunfire, but I had to get us moving before the next set of cars came through and scored bonus points for disabling us.

Shifting from reverse to forward, I rocked us back and forth, slowly moving us away from the barrier enough that we didn't hang up against it. I floored it and the car crept forward at first, then lurched forward, the driver's side door ripping away as we pulled away from the barrier.

Reaching up, I smacked the button to recenter and lock the turret into place, putting us back into the race.

I just needed to make sure no one had a clear shot on the driver's door or I'd be seriously screwed. There was nothing like missing an entire door to paint a great big bullseye on yourself that just begged for the other teams to remove you from the gene pool.

With the lack of two of the drive motors and the power supply system being fragged, the best I could do was get her up to forty-two miles an hour, but at least we were still moving. At this rate though, there was no chance of hitting the ramps on any subsequent passes and having a chance at clearing the jump with any sort of success.

Thank the racing gods that the helmets and suits had built-in neck support. No sooner had I cleared the infield onto the straight way for the next turn than something slammed into us, hard. Our rear end suddenly kicked right, rounds peppering it.

The tires barked when we hit the pavement, and I had to fight to get us back under control. One of the other cars pushed past us on the left, then veered into our driver's side.

The rear of the pack had apparently caught up to us because they shot forward, passing us, pushing us to the side. I slammed the brakes, dropping back behind them as soon as I saw their turret turning in our direction. Staring down the barrel of a live machine gun was really not on my list of things to do today.

No sooner had I floored the accelerator, the first car locked up its wheels, slamming into the second, which slammed on its brakes, causing us to bump into their rear. Luckily the impact was nothing more than a love tap.

I dropped back enough to line up a shot, hoping I had the range right, and tugged at the cable. The light machine gun barked out a three-round burst for each tug of the cable. Rounds peppered the back of the second car, tracers sparking upon impact.

Our car struggled to keep up as the other two vehicles pulled away, but I kept up the burst fire until they were finally out of range. Checking my six, I didn't spot any of the other teams, but there was another thick black cloud of smoke billowing out from near the intersection of the infield.

Tracer fire preceded the cars ahead of us as they came out of the turn and onto the straight-away into the infield. The lead car swerved, dodging fire from the car behind. Skidding sideways, they turned, firing on the second car as they continued in a wide sweeping arc, attempting to get behind them.

Adjusting course, I scored at the last set of markers before turning into the infield. The second car had slowed down considerably, jerking and jinking around the newly raised obstacles in the infield.

Hitting the ramp sideways, the first car skidded out of control. I could have sworn I saw one of their team members go flying out of the passenger's window when their tires caught on the packed earth and the car started to tumble.

Rounding the first barrier as I neared the intersection, I could see that three of the other cars had gotten into a pileup of crossing paths. With the core of the power packs fueling the fires, it wouldn't be long before the entirety of the vehicles was nothing more than a molten puddle of slag.

Swinging my path around the ramp opposite the fire, I limped my beaten and bruised hatchback toward the finish line.

It wasn't the worst match I'd ever had by a long shot but still wasn't one of my favorites. Maybe I had at least scored enough points to rate one of the lower pots on this match.

Chapter 6

"Can you believe that match, Alex?"

"The outcome of this afternoon's autoduel defies the odds of probability, Chuck. Really, what could the odds possibly be for a match that is designated as nonlethal, to turn into a raging inferno of destruction?"

"I couldn't tell you exact numbers Alex, but I'd say it was near to impossible."

"Well, why don't you go ahead and do a quick recap of the match for those viewers just tuning in so they know exactly what we're talking about, Chuck."

"In the latest amateur doubles match held this afternoon here at the Atlanta Motor Speedway, eight teams faced off in an Aces and Eights competition. Designated as a non-lethal competition, the goal of this race was to score as many points as possible by the end of five laps while avoiding disabling fire from the other teams."

"That's what was supposed to happen, Chuck. But how about you tell our viewers what *did* happen in today's extraordinary match."

Chuck Spiegel turned to his co-host, "I was just getting to that part, Alex," he said, annoyance thickly layered in his tone before turning back to face the camera. "The match turned into the farthest thing from non-lethal. It turned into a hellish inferno of death and destruction. Of the sixteen Autoduellist entering into the race, only four walked away with their lives intact."

"I sure hope they had their Gold Cross accounts paid up in full," Chuck added.

"No doubt, Chuck. And to top it all off, this has turned out to be one of the strangest conspiracies in racing history to emerge in decades, placing blame for the carnage on none other than Ricky 'The Ripper' Turner. Message boards across the net have been inundated with speculation that he and his gunner, Darius 'The Dealer' Graves, entered this match, and were out for blood against the autoduelling community. Unfortunately, Mister Graves could not be questioned because he lost his life during the course of this competition."

"That's right, Alex. A number of online communities have speculated that it all stemmed out of a need for retribution for Ricky Turner's previous incident with The Vixens race team."

"It is so hard to tell these days what might set someone off or what they might do when they are. Only time will tell, Chuck."

"So true, Alex. So true. And in other news, for those of you keeping up with the rookie circuits, two Rookie Autoduellists out of West Palm Beach are being highlighted in this week's rookie spotlight. Considered as this season's fastest up-and-coming race team, Luca Tassin and Jimmy Visoth are projected to decimate the competition in the South Florida race circuit."

"Especially with the backing of his uncle, Oscar Visoth of the Ironworks corporation," Chuck added.

"No doubt, Chuck. No doubt. Don't forget to tune in tomorrow night for the highlights of that race, folks. You won't want to miss all of the action."

It had been one hell of an extra long night. I was beyond tired and just wanted a hot shower and my bed. Parts of me that I never knew existed ached with even the slightest of movements. It was well after two in the morning when I rolled back into Henry's garage to park Fergie and drop off the keys after the awards ceremonies.

After it was all said and done and the bonus points for extraordinary moves and memorable moments had been allocated, I'd managed to come in third place. Darius, unfortunately, wasn't able to share in the limelight. The Emergency Medical Technicians speculated that one of his numerous impacts to the head had been enough to crush three vertebrae in his neck and sever his spinal cord with the shards. It really sucked that he couldn't be up there with me to accept the medal. Apparently, the crowds loved it when he climbed out of the window and managed to disable the car behind us with his hand cannon.

The feds and the officials at the AADA on the other hand didn't like it one bit. Considering the spike in ratings, and the fact that Darius had passed away, they played it off as a gunner going rogue and acquitted me of all disqualifying charges.

And while the medal was nice, it was probably a brass-plated chunk of steel worth about five bucks in scrap value. Winning a pot worth a few thousand dollars would have been much nicer to come home with.

Since Dave and Buster had ridden along with Darius to the arena, they had to wait for me to finish up and ride back with me.

After parking Fergie in her bay, Dave plugged her in to charge while I secured the garage door. I really didn't feel like trying to cook something when I got back to my apartment, but I needed to get something in my stomach. Dave suggested some leftover sandwich stuff he'd gotten earlier in the week, but considering Dave's own luck with leftovers, I passed and decided that something from the vending machine would be good enough to drop down my gullet.

I exited the back of the bay into the hallway that connected to the office and heard a snore loud enough to rattle windows. It echoed along the dark, unfinished halfway from behind the break room door.

I stopped and looked back at Dave. "What the hell is Henry doing here?"

"Maybe he hung around to watch the race and drank a few too many?" Dave guessed then looked down at Buster. "What do you think?"

Buster grumbled, tilting his head sideways he sniffed in the direction of the noise.

Dave reached down and gave Buster a scratch across his back. "You don't know either, do ya, buddy?"

Quietly I opened the door to the break room and the decibel level of the snoring seemed to double. When I looked back at Dave he mumbled *what the hell* under his breath. I motioned for him to be quiet and follow, then stepped through the doorway.

There was Henry, kicked back in his recliner, feet up, and snoring away. I'd made it three steps into the room when a floorboard creaked and Buster started barking his head off.

Henry immediately came to life, pushing himself up in his recliner. "What the hell is going on," Henry shouted, fighting to close the foot of the recliner.

"It's just us, Henry," I said. Dave flipped on the lights, and Henry recoiled like a vampire from the sun.

"Did you two lug nuts really have to go and do that? I was sleeping!"

"Then go home and sleep." Dave dropped Buster on the break room sofa and made his way to the fridge.

Henry kicked the foot of the recliner out and leaned back. "Nah, I'd rather not. This is just as good. And at least if I'm here, I don't have to hear the old bat nag at me for being out at all hours of the night."

Dave grabbed a beer out of the fridge and popped the top. "Either of you want anything from in here?"

Henry picked up a can of beer from his side table and swirled it, checking to see what was left. "Yeah, sure. Grab me another one," he said, then knocked back the can, chugging what was left of the beer in two gulps. He let out a wet burp, crushed the can in his hands, and threw it toward Dave. "So how did it go tonight?"

"At this rate, I'll never get out from under Johnny B's contract."

"That sure doesn't sound too good."

Dave let out a chuckle.

I grabbed a candy bar out of the vending machine, then pulled up a chair. No sooner had Dave handed Henry another beer and plopped on the couch than Buster had jumped up on the couch with him, grumbling for attention.

"God dang that dog sure as hell is ugly."

"Eh," Dave said, shrugging. "I think he's starting to grow on me."

Henry took a long pull off his beer and turned on the vid display. Flipping through the channels he stopped on a rerun of the local 'AADA Tonight!.'

The cameras flashed from an opening race montage to the top three winners of the Atlanta Motor Speedway awards ceremony from different angles, then focused in on Ricky.

"Ricky 'The Ripper' Turner has lost yet another gunner, folks," the announcer said before the view shifted back to the studio. "He just hasn't had any luck with teammates, has he?"

"No, he hasn't, Chuck. And considering his recent streak of bad luck, he's going to be hard-pressed to find anyone who would want to team up with him again."

"You are so right, Alex. I know I wouldn't want to climb into the car with him."

"It wouldn't be the first time an Autoduellist was perpetually stuck in the amateur singles class."

"At least the cameras love your ugly ass," Henry commented. "That's something in the grand scheme if you're going to make good in the business."

"And they're talking about you," Dave added.

"But it isn't good talk." I motioned toward the screen. "They named me 'The Ripper' for frack's sake."

Dave let out a long burp. "You can't beat free publicity, man. It might even be enough to get you noticed by a real sponsor." He held his beer up in salute and winked at me before taking another swig.

Buster whimpered and let out a low grumbly bark.

"What," Dave asked. "You want a drink?" Buster barked, then licked his chops. Shrugging, Dave held the can up to Buster's lips and tipped it just enough for him to taste it.

"Just keep at it kid," Henry continued. "If this is something you really want, you can't just quit. You have to keep working at it and push through those doubts. It'll eventually pay off, and you can get out from under your daddy's debts."

Considering the contract issue I had with Johnny B, quitting wasn't exactly an option. He'd just have a new copy made and tack on the cost of another reboot for me to work off. But neither Henry nor Dave knew anything about that yet. I'd finished paying off my father's medical debts more than a few races ago and just kept going cause I loved being behind the wheel.

I didn't really know if I wanted to tell them or not. To be honest, I hadn't really taken the time to think about it one way or the other. But letting them think that Dad's medical debt was a lot worse than it was would work for now.

"Calling all racers!" blared out from the vid with speeding guitar riffs loud enough that Henry spit out his beer at the sudden excitement.

"Dammit all to hell!" he fumbled for the remote. Why in the hell do they have to do that? I hate when they do this crap!"

"Herolutions, along with Uncle Albert's and top tech industry companies from across the country have partnered up for a new and exciting event just in time for the fall broadcast season! With a $15,000,000 pot at stake, the competition is expected to be fierce!

"This will be a no holds barred event. Teams will be allowed to enter any vehicle without limits of loadout as long as it can qualify as a Division 6 vehicle.

"Selected teams will race as a pack from Atlanta to predesignated checkpoints, earning points and trying to stay alive in the latest cross-country rally race, *Dead Man's Run!* Teams will compete against packs from other starting cities to complete the *Final Challenge.*

"All interested race teams should contact their local AADA office immediately to apply.

"Don't wait!

"Applications are filling up fast! Don't be left in the pits!

"Call now!"

Dave enthusiastically grunted and pointed at the vid screen. "Hey, Ricky! Maybe you ought to sign up for that one?"

"It'd sure as hell knock out any debts a man owed," Henry added.

"Yeah, it would. And then some…"

Chapter 7

I'd hardly slept after getting back to my apartment. The thought of getting free from the contract with Johnny B and back to enjoying myself in the arena kept the evil mind squirrels chittering all night long. So I pulled up the official rules for the Dead Man's Run road rally, reading as much of the fine print this time as I possibly could.

It was a simple cut-and-dried event, only that it took place over a span of almost two weeks across major highways and interstates instead of in a closed arena. It did state that there would be standard challenges held in the host city's arena of choice to add another level of engagement for the viewers at home as well.

It was a *lot* of money. And no doubt that it would be enough to pay off Johnny and to set me up as a professional driver. So as morning brightened the horizon, I clicked send and submitted my team's application as an independent entity without a sponsor. Knowing how most of these special events went, bringing in the big named pros and such, I didn't expect much to come from it, but it sure as hell doesn't hurt trying.

I figured that it wasn't exactly Dave's fault for Darius being just a little bit on the side of psycho, so I decided he might be my best chance to find someone else willing to be my gunner for this event if anyone was willing to climb in the cab with me.

I found Dave under the hood in Fergie's bay, ratcheting away on something. He bent a thick gauge wire around in a spring-like coil. Sparks flew out of the compartment and Dave jerked from the electrical arc when he touched the wire to a grounding lug.

"Fracking stupid engineers," he yelled, throwing a wrench across the bay.

Buster grumbled at Dave, stretched, and rolled, laying on his back.

"You know Henry isn't going to replace your tools if you break them." He glared at me for a long moment before diving back under the hood. "What did *you* think of the Dead Man's Run?"

He opened a small electrical box and removed a series of fuses. "Go ahead. I'd like to see you bite me now," he said to Fergie. Wiping his hands on a red rag he'd pulled from his pocket he turned back to me.

"To be honest," he laughed, "it's a lot of fracking money."

"Do you think there's a chance I'd qualify?"

Dave shrugged. "I dunno."

"But do you think there's even the slightest of a possibility?"

"It's possible, I think." He nodded. "We know that when they do these special events it's more of a popularity contest than anything else. I'd guess that either the ratings are down or they're trying to hook the next generation of viewers with something a little different. So, they'll want showmen, drama queens, and any others that will gain them viewers and boost the ratings. Doubt they'll take just any random teams. Why…?" He asked.

"Because I filled out the application this morning and submitted it."

"Oh…," Dave said and dropped back under the hood once again. "You know that was a team event, not a single-driver event."

"Yeah, that's kinda why I was looking for you. I'm going to need to find someone willing to team up and be my gunner. And, I'll need a car that can make a cross-country trip."

He finished tightening the bolts under the hood and replaced the fuses before closing Fergie's hood. "Okay. I'm listening."

"Do you know anyone else who might be interested in gunning for me for a cut of the prize money?"

Dave nodded and leaned against Fergie's fender. He sucked in a deep breath when he came out of his deep thought and looked up at me. "Yeah, I think I might know someone willing to jump on board with *'The Ripper'*."

I was really starting to hate that name. But it honestly might be just what I needed to be selected.

"Would you mind finding out for me? I don't have much, but I can toss a little finder's fee your way." I pulled out my wallet and handed Dave a $100. "I know it isn't much, but it's at least something. What kind of beer do you prefer?"

"Cold"

"Cold beer I can do. Anything else?"

He shook his head. "Nope. Nothing that I can think of."

"Well, if I get accepted and your guy is in, that just leaves finding a car to use." Dave shifted uncomfortably for a moment, tapping out a beat on the sides of his legs.

"I might have something that'll work. You got a few minutes?"

"Yeah. I guess. I was getting ready to go out on my route."

"Well…Henry went to deliver some parts, so come on back to my place for a minute. I've got something you might want to see."

I followed Dave through the stacks of junk cars, rotting appliances, and miscellaneous detritus to the back of the property. Dave explained that Henry had turned an old barn into his own personal storage facility for the things he wanted to hold onto.

When we came around the last bend, it looked like something out of the grim dark movie set of a horror vid. The place looked ancient. Like one of those old country barns that were supposed to be painted red. This one didn't look like it had ever had the first drop of paint on it and was probably older than anything else in the junkyard with its rusted tin roof and graying wood walls.

"You really live back here?"

"Yeah, man." Dave chuckled. "It's great. No one bothers me, and Henry doesn't charge me rent since I'm back here guarding his retirement fund."

"That's nice of the old curmudgeon, at least."

Dave fumbled with a wad of keys and unlocked the three padlocks installed on a smaller personnel door built into the larger double barn doors. With the click of the last lock, creaky rusted hinges popped and squealed when he pulled open the door.

Buster barked and dashed through the opening, sniffing at everything.

"After you," he said, motioning with a bow and horribly executed flourish. A mixed scent of old oil, polishing compound, and stale beer struck me in the face like a sack full of bricks when I stepped through the rough lumber door. It was seriously dark inside. I half expected it to look like a creepy horror setting inside, with rays of light seeping through cracks in the walls, highlighting the decades of dust motes trapped inside. It was just the opposite. Very little light seeped through making it hard to see, especially after Dave pulled the door closed behind us.

"One sec. Let me get the lights."

He stepped to the side, fumbling around with what sounded like a metal box. Then the lights burned with that orange glow of warming incandescents. What he'd done was step to the side to screw in an ancient fuse into a panel mounted near the door.

Down the center of the structure was a long corridor that ran the length of the building and ended at another set of double barn doors similar to the ones we'd just passed through. Along the middle sat a large tarp-covered something blocking the path. To either side along the length of the building were what looked like horse stalls. The first four such stalls to the left held other large covered somethings.

"I'd like you to meet Henry's mistresses," Dave said playfully, then chuckled. "His grump of an old lady gets so pissed that he spends more time in here than he does with her. Can't say that I blame him any. When she gets on a roll, no one wants to be around."

He motioned off to our left in the first stall and pulled away a tarp made of a soft cloth. Continuing from stall to stall doing the same as he rattled off the names. "Meet Aileen, Carlota, Cherrie, and, Salina."

The stunning beauty of what sat parked in the stalls was almost beyond words. "Aileen," Dave started to explain, was Henry's pride and joy. If any man had ever had an affair with a vehicle, it would be Henry and Aileen. She is a 1956 Ford pickup that he pieced together a little at a time, scrounging every originally manufactured piece, no aftermarket parts at all.

Then there was Carlota. A 1972 Plymouth Duster with the original 340 cubic inch LA series V8 in a beautiful midnight black with a golden hood, roof, and racing stripes.

Cherrie was a 1966 Lamborghini Miura in a deep dark cherry red that drew the eyes to the point of being mesmerizing to the weak-willed onlooker. Myself included.

Then there was Salina. Dark, mysterious, and masculine. She was a 1987 Chevy Silverado step side 4x4 in charcoal gray. According to Dave, Salina even had the original numbers matching 454 cubic inch big block she'd rolled out of the factory with.

"Okay, so what was the point in showing me those? Henry isn't going to let me use one of his collection."

"That was just to show off something cool that you don't see every day," he said then continued toward the mounded tarp at the other end of the barn. "Now, for what we really came here to see. She isn't much, but I've been piecing her together bit by bit from salvaged parts as things come into the junkyard. Henry's never minded me snagging a little something here or there for myself since I'm on call twenty-four-seven and all."

When he pulled away the heavy canvas tarp, I was stunned?... No that wasn't the word. More like, confused.

Yeah, that's the word. Confused. It hurt my eyes to even attempt to comprehend the meshed-together lines of the monstrosity. It looked like a meld of about three different supercars from the last forty years that had been manhandled and forced into the somewhat smoothed-out body lines thanks to pounds upon pounds of welds and bondo, then mounted onto a lifted off-road chassis.

"What in the hell is that," I asked. My brain ached and sort of felt numb all at the same time. It felt like what I imagined it would be like to be one of those mouth breathers that lived in the trailer park who huffed paint fumes all day.

"Eh," Dave grunted. "Be respectful in the presence of a lady. Besides, you might hurt her feelings." Dave ran his hand along the top edge of the front fender, then scratched at a small imperfection in his bodywork. "Her name is Sally."

"Why does *it* hurt my eyes?"

"Because *her* beauty is unmatched by anything in heaven or on earth."

"I was thinking something more along the lines of unholy and not meant for this reality."

"Don't talk about Sally like that. She's sensitive."

"Sensitive, my ass. Are you sure the hood isn't going to pop open and gobble me up as soon as I get too close? *It* is hideous."

Dave lazily slid his hands into his pockets and glared at me with one of the smoldering looks. "Are you interested or not? We can go back to you needing a gunner *and* a car and Sally can chill here with me until I find a buyer for her."

Buster hopped, bouncing his front paws against the driver's door while doing that grumbly bark of his.

"You want to go for a ride, little buddy?" Dave opened the driver's door and Buster hopped right in, barely able to make the jump into the lifted chassis. He darted from the front to the back to the passenger seat where he proceeded to spin in place and plop his rear, making himself comfortable.

"Yeah…" I moaned, then I stepped over to the passenger side and opened the door, sliding in against Buster's protestations of my invasion. The dash was a crazy mix of buttons and switches like something out of a spy movie with two additional screens mounted at the center of the dash and a gunners station with a jump seat installed laterally where the back seat should have been. I caught myself letting out a long whistle at the setup. "But does she run?"

Dave smiled, letting out a condescending grunt, "She shakes the ground." He flipped three switches vertically mounted to the dash just behind the steering wheel, waited a moment, then hit the push button start.

Sally rumbled to life. Thick black smoke billowed out of the exhaust initially, clearing up as she settled into a steady idle clatter. Dave grinned wide and revved the engine, causing Sally to sound like a roaring beast.

I sat there, frozen. Dave wasn't lying. Did she ever shake the ground. Something about the guttural reverberation of Sally's revving engine awakened a bestial desire within me. I wanted nothing more than to be behind her wheel with the pedal buried to the floor.

"She isn't a torque hog, nor will she take the fastest of the pack, but she'll get you there. Her gearing is good for a wide range of use, but with the manual transmission, doubler transfer case and an aggressive tread on the thirty-three-inch hardened tires and run-flat wheels, we'll be able to creep out of nearly any situation."

"Okay, so then what unholy beast have you managed to strap under the hood?"

"A refurbished military grade turbo-charged all-fuel power plant with gaseous secondary injectors. Hell, as long as it'll burn under compression and you can get it into the combustion chamber, it'll work as fuel." Dave climbed out and walked toward the front of the rig before kicking the nose. "Not much is going to stop her from pushing her way through with this cattle catcher push bar either. Sally has two forward-firing heavy machine guns mounted to the hood. One forward-firing rocket pod mounted to the roof," he said pointing. "Mini rocket launchers mounted to either door on pivot mounts that can fire at anything within roughly a one hundred and thirty-degree firing arc on either side. I might could get a full one hundred and eighty degrees if I changed out the mounting, but that would take some time to fabricate."

Dave continued around to the rear of the car. "The spare parts rack can double as a junk drop and the flaming oil jet outlet right here," he said, pointing to a nozzle that protruded from under the rear bumper, "will help us keep those pesky tailgaters to a minimum."

"Okay, but what about that," I asked, pointing to the large protrusion from where the rear window should be.

Dave smiled wide. "Saving the best for last, baby. That is a defensive turret I managed to salvage from a wrecked fast-action strike vehicle Henry had won at auction. Three hundred and sixty degrees of mow-down madness are available at the crew's fingertips. It just clears the upper rocket pods, so it can be aimed at anything just ahead of the front bumper or up to seventy-five degrees of upward arc. Plus all weaponry can be controlled from either the driver's seat or the gunner's station."

"Well, what about food, fuel, and other supplies?"

"The trunk is still intact and can hold at least a few bodies worth of stuff. Worst case I can rig up extra cargo netting and just strap it to the outside."

"Is she compliant with AADA rules for the race?"

Dave shrugged. "Maybe…I might have to make a few tweaks once I get the specifics for the rally."

"You know I don't have much to work with. What do you want for her? Or how much to rent her knowing she's going to get shot at and possibly destroyed?"

Dave shuffled a foot on the floor, rubbing at an ancient oil stain with the tip of his boot then shrugged again. "Slide me a little something from the pot when you win."

"What if I don't win?"

"Even if you don't take the main pot, there are other prizes along the way."

I hated something for nothing, even if it were on the promise of payment. Hell, I might not even make it a hundred miles outside of Atlanta before being eliminated. But I didn't really have any other choice. A combat-ready vehicle wouldn't come cheap and time was limited. I held out my hand and Dave eagerly took mine in his to shake.

"Deal."

Chapter 8

"Welcome to all of the viewers just tuning in to the first annual Dead Man's Run road rally! We are here at Sweetwater Creek State Park, the starting point for the Atlanta pack, and the opening ceremonies of the rally are about to begin," Chuck Spigel announced.

"Each of our teams have been supplied with the three primary checkpoints that they must reach in time in order to compete in the final challenge being held in Sturgis, South Dakota. While each pack will be entering the event from a multitude of cities, they will be running the race via different routes, and at times crossing each other's paths. While the primary goal is for each of the packs to reach their designated rally point outside of Sturgis before the final fight, there will be a number of challenges they'll have to overcome beforehand. For the Atalanta pack, each of the teams must first reach Toledo, Ohio no later than seventy-two hours after the start of the race to avoid incurring major points deductions."

"Seventy-two hours seems like much more than they'll need, Alex."

"You would think that, but with the number of roving gangs that raid and pillage the highways of this great nation, our teams may be lucky enough to arrive in time. And remember, Chuck. The teams are not so much in competition with each other as their packs are in competition with the packs sponsored by other major cities. The teams must work together to eliminate threats and to complete challenges in order to score the highest number of points possible in order to win the top prize and be crowned Champions of the Dead Man's run."

"And man, do they ever want to win that prize. Not only does the winning pack split $15,000,000 between the survivors. The team with the highest accumulation of points will also take home an additional $10,000,000 for themselves, $5,000,000 for the second-place winner, and $3,000,000 for the third-place winner. Then to top it all off, each team that survives the final challenge at Sturgis will receive a $1,000,000 bonus for completion of the rally."

"And that isn't even counting the potential bonuses and sponsorships the teams may earn along the way, Alex."

"Now, back to the Atlanta team's course, Chuck. They will have another seventy-two hours to traverse the warzone between Toledo, Ohio and Minneapolis, Minnesota for their second challenge, then seventy-two hours from that for them to go from Minneapolis, Minnesota to Rushville, Nebraska, the Atlanta team's rally and repair point before continuing to Sturgis and the final challenge."

"It's so exciting to be part of history in the making, Alex. I can't wait to see what happens in this race to Sturgis, South Dakota.

"You can say that again, Chuck. Joining us for coverage of today's historic event is Autoduelling legend Devon Varady, better known as TranceRacer and the madman behind the wheel of the Cosmic Eagles race team. He has been selected by the AADA-sanctioned event organizers as the event Overseer, or lead referee who will, when required, convene with a team of his peers who have been hand-selected for this event. If any actions, methods, or outcomes of an Autoduel team are in question for any reason, the Overseer will have the final say.

Welcome back TranceRacer! The Autoduel world has greatly missed you."

TranceRacer's image between the two announcers flickered momentarily before the hologram projection stabilized once again.

"For those of you too young to remember the exploits of the Cosmic Eagles race team, Mister Varady and his partner Mojo retired after a fifteen-year winning streak and never once using their Gold Cross membership."

"Amazing, isn't it, Chuck?"

"It's as insane now as it was then, Alex. So, welcome TranceRacer. Welcome. What have you been doing the last twenty years to stay busy since your retirement?"

"Please," TranceRacer said, nodding to both of the announcers. "You can just call me Devon. It is great to be back. And thank you for having me on. Well, as most of you know, I'm the announcer for the AADA Nationals Championship race circuit as well as I manage TransTank. A small franchise of offensive driving schools for new drivers. You can find our offices in most major cities across the eastern seaboard."

"That's great, Devon. And might I add that I'm a huge fan of your work. I followed every race up until your retirement," Chuck added. "So, what are your thoughts on a rally race of this type in today's racing community?"

"The Dead Man's Run is not your average challenge. There are factors that the average arena duelist will not even consider because they've gotten too comfortable in the way that they operate. The first being, endurance. A road rally race of this magnitude has never been attempted. These teams will need to not only stay vigilant but sustain themselves for days while fighting off roving gangs and unsanctioned autoduellists who are out to make a name for themselves. "

"The highways are not for the faint of heart, that is for sure," Alex said.

Devon chuckled. "No, they are not. What I think is the most amazing part of this event is the sheer number of applications received by the event organizers from all participating cities. Once the announcement went out, the applications began pouring in."

"From the literally thousands of submissions," Chuck interjected, "our dedicated and diligent project members have selected the best of the best, for your viewing pleasure. Assembling each pack of Autoduel teams, ensuring the greatest balance of skills, increasing the potential success rate of each starting pack to complete the rally."

"One possible cause of the flood of submissions," Alex added, "are the incentivized sponsorships being offered to the teams by both local and national businesses alike in each of the host cities. Not only could the teams land a paid Gold Cross account or corporate sponsorships, but if they manage to score enough points in each of the three major legs of the rally, they could walk away earning up to three Aces and Eights Rally badges."

"It is a beautiful badge, no doubt, Chuck. A laughing skull in front of a dead man's hand, three cards showing ace cards, and two cards showing eights."

"Each team selected for the event will earn the permanent right to carry a Dead Man's Run entrant badge on their car, and will be paid $1,000 every time that car participates in any other AADA-recognized event. There are different colors of Dead Man's Run badge, from the gold Winner to the black-bordered Died Trying, but we won't get into all of that right now."

"Those teams not blessed with deep bank accounts or pit crews following behind will need to be resourceful in order to keep their vehicles running and gunning. But then there's nothing stated in the rules that a team can't commandeer a new vehicle after leaving the starting line. The organizers realize how hard this rally will be on teams and their equipment, so as long as a team starts with an AADA-approved vehicle, they can cross the finish line with whatever they so choose.

"The next major challenge these teams are going to face," Devon continued, "will be the need for repairs and resupply between major checkpoints. While each leg of the race is expected to take the packs up to three days, a whole lot can go wrong in the blink of an eye."

"So true, Devon. So true," Alex added. "And that's where sponsors or even viewers can donate to the AADA race account of their favorite team, or consign supply drops that may be delivered to a predetermined location along the projected race path, or air-dropped directly to the team in under an hour for an additional premium fee."

"Which may be what keeps some teams in the race," Chuck continued. "That's why it is important for our teams to remember that good deeds or even extraordinary moments could endear them to the viewers at home. Another aspect to take into account are the cars themselves. While a standard vehicle built for the arena is tough and swift, that doesn't mean it has the days worth of staying power that will be required for this event. I expect that we'll see a wide range of highly modified vehicles to cope with the challenges of a long-distance trek across a lawless, gang-infested country."

"Would you like to introduce us to the ten starting teams from the Atlanta pack, Devon?"

"Gladly. It would be my pleasure." Devon started forward into the cameras. First off, we have Smog and Vision known on the veteran circuit as the Miracle Mutants in their heavily modified Grenadier manufacturing police cruiser, representing Odinetworks."

"These guys also seem to be the fan favorite and are expected to make it all of the way to the final challenge in Sturgis," Alex said.

"Next up," Devon continued, "we have Ruth Lezz and Freya Domme of Queentastic in their modified Crane Industries battle camper."

"As one of the most recent rising stars in the Atlanta specialty circuits," Alex said, "it'll be interesting to see how they do in this long-haul challenge."

"Next up are the bad boys in black," Devon said, jumping back into the flow. "Vincent 'Pretty Boy' Petrone and Sam 'Dozer' Donovan known as the Blackskulls, in

Vlad the Impala, their luxury assault sedan from Kane Industries."

"These guys have never sat right with me, Chuck. There's always been something fishy about them in my opinion."

Chuck laughed. "That might have something to do with their alleged ties to known criminal organizations, Alex. Regardless, they'll be a formidable force to be reckoned with as their track record in the arena proves beyond a shadow of a doubt."

"Next up is Ibis and Rose Budd of team Burning Foxes in their Tiger D drag special from Imperial Motors."

"Their showmanship and stage presence in the arena has been second to none, Alex."

"That it has," Devon said. "And so many don't understand how that aspect of a team can cause their ratings to skyrocket. Next up we have Payne and Razor of Disaster Force in their low and slow luxury sedan that I have a feeling are going to be a dominating force in this event."

"These two have had nothing but a bad rap from the moment they left the American Wrestling Federation after allegations of premeditated murder and arrived on the amateur Autoduel circuit."

"I wonder if they'll pile drive the competition into the dust, Chuck?" Chuck forced out a laugh before Devon could continue.

"Good chance, Alex," Chuck agreed. "A very good chance I think."

Devon looked back up at the camera. "Next on the list is Digger and Blaze, the Rust Brothers who'll be riding along in style in their Tequila Slammer luxury battle wagon.

Followed closely behind by the Booze Reapers, Jane 'Thunder' Cooper and her companion, Bullseye, cruising along in their high-speed Venom street racer that's just as hot as the pair of them."

"With that resting 'I'll rip your head off' look that Jane is so famously known for, I'd hate to see what she looks like when she's truly angry."

"No doubt, Alex."

"Team Inferno," Devon continued, "brings the Ace Vehicles Unlimited battle bus. Between four-time regional winner Chaz 'The Bug' Haimes behind the wheel and Amber 'Grace' Wolfe gunning to eliminate the competition, they'll be a tough pair to compete against. But then again if the Mental Berserkers, Carnage, and Maneater in their Delta Automotive Vanguard II battle van named Van Helsing have anything to say about it, Team thas their work cut out for themselves."

"For the sake of full transparency," Alex broke in, "we should remind our viewing audience that Carnage was only released from his death row sentence yesterday, so that he might compete and carry out his own sentence with dignity and honor in the arena. And for those who have been living under a rock, Carnage was incarcerated for the dismemberment and butchering of Nickolas Schrott, better known as Phase, a fast-tracked amateur that found himself on the wrong field at the end of last season's national championships"

"It really is amazing what strings the organization will pull to give us the most incredible match possible, Chuck."

"It really is, Alex. Back to you Devon."

"The Grim Aces, Trip, and Holeshot in their Indra motors Sedan, and The Born Destroyers, Bingo, and Bash in their classic Acme pickup truck are two of the up-and-coming amateur teams to keep a close eye on. They have been climbing the ranks enough to just barely make the cut."

"But," Alex added, "they managed to make the cut, and that's the important part."

"Yes, it is, Alex." Chuck laughed. "Last on our list, but in no way least is the JunkYard Dawgs, led by none other than the most infamous driver of the season, Ricky 'The Ripper' Turner."

"I'm curious to see who the unlucky or suicidal gunner is that has joined forces with 'The Ripper' this time, Chuck."

"It doesn't list a gunner at all."

"Could 'The Ripper' have decided to go it alone?"

"There isn't anything specific in the rules against it. By the race bylaws, teams of *up* to two members maximum may enter the event, with no exemptions, and no minimums. And, just as surprising as no gunner listed is that he is the only amateur entry to have a sponsor."

"That *is* a surprise, Chuck. Who has that much faith in 'The Ripper's' skills?"

"A local company, Alex. Henry's Spare Parts Emporium and Towing for all of your rare and spare parts needs."

"Well, there you have it, folks," Alex said, turning back to the camera. "I'd like to thank Devon Varady for taking the time to come out and help us to kick off this event. And I'd like to take a moment to thank the lead sponsor for the event. Herolutions, *Supplying all of your security and surveillance needs.* Without them, this rally wouldn't have been possible. And our other diamond-level sponsors, Starlighting, Ridgewares, Bluetronics, Marscast, and Daydream Corporation."

"Good luck to all of our teams," Chuck interjected. "And don't forget that the first thousand viewers that sign up for the premium event package will also receive access to the in-cab camera and microphone feeds."

It was a madhouse when we arrived at Sweetwater Creek State Park. Between racers and their crews, news teams, and fans, it was like parting a sea of bodies as we rolled into the pit area.

I left Dave and Sally in the pits to find registration and get us signed in. It had taken me over an hour to get through the crowds and what felt like an eternity waiting in line before I found somewhere to change into my race suit and armor.

Henry insisted on being my official sponsor for the event. Granted that only amounted to a new race suit and a decal of the same Henry's Garage logo across the hood. I'd honestly wondered if he'd lost it when he first mentioned it, because Henry doesn't give up good coin to anyone that he doesn't have to, but then I realized what sort of exposure he'd be getting out of the deal and the company moto, *for all of your discount spare part needs,* came to mind.

I found Dave under the hood wrenching on something when I made it back to the pits.

"All signed in and ready to go on my end. Is Sally ready to go?"

Dave eased himself back to the ground and took a moment to admire Ricky's outfit. "Good, the suit fits. I used your last set of measurements from before the reboot when I ordered it. I figured you couldn't be that different between before the reboot and now." He chin nodded as he stepped closer, wiping his hands on an already greasy rag. "How does the armor feel? Any pinch points that need to be adjusted?"

"Not really," I responded. "It fits so well that I really can't tell it's even there when I move. Henry really went all out on these. You'd think he actually liked me or something."

"Not really." Dave turned me around and adjusted one of the rear shoulder straps that was still slightly loose. "He just wants you to look pretty for the cameras. Nothing sells parts better than a nice dressed underdog with a shit ton of drama and controversy attached to them." Dave stepped back and raised his right hand. "Swear to God, his words to a tee."

"Sounds about right," I said. Nothing like working for an opportunistic curmudgeon.

"Henry even had me set up a Clutch streaming profile and install a live chat display for your Clutch fans. He's already signed into the stream as FishKiller2000. He'll be easy to spot. I set his comments to an animated red font that you'll be able to spot out of the chat without much trouble."

Dave went back to what he was doing as I started my walkaround. I went to drop my backpack in the driver's seat only to find Buster, in all of his bug-eyed glory sitting in my seat with his tongue lolled out to one side, dressed in a matching race suit sized to fit him.

"Um…Dave?"

"Yeah."

"Why is Buster in a race suit?"

Dave did his, *I really don't give a frack shrug.* "Honestly, I think Henry might be getting close to a mental breakdown or something. He thought that the poor little guy was feeling left out and should be included in what we were doing."

"Probably more like he didn't want to puppy sit while we were out here today," I said, then slid into the driver's seat, displacing Buster to the passenger's side.

"Yeah, that's what I kinda figured too. I've got all of the AADA-supplied cameras and microphones installed. Maybe we'll get lucky and pick up a few sponsors desperate enough to want to look at your ugly mug."

I flipped the three activation switches on the dash and did a quick systems check. Sally didn't have a lot of automation built in, but I'd much rather have Dave look at it now before I hit the road instead of being stranded with no way to fix a problem. That in itself was going to be problematic unless the gunner he'd found could turn a wrench as well as Dave could.

"Climb out of there real quick," Dave said, placing a box he had taken out of the trunk onto Sally's hood. "I've got two weeks' worth of supplies stashed in the back plus five individual gallons of fresh water in different locations of the trunk and cab just in case the armor gives. You also need to go easy on the ammo at first. To keep her legal for the start of the race and give you the best possible chance I had to go light on the ammo carried and what weapons she could have."

Dave must have noticed the worry building in my gut showing on my face because he held up a hand and started to shake his head. "Don't worry, she's AADA legal. I checked the rules. After you get on the road, it's anything goes. You can salvage and install whatever you want out on the road without any penalties. Remember, it's all about the show. They want the viewers to keep tuning in. As long as you keep it interesting, the viewers will."

Dave handed me a gorgeous-looking revolver holstered in a beautifully worked hand-tooled leather holster and gun belt.

"What's with that?" I asked.

"Since Henry decided to *sponsor* us," he said, flexing his fingers in air quotes at the use of the word sponsor, "he wanted to give us the best chance possible. So he pulled a few of his nicer guns out of the safe for us to use. That right there is a true to the title of hand cannon and will do some serious damage. It's an Iny Tribunal revolver. She's heavy, but the lower chamber firing design puts the recoil more in line with your arm and greatly reduces the kick of the .50 caliber armor-piercing rounds."

The warning horn sounded over the giant voice loudspeakers erected near the registration tent. "All racers, report to the rally line!"

"Where's the new gunner," I asked Dave. "We're going to be disqualified if we don't get up to the rally line."

"You know what Ricky? You worry too much." Dave unzipped his coveralls, then removed them, tossing them into the gunner's back seat.

"What the hell are you doing, Dave? You're in your underwear!"

He did his *I couldn't really give a frack* side shrug that got on my nerves. "So? No one is paying attention to anything down here in the pits."

Two camera drones suddenly slid slowly sideways, panning from Dave to Ricky before continuing along pit row. Digging around in the back seat Dave pulled out another set of body armor that he dropped to the ground beside himself and a racing suit that he shook out before sliding it on.

"What the hell are you doing?"

Dave turned and moved, flexing to get the feel of the suit, then slid the armor over his head and cinched down the side straps.

"I'm doing my job, is what. What the hell did you think I was doing?"

I shook my head. "I thought you said you knew a guy."

"Yeah," he said, nodding before pointing his thumb back at himself. "Me."

"You? But…"

"Yeah, man. Why not? I don't see you coming up with any better ideas." Dave climbed into the back, displacing

Buster long enough to get by, he moved the passenger seat back into place. No sooner had he laid a thin lap blanket down for Buster than the ugly little shit jumped back onto the seat, spun in place, and plopped down.

After strapping in, Dave reached back toward the trunk and opened the door to what looked like a fridge, grabbed a beer, popped the top, and took a long swig from the bottle.

"What the hell is that?"

"What?"

"That," I said pointing back toward the door he'd opened.

"Beer fridge," he said then smiled, waggling his eyebrows as he took another long pull from the bottle. Reaching down he picked up his helmet, which had what looked like a camouflage-colored crocheted octopus attached to the top. He slid the helmet over his head and brushed the dangling tentacles out of his face before finishing his beer.

"Why do I have a bad feeling about this?" I climbed in and buckled the five-point harness.

I flipped the three activation switches on the dash then stared into the dash camera and smiled before saying, "Let's shake the ground."

Sally roared to life when I pressed the start button. I slid my helmet on, securing it before tapping at the radio. "Check, check, this is the JunkYard Dawgs."

"Copy that Dawgs, Arena Control has you loud and clear. You are cleared to move to the twelfth pole position at the starting line and go hot on all weapons once in position. Good luck JunkYard Dawgs."

"Copy that Arena Control," I replied, then shifted into first and let the clutch out slowly. Sally roared, belching black smoke as I revved her forward.

"Don't look now, but the puppies are on fire," someone said over the Atlanta Pack radio channel.

I revved her even harder, loading up the exhaust just because I could. More shit talk and banter filled the airwaves as all teams found their designated position at the starting line.

"I should probably check in with Arena Medical before we leave," a gravely female voice said across the comms.

"Why's that," someone else asked.

It was a split second before the first voice chimed back in. "Because it might be smart to get a tetanus shot if I have to look at the JunkYard Jokes any longer."

Dave snatched the handset and keyed the mic. "Don't you folks worry your pretty little heads none," Dave said with a heavy slathering of exaggerated Southern. "We'll be so far ahead that you won't see nothing but our dust."

I turned and looked back at Dave. "Sure you want to do that?"

"Do what?"

"Provoke a pack of rabid killers and racers?"

He shrugged and turned up his beer, finishing it. "I've had to deal with worse before," he said before letting out a wet burp.

Figures it wouldn't be a problem for you, I thought, then brought up the map on the main dash screen and started double-checking the few readouts that we had. The Global Positioning System gave us a drive time of just under twelve hours nonstop from the starting point to the arena in Toledo, Ohio, our first checkpoint. I'd heard that some of the highways out there in the wastelands were pretty rough, especially in the lawless zones, where the law was made by whoever had the biggest guns. If they gave us three days to get to Toledo, then they must have been expecting something to happen in between.

The oily scent of fuel suddenly filled the cab. I looked, but couldn't find any leaks from under the dash.

"Dave, you smell that?"

"Yeah."

I turned back to find him pouring something from a plastic jug into the beer bottle he'd just emptied, before stuffing a premade cork and cloth thing into the opening.

"The hell are you doing?"

"Backup plan."

He opened the fridge and placed it in the small rack in the door and closed it again. He clapped, rubbing his hands together. "Are we ready to get this shindig started or what?"

"Just waiting for the signal."

And of course, that's exactly when the *go* horns blared across the State Park. White smoke billowed out from beneath several of the pack vehicles. The first three shot out from the pack, bumping each other, fighting for that first-place position.

Dave let out a sarcastic chuckling snort. "Idiots."

"I know. We're supposed to be working together, not against each other. I guess old habits from the arena are hard to break."

"I guess," Dave said, then leaned forward, tapping at the GPS map on the screen. "Hey, Ada."

"Yes, Dave," the automated assistant replied.

"You installed Ada?"

"Yeah, why not. I figured she might come in handy, if for nothing else than to have someone besides you to talk to."

"What is the most optimal route to Toledo Ohio, avoiding reported locations of gangs or disturbances?"

"Well," I started, "from here, the fastest way out of town is to take I-285 to the outer defensive walls.

"It'll probably take us up I-75 through the lawless lands of Tennesee and almost the rest of the way, but I'm just curious about what comes up on her route."

"Is I-75 even still viable? I thought sections of it were cratered by bombs back during the war?"

Dave shrugged. "Dunno, that's why we have Ada."

"You of all people should know better than to trust a corporation-controlled software."

The console beeped. "Potential routes and interferences calculated, Dave," the computer voice said in a sultry tone. "What else can I do for you, big boy?"

"That'll be all for now, Ada. Thank you."

I glanced over at the map as much as I could, keeping most of my attention on the road, trying to avoid being run over by our pack mates.

"Looks like there have been lots of activity with tractor-trailer caravans between Atlanta and Chattanooga being hit almost constantly."

"Is there any way around it," I asked, glancing over, the long red line on the map representing the danger zone along I-75 almost glowed compared to the other potential routes.

"It really doesn't look like it. All other viable routes will take us way out of the way to the east or west before we hit Chattanooga."

Well isn't this just going to be a load of fun, I thought.

Chapter 9

"Can you believe the cajones of those highwaymen, Alex? To completely block off all six lanes of traffic is just begging for the national guard to be called out to execute a scorched earth initiative on them. Cartersville may have been abandoned decades ago, but along this stretch of I-75, the teams are barely outside the defensive walls of Atlanta."

"The Miracle Mutants didn't even have a chance against the mines the highwaymen placed in the median between the north and southbound lanes of traffic. That cruiser of theirs may have been heavily armored, but rarely if ever is the undercarriage of most competition vehicles armored to withstand mines."

"No, it doesn't, Alex. I bet more than a few of the teams are reconsidering their load-outs exactly because of that."

"Ohhh," both announcers shouted, flinching at the massive explosion flashing on their monitors.

"And there go the Mental Berzerkers, Chuck."

"They should have thought twice about reducing their rear armor over the extra ammo."

"No doubt, Chuck. No doubt. I don't know if we're seeing the beginning of the end for our Autoduellists."

"What do you mean, Alex?"

"Unless the Autoduellists can break through that barricade, the Dead Man's Run is over."

"Oh, ye of little faith, Alex. You're talking about a pack of professional Autoduellists with a mission. I have no doubt that they'll take out the competition and breakthrough, collecting points all the while."

"I sure hope you're right, Chuck. Because if you aren't, this rally is over before it even got started."

I downshifted into third gear, dumped the clutch, and cut the wheel hard to the left, drifting the long arcing turn to stay on the move. Dave took sure shots where ever he could but didn't just blast away at these guys. He did what he could to conserve ammo. I wasn't the only one with that idea. At least three other pack vehicles had fallen in line with us, drifting right along and firing at the barricade. The fog of war was becoming thick though. Billowing white smoke from the screeching tires began to obscure our view.

The highwaymen had blockaded the roadway with what looked to be whatever they could find. Trucks, cars, heavy equipment, and shipping containers. Hell, I thought I even spotted a few bicycles tossed onto the pile for good measure.

"Yeah, baby," Dave yelled, then let out a whoop. "Get some! That's five bad guys for us. How many points per were they giving us?"

"These guys aren't even in cars, so I don't know. Maybe a point each for bad guys on foot?"

"Then make up for it with some of your fancy driving," Dave said, letting out an excited chuckle. "Is my boom boom too much for you big babies?" he said in a sarcastic baby tone. "You asshats should have really reconsidered staying in bed this morning."

Rockets slammed into one of the weaker spots in the barricade where only a small sedan with other bits of junk piled on top of it blocked the road. I cut the wheel hard to the right, shifting our drift and swinging our tail around for another pass. I watched two more bad guys shake and tumble from the top of the barricade in time with the rat-a-tat-tat of Dave's burst fire.

A massive boom rocked the air around us. Team Inferno in their battle bus had rolled out their big gun, a massive mobile artillery piece mounted to the top left corner of the bus's roof. The van recoiled once more in time to the flash and concussion of the shot, followed by the fiery destruction and removal of the sedan from the blockade.

One vehicle after another turned north and made for the open hole, taking what potshots they could on their way through the opening. I brought us around, following behind the Blackskulls and team Queentatstic.

"Hey," Dave shouted. "Hold up, man!"

I looked back, confused at what was going on.

"I said, stop!"

I slammed the brakes, skidding Sally to a complete stop. Buster yelped, sliding from the seat into the passenger side floorboard.

"What the hell are we stopping for?"

Rounds plinked off of our passenger fender.

Dave turned back to the turret controls. "Hold that thought." Three bursts pounded out quickly from overhead before he released his seat harness and pushed the passenger seat forward.

"Where the hell are you going? The rest of the pack are getting ahead of us."

"Salvage," was the only thing he said before climbing out and sprinting toward what was left of the Mental Berzerkers combat van.

Buster grunted. When I looked down at him he licked his nose and started to do that nervous dog panting thing of his.

"I know. I'd rather be on the move too. It's better than being a sitting target." Two handgun rounds rang out from the direction Dave had gone. Before I could unbuckle and climb out, I saw Dave dragging the body of a highwayman from the barricade to the ground before searching him. He stuffed everything from the dead man's pockets into a sack he pulled from a cargo pocket on his right leg.

I climbed out and hurried over to what was left of the Miracle Mutants' modified police cruiser. It had come to a smoldering stop on the pavement in the northbound lane. The rear passenger quarter panel was a tangled mess of scorched metal. The previously mirror-like finish of the candy apple red paint had been flash burned across the passenger side by the incendiary mines they'd struck.

As I neared, I could hear a gasping wheeze over the tinking sound of cooling metal. I started forward then froze in place, the thought of one of the mutants waiting to take down the competition flashed through my mind.

Drawing my revolver I pulled the hammer back and approached the passenger door slowly, sidestepping to the right till the driver came into view.

She'd managed to remove her helmet. Her shoulders rose and fell with each ragged and labored breath. Blood soaked her bright neon green mohawk from what looked like a gash across the crown of her head.

Continuing around the front of the car I could see the scorched and mangled remains of the gunner who was leaning back in what was left of the passenger seat. I continued around to the driver's door, lowering my weapon, I decocked and holstered it.

She was banged up something awful. Not only had shrapnel made it through her helmet, but it also looked like she leaned onto the center console because her right side had been shredded by shrapnel from the mines. From this perspective, I could see a gaping hole in the rear floorboard of the passenger side of their car. I could only guess that more than a few pieces had torn into her and punctured a lung or worse.

Glancing around, I spotted Dave removing ammo cans from the back of the Mental Berzerkers van. "Dave!"

"Kinda busy right now," he yelled back to me.

"We've got a problem."

He loaded the ammo cans into Sally's trunk and hurried over.

"What?"

I pointed at the driver as he rushed over. "She's still alive."

"Oh… Sucks to be her," he said, opening the driver's door and leaning down to examine the driver before rifling through her pockets.

"Dude!" I pulled him out of the car and pushed him away.

"What the hell was that for, Ricky?"

"What do we do?"

"Exactly what I was already doing. We take what we need and roll on."

He started to step past me but I blocked him, placing my hand on his chest. "But what about her?"

"Please…"

That's when we both turned at the sound of her plea. Her voice was a weakly whispered rasp. She reached out from the opened door with a bloody, shaking hand and pleaded again in that almost inaudible whisper. "Help."

"What do we do about her?"

"Nothing. We aren't field medics." Dave climbed onto the hood, then stepped from the hood to the roof and began removing the turret-mounted machine guns with the ease of an experienced salvage thief.

I stepped back to the door and knelt down, taking her hand in mine. Her fingers were already ice cold to the touch. The blood was sticky where it had started to coagulate. I was way outside my realm with this. Besides the occasional cut or scrape, I'd never dealt with anything major. Do I move her to maybe make her more comfortable? Or would doing that cause more damage and pain? I had no doubt that she wouldn't make it through the night in the shape she was in without some serious medical help.

Leaning in close I spoke softly. "Do you have Gold Cross?" She slowly nodded, wincing in pain at the motion.

I turned to the dash-mounted camera that had been knocked loose from its mounting and sat cockeyed in its cradle. Removing it from the mount I aimed it at myself.

"Someone out there, I don't care who, an announcer, a fan, someone from their family, make sure that they see *all* of the footage leading up to this moment. They need to know what happened. I happen to know that there is nothing fun about the cold emptiness left behind after a reboot."

Pulling my sidearm, I cocked the hammer, stepped back, and aimed the revolver between her eyes. The crack of a smile appeared at the edges of her mouth before she mouthed the words, *thank you*, tears streaming down her blood-caked cheeks.

This was the only way, I told myself, placing my finger on the trigger. This way she wouldn't suffer. There really wasn't any telling how long she might be stuck here if we just left her. It could be hours, days, or even never. Her blue eyes seemed to glow with hope at the prospect of a reprieve.

Her deep blue eyes…

Three rounds popped off in quick succession, pulling me out of the hypnotic stare of those eyes. I turned, glancing behind myself. Dave stood there staring at her, chewing on his lower lip. He holstered his sidearm.

I turned back to her and those once deep blue eyes were now milky and grey.

"What did you do?"

"What you couldn't," Dave said solemnly. He glanced at the driver and then back to me before he turned and picked up a sack from the ground beside him. "Let's get out of here. We need to catch up to the rest of the pack."

He was right. We needed to get moving again. Sitting still was just asking to be an easy target for someone. The rest of the way back to Sally he didn't say much more other than that other than to call Buster back. It was that awkward sort of silence that the longer you wished it would end, the longer it seemed to take.

We buckled in and turned north, hoping to catch up to the rest of the pack preferably sooner than later.

Chapter 10

"You're good with reading people, Chuck. Do you believe that is pain showing on his face? The man may not be showing much outward emotion, but I'm telling you, Ricky The 'Ripper' is torn up inside about it."

"How could anyone in that situation not be upset about it? The arena is one thing, but up close and personal, that's something different entirely."

"But what about Ricky's Gunner? He pulled the trigger like it didn't mean anything to him, and he's been as stoic and unaffected by it as if he were some kind of professional killer."

"Maybe he's just that, Alex. Could The 'Ripper' have hired a professional as his gunner? We don't have any information on this man, other than we've heard Ricky call him by the name of, Dave."

"Could be his actual name, could be a code name. We may never know, folks."

"We may not, Chuck. We may not. As the fan choice favorites for that little encounter after the Cartersville barricade, Ricky and Dave have been racking up bonus points from sponsors and viewers alike."

"They've earned my vote, Alex. Let's just hope these two unlikely heroes can survive crossing the I-75 stretch of the Lawless Lands through the great state of Tennessee. Not only have they lost a number of pack members by this point, but the remaining teams have split up, dividing the pack's strength against any oncoming challenges."

"I have no doubt that this will be an interesting fight to follow, Chuck."

Dave had pulled up an overall map of the east coast after we cleared the barricade to get a better look at the existing boundaries for the Lawless Lands. The encounter we had near Cartersville was maybe ten miles or so south of the border on the map; so with our general routes known to the public, it wasn't a surprise to find a gang of highwaymen set up and waiting for us.

What was a bit of a surprise to me was the lack of resistance we'd encountered over the last sixty or so miles. We were both expecting to find raiders waiting on top of every overpass and hidden behind every tree. But it turned out to be an eerily silent nothing.

At least until we crossed the state line from Georgia into Tennessee. It wasn't hard to spot our pack members pulled over at the old Tennessee welcome center just before the I-24/I-75 split. They were parked alongside a caravan of twelve tractor-trailers surrounded by what looked like several smaller guard vehicles that were parked in a defensive arc around the rigs. I spotted the combat camper of Queentastic and the unmistakable black luxury sedan of the Blackskulls. Parked a little further back from them were The Rust Brothers, The Born Destroyers, and Team Inferno's battle bus.

Dave woke with a snort from his light snooze when I let off the throttle and we started to slow. Rubbing his face, he activated his console and tried to get his bearings.

"What do you think is up?" I asked, pointing at the gathered vehicles as we slowly cruised by the rest stop.

Dave huffed, pulling his cap over his eyes before attempting to get comfortable again. Crossing his arms he leaned back in his seat as far as it would go and squirmed, shifting his shoulders. "Dunno. Might be none of our business either and we could just keep right on going." Buster grumbled, stretched then hopped back into Dave's lap.

"What if they need help?"

Dave pulled the brim of his hat up and glanced out the window over his shoulder before settling back in. "Looks like they have plenty of help to me. The Queens and the mob boys are both there. I'm sure if it's really that bad, someone will come along soon enough to help them with repairs."

I downshifted, turning onto the onramp from the visitors center to the interstate. Dave let out a disapproving groan and sat up, retrieving a fresh bottle of beer from the fridge. "You want one?" he asked, thrusting the bottle forward where I could snag it.

"Thank you, but I'm good right now."

I saw him shrug in the rear view then pop the top and take a long pull from the chilled bottle. "You're loss." He smacked his lips and burped. "Just means more for me I guess."

Buster grumbled and let out a quick whimpering bark.

"Oh, I'm sorry. Did you want some too?"

Buster barked again. His bobbed nub of a tail gyrated with excitement. "Here you go, little buddy." I glanced up into the rearview and saw him pour a little bit into the palm of his cupped hand for Buster to lap up.

"If you two are about done making out, you might want to get ready in case something's up."

"Fine…," Dave groaned, then finished the beer in two long gulps. Tucking the empty bottle into the fridge he shoved Buster back into the front seat before activating the gunner's station.

Easing us forward, I pulled up in front of the Blackskulls' sedan and came to a stop. I easily recognized Vincent 'Pretty Boy' Petrone. I'd been a fan of his and Sam 'Dozer' Donovan since they'd come onto the Autoduel scene two years ago. They were known for their straightforward offense, only defending when they had no other choice.

Vincent started walking over when he'd seen we were pulling up toward them.

"Do we have a problem here," I asked.

"Nope, no problem at all. Ain't that Right, Sam?" Vincent asked over his shoulder to his partner.

"No problems here," Sam parroted.

"Then what's with the caravan?" Dave gruffly asked, interrupting.

Vincent let out a laughing hiss, then pulled the toothpick he'd been chewing on out of his mouth and used it to point toward Dave. "Haven't finished training your *dog* yet, have you?" He laughed, then waggled his bushy black eyebrows. A wide shit-eating grin crossed his face.

I'd managed to head off extra trouble, reflexively holding up an open palm toward Dave before I even heard the click of his harness releasing.

"What's with the caravan," I asked.

Vincent glanced over his shoulder and then turned back to me. "They had…a little breakdown."

"Doesn't explain why you bothered to stop," Dave added.

Vincent leaned in closer, looking past me to Dave with an annoyed glance then looked around at the other vehicles before turning his attention back to me. "I cannot speak for the other members of our illustrious pack, but it is in our best interest," he said, motioning between himself and Sam, "to ensure this caravan of trucks is safely back on the road for the good of…*society*. Those of us present have decided to escort these fine, hard-working long-haul crews as far as our paths will cross since they too are en route to Knoxville, as are the rest of us."

"Vincent, report," a voice said over the speakers from the Blackskulls' car. Sam climbed in and rolled up the windows.

A wide, sharklike grin crossed Vincent's face when he turned back to me. "Business," he said, "I'm sure you understand."

"I think I'm starting to."

The rumor was that these guys worked for one of the more powerful crime families on the eastern seaboard. I smiled back and put Sally in park. "Any idea how long it'll be before they're ready to hit the road?"

"Shouldn't be too long. The sisters," he side nodded toward team Queentastic's combat camper, "were on the job and didn't think it would take much more than an hour. That was also three hours ago." He shrugged. "So, who knows? All's I know for sure, is that if I'm here, and those rigs don't get to get to where they're supposed to be, I might as well drive off a cliff now."

"What do you think?" I asked Dave over my shoulder. He stretched his neck, looking over my shoulder toward the interstate. I spotted several wrecks on the shoulder that looked like they'd already been picked clean and one that still smoldered from an engine fire. You never know what someone might leave behind. One man's trash can be another man's treasure.

"If we're going to hang around for a bit, I think I'll see if I can snag something useful from those wrecks over there."

"Sounds like a plan to me." I slid out of the seat and stretched, loosening my sidearm in its holster. Dave didn't wait. He climbed through the passenger side window, taking a small tool bag with him. Buster didn't waste any time either. He hopped out, barking with every bounce as he chased after Dave.

Climbing back into the cab I reached for a beer, popped the top and took a long drink before turning around to face the cameras. A simple message in angry red letters flashed on the Clutch stream From none other than Fishkiller2000.

Get to it already!

"Well thanks for the comment, Fishkiller2000. I appreciate you keeping an eye on us out here in the wild."

I continued talking through the comments, thanking our two other Clutch fans who'd started a pissing contest with Henry about what the best fishing lure was for crappies. If I didn't know better, I'd think he was enjoying himself because it looked like he'd found someone new that he could argue with.

Chapter 11

By the time we'd reached Knoxville, the team chat had blown up with new viewers talking about how the Atlanta packs assistance to the disabled caravan was easily the most humanitarian deed yet in the rally. Apparently, the trucks we'd escorted from the welcome center had been loaded with algae and medical seed stock donated by the city of Mobile Alabama to replenish the city's supplies after a mutated blight ran amok throughout Knoxville's control farms.

After being approved to enter the city's outer defenses, the Blacksulls led the convoy into Big Bill's Dine and Dash, previously known as the Brown Squirrel Furniture warehouse on I-40 heading into downtown. The new owners had kept the huge thirty-seven-foot tall squirrel on the sign outside since it had been a highway icon for over a century and just renamed the joint based on the local's nickname for the Squirrel.

We'd had a few minor scrapes along the way from the rest stop, but nothing that was noteworthy. After ensuring the convoy was good to go, Vincent invited us along to a private dinner arranged by his 'employer' in thanks for helping to escort the caravan safely to Knoxville.

Since we were in the safety of the city and it was already late, the entire pack decided to accept the offer. The Blackskulls led us into downtown where we pulled up into the circular drive of the Volcue, a massive hotel complex, and were directed to park. The way that the front of the building jutted out, each higher level more than the previous, it felt like it loomed overhead, ready to topple over on top of us.

"Catch everyone on the flip side," I said, then waved at the cameras before climbing out. Dave grabbed Buster, tucking him under his arm and we followed close behind Vincent as he led us into the building. The doorman wrinkled his nose at us when we walked past. I guessed he was fighting against his natural urge to toss the riff-raff out on our asses.

No sooner had I turned to thank the doorman for holding the door for us than the broadcast drone following us from our vehicles dropped, crashing against the white marble steps of the entrance. Dave turned at the sound of the crashing drone but before he could get out the first word, Vincent stepped up and interrupted.

"We prefer to keep our affairs private, if you know what I mean." Vincent flashed that shark-like smile again. Both Dave and I nodded before continuing into the lobby at his urging.

The place was amazing, beyond fancy even. The floors and columns of the joint were made of highly polished marble. We were directed to the hotel restaurant where the lights were turned low and lit candles cast eerie shadows around the room. We were seated at a long cloth-covered table with polished silverware wrapped in real cloth napkins. Crystal wine flutes and large candelabras decorated the dark hardwood table. Music thumped, resonating lightly through the large room from somewhere deeper in the building.

Before we were fully seated a flurry of activity rushed at us. Several of us gagged at the overwhelming scents that preceded the wait staff. Servers in starched white uniforms flooded into the room toting platters of what looked like roasted meats, pasta with meat sauces, ears of corn, sausages, platters of meatballs, vegetables, bowls of fruits, baskets of pastries, and fresh loaves of bread. It was a cornucopia of guilty delight beyond anything I had ever seen in my life.

"We sure aren't in Kansas anymore," Dave said as we took our seats at the table. Buster dropped to the floor and sat next to Dave's seat.

Jane 'Thunder' Cooper from the Booze Reapers started to say something, but stuttered, fighting to get her words out. "Th…This must be a dream."

Digger, the Rust Brothers driver pulled his wrap-around sunglasses down to the end of his nose and stared at the steaming foods that floated past him. "Someone pinch me, I think I've died and gone to heaven."

"Gotta be something from one of those novelty algae farms," Digger's partner Blaze added.

"I can assure you all that what you see before you is not designer, novelty, or otherwise fake in any way," Vincent said loudly, interrupting our individual paths of speculation. "What you see before you is truly a wonder and delight. Meat, vegetables, and fruits, fresh from the Family ran farms. Some of which you helped to guard and ensure its delivery. So, on behalf of the Family; please, eat your fill, relax, and enjoy the bounty offered this evening as a token of their appreciation."

Motion to my left caught my attention. Dave had removed the silverware from the rolled napkin and began sliding it into his left sleeve cuff. I placed my hand over his and glared at him, quietly shaking my head.

Sam chuckled. "That was beautiful Vinny." He clapped. "I couldn't have come even close to saying it better myself."

"You've got to be kidding," Ruth Lezz of Queentastic muttered.

"Do I look like I'd lie to you, doll? There's not a speck of algae on the table."

Ruth Lezz mindlessly smacked her lips as she stared at the smorgasbord. The other team members stared at each other in confusion, the anguish of temptation written clearly on their faces.

Dave picked up the glass of wine in front of him, studied it, then shrugged and downed the glass. All of the other team members stared at him, horrific anticipation painted their faces like a crowd waiting to watch a train crash.

"What?" Dave looked around at the concerned faces. "None of it's poisoned."

"How do you know," one of the Queens said.

"A bullet in a back alley where the cameras aren't is a whole hell of a lot cheaper than this spread. Meat is too precious to waste on a last meal." Dave didn't waste any time. He dug in, forking over large chunks of meat, potatoes, corn, and anything else within his reach that would fit on his plate.

"Exactly my thoughts," Sam said before taking his seat. Vincent slid into his seat and immediately started filling his plate, forking over bits of this and that onto his plate.

"What are you's waiting for? Dig in!"

Most followed the Blackskulls' lead. No one really took the time to talk amongst themselves. We were entirely too occupied with making ourselves sick, gorging ourselves on the finest that the Family had to offer.

I watched as Blaze slowly paced, studying the small, intricate details of the furniture, decorations, and more as he worked his way around the room. I caught him tapping at the side of his wrap-around sunglasses before he slowly turned like he was scanning or recording the room.

Freya Domme of team Queentastic anxiously pulled a concealed pistol and placed it on the table in front of her before taking her seat.

"There's no need for that," Vincent said, talking through a mouthful of food. He forcefully dropped his fork and knife into his plate, acting as if he were personally insulted. "We're all friends here."

"I'm not picking up any transmissions at all in here," Blaze announced to the room, continuing his sweep. "It's like the room has been completely sanitized of any transmission sources."

Almost everyone pulled out their phones or activated their wrist computers to confirm that there was no signal at all available in the room.

"What's the deal, Vincent?" I asked. "What's with the signal blackout?"

"As I said before, the people I work for prefer their privacy."

"Uh huh," Digger added. "I'd be willing to bet that it means you want something. So, spill it, Vincent. What is it that the Family wants with us?"

"No," Dave mumbled around a large hunk of meat. He gnawed another long moment and swallowed before continuing. "It isn't even that." He dropped the meat-filled fork and started to refill his glass, but instead took a long swig from the bottle. "It's a matter of what his bosses want." He picked up the hunk of meat again and shook it in Vincent's direction before continuing to gnaw on the morsel where he left off.

"Ha!" Vincent laughed. "Will you get a load of this guy," he said, pointing his thumb in Dave's direction. "You know you got some seriously big cojones my disgustingly barbaric friend. Even though you are also correct." Vincent dabbed gingerly at his mouth with the heavy cloth napkin. "I have been asked by the family to convey their sincerest gratitude for ensuring the supply caravan arrived on time and unharmed." He stood and took a step back so everyone could easily see him.

"This," he said, motioning at the expansive spread on the table, "is a measure of good faith for future luck and endeavors."

Everyone glanced back and forth at each other, a little confused at the words. Dave chewed off another chunk of the marbled meat. "He means something about good health and good business to all."

Sam nodded, sincerity painting his face. "That's it, exactly."

"There's got to be some sort of catch," Freya added, breaking into the conversation.

"No," Vincent defensively argued. "No catch at all. It is literally an eat, drink, and be merry situation. But…"

"Ahh, there it is," Blaze added, excitedly. Vincent continued after a side-eyed glare.

"You've impressed more than a few of the family. Should you wish to move into a more… shall we say, lucrative business in which to utilize your skills, it could be made available for you."

Freya laughed. "You're offering us a job? Well, honey, that's all well and good, but those sorts of ties don't usually come lightly." Her head bobbed side to side, and her finger wagged as she talked.

Vincent shrugged. "That may be so, but the offer is still available should you ever want to take advantage of it."

"Why the serious faces?" Sam shouted. "This is a celebration, already."

"I'll drink to that," Dave mumbled around a mouth full of mashed potatoes. Everyone dove back into their plates and quietly stuffed themselves to the point of being sick. We didn't rush but we didn't take our time either. Then after the main meal, they brought out the desserts. Cakes, pies, puddings, and all sorts of other confectionery delights.

Vincent gave everyone a long moment to let their bellies settle before inquiring about drinks to wash everything down. We were all leery. No one really wanted to trust Vincent, but the food was like something out of a dream come true.

"Trust me." Vincent flashed that shark-like grin at us again. "I have no doubt that you're going to enjoy yourselves tonight. The Cathedral is the only place to be in this town."

Vincent wiped his mouth and tossed his napkin onto the table before buttoning his suit jacket. Reluctantly, we all followed him toward the back of the complex and down a set of winding spiral stairs of marble to the club entrance.

The floor resonated with the electronic beats emanating from within. The neon sign over the entrance bathed the area in a soft-colored glow of pinks and blues. Vincent was nice enough to hold the door open for everyone as we entered and Sam rushed ahead leading us to our tables.

The club was bouncing.

Dancers dressed in flowing silks, glow-in-the-dark body paints, and elaborate costumes bounced and flowed to the hypnotic, trance-inducing beat of the music. Between the thick fog that crept across the dancefloor, illuminated by strobing laser lights, the room looked like a glimpse into some other dimension's demonic hell.

Over half the pack rushed for the stage to join in the fun, Dave included. I slid into the booth next to Vincent, ordered a drink, and watched everyone enjoying themselves.

Vincent leaned over and talked directly into my ear to overcome the noise of the music. "Working for the family isn't as bad as all of you might think it is. There are many benefits to being in the position I have found myself in over the last few years."

"Not what I've heard that goes on," I said, "what I've seen is that you are at the beck and call of these people."

Vincent nodded, smiled, and took a slow sip from the martini he'd ordered. "You aren't wrong," he replied. "But to have the backing of an organization as large and powerful as this is something to be considered and not taken lightly."

My only response was, "No, it isn't something to take lightly." I went back to sipping my drink and watching the others.

"There are other benefits to working for the family as well," he continued. "How about the reassurance of immortality."

I must have been glaring at him because his visual demeanor changed. "If you're talking about a reboot through Gold Cross, then no thank you. Been there, done that, already got the shirt, or haven't you been keeping up with the news?"

He tapped out the beat of the music on the table with his fingertips, almost like a nervous afterthought before leaning in once again. "There are still many benefits to this mutually beneficial arrangement that you do not know about. Most of which, an individual isn't privy to until they become part of the family. To each their own my friend. To each their own," he said, holding up his martini glass in salute.

The rest of the evening went by surprisingly well after that little conversation. I don't know if he hit up anyone else with the offer, but from that point on he at least left me alone.

Chapter 12

"You know, Chuck, too little sleep and too much alcohol could seriously affect the outcome of the race."

"I do, Alex. And you never know, it might not affect them at all. But I'm sure we all know that *one* friend who is miserable for days after an all-nighter…"

"And that might be exactly what we're seeing here, Chuck. The JunkYard Dawg's Gunner looks a little worse for wear in my opinion."

"That he does Alex, that he does. He looks so rough, I'd guess they must have dragged him across the floor of the seediest bar in town. I don't know what he has all over his race suit but it sure does look rank."

"I couldn't imagine the stench coming off of him and being stuck in a car with him for the next 2 days, Chuck. Let's just hope that Ricky the Ripper doesn't have a sensitive nose."

"Oh my God, kill me now," Dave moaned into his folded arms. He'd spent most of the night trying to woon and swoon a few of the other pack members and ended up drinking way too much in the process. He sat up and glanced at the Clutch feed. Flashing in big bright angry red letters was another message from FishKiller2000.

Do something useful already! You're boring my ass off!

"Yeah, yeah." Dave let out a painful-sounding burp and groaned. "I'd like to see you get out here doing something useful."

Laughing and burned emojis tagging Henry's username appeared on the screen. He immediately replied with an emoji middle finger.

"Hey, now," I said, glancing between the chat and the road. "There's no need in having an attitude like that. Be nice or I'll boot everyone of you from the chat feed and start over." I glanced back at Dave and whispered over my shoulder, "I can do that, can't I?"

He shook his head slowly, grimacing with the motion. I handed him a bottle of water from the floorboard. "Drink this. I can't afford to have you as worthless as snow chains on dry pavement. If we run into trouble I need you at your best."

He drank it down, crumpled the bottle, and tossed it back into the floorboard. "Where are we exactly?"

I glanced at the GPS display in the lower section of the center console. "Looks like we're coming up on mile marker ninety-five. Getting close to Lexington. We're roughly fifteen miles out from the city's outer defenses."

"Anything on the radio?" Dave asked. "Either I slept through it or it's been quiet."

"Complete radio silence from the other teams since we left Knoxville. All in all, it hasn't been a half-bad trip so far." The words had barely left my lips when something hard smacked the back of my helmet.

"Don't ever say anything like that or you're going to jinx the shit out of us!" When I glanced back through the rearview mirror, Dave pointed the wrench he must have just hit me with at my reflection in the mirror.

"The hell are you going on about?"

"Don't ever say things are going good. That's a surefire way to piss off the racing gods and ruin our streak of luck."

"When did you get all superstitious?"

"There are certain things in life that you just don't question," Dave said. Anger started creeping into the edges of his voice. "And a jinx, I take almost as seriously as half-price wing night down at Oddities."

Dave really did take his half-price wing night seriously. Any time that they ran a special down at Oddities sports bar, Dave would be the first in line, even if that meant he'd be in line hours before happy hour began. He claimed it was to get the freshest wings possible instead of the soggy, burnt oil-flavored wings that came later in the night. I think he just used it as a convenient excuse to get out of work early, but he'd never admit to it.

Dave snapped his fingers as if an epiphany had just struck him. "Hang onto that thought for one freaking second. I've got just the thing to take care of it." He fished around in the fridge for a moment before handing me a salt shaker.

I noticed a message flashing red among the others in the Clutch feed.

Hit him again! 😂 😂 😂

"You aren't helping things in the slightest, FishKiller." A new stream of emojis flooded the chat feed from Henry's end. He was having entirely too much fun messing around with his new toy. With the way that he normally was, he'd tend to hyperfocus on something shiny and new. I'd be willing to bet that he wasn't getting anything done around the shop, and he'd end up blaming us for that later.

"Here, take the damn thing," Dave groused, waggling the salt shaker at me.

"What am I supposed to do with it?"

"You shake it over your right shoulder to counteract the bad juju."

"Do, what?"

"Just do it and it'll be alright again."

Reluctantly, I humored him and took the salt shaker. "Why do we even have a salt shaker in the car?"

"Tequila shots. But that's for later. For now, shake it over your right shoulder so we can clear the air."

"You'd better not be farting back there again," I teased. "That last one could have made the dead wretch."

"Quit stalling and just do it already."

"Fine," I grumbled, then shook the shaker over my right shoulder.

"Dude!" Dave screamed.

I looked into the rearview mirror and saw him wiping his face. "What?"

"You just shook that into my face ya lug nut."

Lines of flashing red letters took over the Clutch chat.

Watching you two numbskulls is sometimes better than watching my shows.

Keep it up and the networks won't be able to cancel you. The viewers will vote to keep you around for the comic relief.

Brake lights flashed to life ahead. The three pack member vehicles ahead of us started to slow. I picked up the radio mic and keyed the channel.

"Break, break this net. This is the JunkYard Dawgs. What's the slow up?"

Chaz, from team Inferno, responded. "We have a scout drone running ahead of us, and something big is going on at the next exit."

The chat stream doubled in speed, and of course, Henry had to pitch in his two cents.

About damned time something happened.

"Can you tell what's going on?" Vincent from the Blackskulls asked, breaking into the radio chatter.

"I'm not entirely sure," Chaz responded. "Lots of military vehicles are staged alongside the road around the exit. Looks like they are setting up tents in the fields around an old abandoned truck stop."

"About how many do you guesstimate."

Chaz keyed his mic, grunted, then keyed it again. "Quick counting I'd say it's over one hundred soldiers on the ground at minimum."

Vincent keyed the mic, cleared his throat, and spoke, "Two questions. Are these guys in uniform and are there any distinctive markings or anything to identify them with."

"There's a mix of civilian clothing, older camouflage uniforms, and at least half of them are wearing black leather vests, but I can't make out any distinctive markings from this distance," Chaz answered.

"Could be a biker gang," I mumbled to Dave. He nodded in agreement.

Freya from team Queeentastic suddenly broke into the radio chatter. "What sort of vehicles are we talking about here? Trucks, trailers, tanks?"

"Transports mostly," Chaz replied. "A few Armored Personnel Carriers, one main battle tank that I can see, and…Hang on," Chaz said, trailing off. "Frack me. They are setting up field artillery just north of the exit overpass. There are seven full artillery pieces in different stages of setup, and they are huge."

Digger from the Rust Brothers, broke into the channel, walking over someone else's transmission. "What the hell would anyone need artillery pieces for?"

"War…" someone else added.

Dave unstrapped, leaned forward between the seats, and grabbed the mic. "The city is under siege. Lexington is under attack."

"It's the only thing that makes sense," Vincent came back with.

I tapped the brakes, slowing us to what felt like a slow crawl behind the lead vehicles. Dave adjusted the GPS map to get a better look at the surrounding roads. "Any ideas?" I asked.

Dave shook his head in an emphatic, "Nope, not yet."

"Me neither." We slowed to an idling crawl of about fifteen miles per hour before Vincent pulled over along the shoulder of the road.

Dave keyed the mic again. "Chaz, is there any way you can pipe the video feed from your drone to the rest of us?"

"Yeah, actually. Hold on one sec," he responded. A new notification came up on our display for the shared data feed. Dave accepted the invitation and an overhead video view of the encampment appeared over the Clutch chat. "I'm also enabling the pack video chat that I just realized we had available." Video feeds from inside the cabs of the other vehicles appeared at the top of the screen.

"That doesn't look good," Ruth Lezz added.

"No, it doesn't," Sam chimed in. "Hey, Chaz…Can you zoom into the upper left quadrant? Right there where those five guys are standing around the front of the pickup truck."

"Sorry, man. That's the extent of the zoom on the camera."

"Can you get us any closer," I asked, jumping into the line of questions and snide remarks from the rest of the pack.

Chaz blew out a heavy breath. "Maybe? I don't want to get too close and get spotted by any of them. There isn't anything cheap about my drone hardware and I'd hate for one of these guys to shoot it down."

"Hey, Sam," I continued. "What is it about those five guys that stood out?"

Sam scratched at the back of his head like he was holding back a secret that he wasn't supposed to tell anyone.

Dave leaned forward and flicked the camera. "There's a reason you brought it up. We've got less than two days to make it to Toledo, so spill it already."

Sam rubbed his face and looked toward Vincent who spoke up first. "If you know anything about these guys, you better not be holding back or so help me the family will be the least of your worries."

Sam started to open his mouth, then pursed his lips, fighting back the words. Vincent drew back his hand like he was about to backhand Sam. "Out with it!"

Sam threw his hands up in surrender. "Alright, Alright. I'll talk, already."

"What was so special about those five guys around the truck?" I asked.

Reluctant, Sam nodded slowly before he spoke up. "There's a chance that those five guys are part of the Vagabonds, a gang from the lawless region of northern Tennessee and Southern Kentucky. I'm not absolutely certain, but the patch on the backs of their jackets look similar at this distance. They sometimes venture out of their normal area in search of supplies, weapons, and such."

"And, how exactly do you happen to know this?" Ruth Lezz interrupted.

Sam nervously rubbed the back of his neck. "Because I might have ran with them for a few years."

"Alright, then why would they have artillery pieces?"

Sam shook his head, waving his finger at all of us through the camera. "That, I have no idea about. That's something entirely new. I'm not even sure where they would get something like that from."

Dave tapped at the camera again. "Hey, spaz boy. Pull it together for a second. I've been looking over the map and we really don't have many choices to work with here. We can backtrack about thirty-five miles to US Route 150 through Mount Vernon and go the roundabout way around Lexington, side track off State Route 627 or we crash their party and head straight for Lexington."

"Staying on the interstates will be preferred to any backroads," Sam added. "There's a better chance the roads have been maintained somewhat and I'd say less of a chance of running into raiders or roadblocks."

"What are they likely to do if we show up knocking at their back door?" I asked.

Sam wrung his hands nervously. "If it is *them*, they'll shoot first and never ask questions. If you get in the way of what they want, they will eliminate you without question."

"I vote we fight our way through," Jane 'Thunder' Cooper from the Booze Reapers proclaimed. Several others quickly joined in with the same adamant opinion that we should just fight our way through into the city gates if they'd allow it. Someone suggested that if the city wouldn't let us in the main gates we could at least hit the Beltway to get around the city quickly, and out of range of those field artillery pieces.

I muted the mic and then looked back at Dave. "How are we doing on ammo? Do you think we can pull this off?"

Dave scratched at the scruff on his neck and did one of those dad head bob nods. "If we hit hard and fast, just trying to get through we shouldn't have too many problems. If we want to rack up extra points on our way through, it'll all depend on what they have, armament and armor-wise."

The more points we could score the better when it came down to it. It was all part of the race in the end. The grand prize winner was whoever could score the most points and survive to complete the final challenge in Sturgis. It didn't look like these guys were heavily armed, well, besides the field artillery. Standard sidearms, submachine guns, and a few assault rifles, but nothing crazy or out of the ordinary. Our biggest challenge would be the Armored Personnel Carriers. By odds, they'd be armed with .50 caliber machine guns at a minimum, and that was something our armor could easily handle. Well, it could at least handle it for a little while.

I looked down at Buster, nestled in his nest in the passenger seat. "So, what do you think? Should we go for it?"

The ugly little shit licked his lips and barked. His nub of a tail wagged frantically, so much so that I was worried that it would fly off at any moment. I looked back at Dave. "What do you think?"

Dave shrugged his non sequitur side shrug. "I say frack it. Let's do this thing and get it done instead of sitting around here with our thumbs up our butts, jabbering about what we're going to do."

I chuckled at that. "I couldn't have said it more eloquently, Dave."

"Then let's get this show on the road," he said, leaning forward to unmute the mic. "Last one through the blockade is a rotten egg!" Dave slid back into his seat and buckled in. Buster grumbled, then burrowed himself deeper into the nest of blankets.

All of the other pack members peeled out, leaving black trails of rubber on the pavement and clouds of white smoke behind them. Dave slapped the back of my helmet. "What the hell are you waiting on? Let's go!"

Shifting into first, Sally leapt forward when I dumped the clutch and floored the accelerator. Buster scrambled to hold his place in the seat, letting out a low, grumbling growl. Other vehicles blew by us, putting us in last place before we could get up to speed with the rest of the pack.

"Why won't she go any faster?"

"She isn't made for speed, Ricky," Dave answered. "She's got the best possible gearing for a wider range of options so we'd have a better chance at winning this damn thing. She may not be much of the line, but she'll get us there."

I minimized the chat on the display and enlarged the video feed from Team Inferno's drone. Keeping the accelerator buried to the floorboard between hard shifts, Sally barked the tires with each sudden clutch drop. She may not have been the fastest vehicle in the pack, but she still had a good bit of power under the hood.

The soldiers must have heard us coming. The video feed exploded with activity. Men scrambled for their rifles, piling into the back of several pickup trucks that peeled out as soon as they were full. Two APC's parked along the interstate on the north side of the overpass lurched sideways, threatening to overturn as they came around, heading south in our direction.

"Heads up everyone," I shouted. "They know we're coming!"

Sprays of asphalt leapt from the pavement ahead of us. Rounds fired from the APC parked on the south side of the overpass impacted all around us. Sparks exploded from the roof of Queentastic's combat camper. They veered left, nearly crashing into team Inferno who were going full bore trying to pass the rest of the pack.

"These guys mean business," Ruth Lezz shouted. "That hit took out our missile targeting system and penetrated our armor. Whatever they are using, it hits harder than a Mack truck."

"I got them," Bingo from the Born Destroyers shouted. The target lock tone coming through his microphone was almost loud enough to drown him out. The Born Destroyers were all but tailgating team Inferno, nearly pushing them out of the way. Three missiles launched from their roof-mounted rack, impacting the side of the overpass.

The steel girders of the overpass sagged under the weight of the parked APC, concrete shattering from the detonation. A moment later the section of the overpass and APC collapsed, blocking the northbound section of the interstate.

"Oh yeah! Follow me!" Chaz shouted. Team Inferno's battle bus hunkered down and launched forward. A heavy black cloud of smoke billowed from its exhaust.

"No way we can bust through that," Ruth Lezz replied. "I'm going around." Queentastics combat camper veered off the interstate onto the offramp at full speed.

"I'm with the Queens on this one," Vincent said before the Blackskulls sedan veered off the highway following behind the camper.

Chaz let out a battle cry roar as they approached the wrecked APC, coming to a full and sudden stop when they impacted the front corner of the transport. The tail end of team Inferno's battle bus bounced into the air from the impact and full stop of forward momentum. The turret mounted to the top of the APC turned and aimed downward in the direction of the battle bus, unleashing fiery hell at point-blank range.

The drone video feed went black at the same moment a massive fireball blossomed from the remains of the battle bus.

Small arms fire from the direction of the truck stop peppered our column of autoduellists. I cut the wheel hard right, following in behind the rest of the pack that raced away up the off-ramp.

Two more APC's appeared on the road at the top of the ramp and turned to block our path to the west over what was left of the overpass.

"We can't go toe to toe with these guys," Vincent yelled.

Gunfire peppered our side. Buster dropped to the floorboard in the back, hiding under Dave.

"Those rifles won't be a problem," Dave said. "But those APC's must be packing twenty-millimeter cannons or better with the way they chewed up Inferno's battle bus. Bob, weave, do a little jig, or something. Just don't let them get a clean shot at us. Those cannons will tear through us like we were armored with tissue paper."

"It isn't exactly like I planned to sit still. You do what you can to take out some of those targets and leave the driving to me."

No sooner had I finished my words that a burst of rounds tore into the front passenger corner of the roof, spiderweb cracks shot out where the hit shattered the corner of the bulletproof windshield and peeled away the thinner metal of the roof."

"Thought you had the driving under control?" Dave yelled over our own gunfire.

"I do!" Cutting the wheel hard to the right I steered Sally off-road, through the drainage ditch, heading for the parking lot of the old truck stop. "How many points do you suppose field artillery are worth?"

I saw Dave do his shrug thing, even though his attention was on the turret display. "Dunno, but any points are better than nothing."

"That is true. See what you can do."

No sooner had he replied with "yup" that I heard a target lock from our own missile targeting systems. Kicking up dirt as we cut through the grass, I fired our forward machine guns, taking out at least two of the gang members who'd been firing at us. Dave launched four missiles, emptying our main rack. Two hit home to each of the field artillery pieces set up in the abandoned truck stop parking lot. Scoring enough hits on one of their pickup trucks that it ignited, I cut hard left, side sliding our rear across a small line of combatants that worked well as speed bumps.

Explosions off to our left caught my attention. Someone had launched a number of rockets at the APC's before turning east on Kentucky Highway 627. It seemed like everyone in the line took a shot at the APCs as they fled, with little success. Both of the APC's turned, following the pack. I caught a glimpse of a mine dropping out onto the pavement from the rear of the Born Destroyers' pickup as they turned onto the highway, racing away from the armored transports.

"Hey," Dave shouted. "Back us up!"

"What?"

"Back us up. Get us within ten feet of those two artillery pieces."

I cut the wheel hard right, side sliding to the left as I brought Sally around in what amounted to a long arching donut across the broken pavement. Dave continued laying down suppressive fire from our turret while I did the same with our forward-mounted machine guns. Coming to a stop behind both of the artillery pieces, I'd angled it so that both were within our rear firing arc.

"Alright, do whatever you're going to do before those APCs get over here and chew us up."

"Already on it." An oily jet of flames shot out from the rear of the car, coating both of the artillery pieces in a burning, viscous fluid.

"Holy hell," I blurted.

"Exactly!" Dave laughed. "Good luck salvaging either of those!"

I turned to look back at him. "Are you done?"

He nodded. "Yup," then turned his attention back to the turret display. I shifted into first and floored it, sliding our tail around into another of the gang members before straightening out, and heading for the northbound lane of

Kentucky Highway 627. Heavy rounds suddenly pummeled our left rear quarter panel.

"Go faster!" Dave yelled.

"I'm going as fast as Sally will let me."

"Then get better at dodging. Those shots were a bit too close for comfort."

"If you think you can do better, I'll trade with you right now."

Buster grumbled and barked.

"See," Dave continued. "Even Buster knows how stupid of an idea that is."

More rounds clipped our rear corner. I released the latch for the side-mounted rocket rack and aimed it the best I could in the direction of the APC. I didn't expect it to do much more than become a distraction, but as long as it let us get away from that beast, it was worth the spent ammunition.

Smoke roiled off the side of the transport from two rocket impacts. The other two went high and wide, completely missing their target. Maybe if we were lucky they hit something on the other side of the ramp that would score us a few extra points, but I wasn't going to hold my breath.

The APC slowed with each wreck they tried to push out of their way. Veering around the wrecked and burned-out vehicles scattered about the highway, we easily outpaced them and were out of range of those cannons in no time and hauling ass into the unknown.

Chapter 13

"**D**o you think that anyone in the Atlanta pack have realized that they've left one of their own behind, Alex?"

"It's hard to say, Chuck. With the amount of firepower the Vagabonds were packing, I'm honestly surprised that they didn't lose even more team members. Barely a third of the way into this leg of the rally and we're seeing some major repairs going on."

"It makes you wonder if the Atlanta pack will have what it takes to complete the Dead Man's Run or not, Alex." Chuck leaned forward, peering deeper into his video display. "What exactly is he doing?"

"Can we get a different angle," Alex asked. The screen cycled through camera displays to a secondary remote drone that hovered a few feet away from the JunkYard Dawgs passenger side door.

"I think I have seen everything folks," Chuck gasped in amazement. The JunkYard Dawgs gunner is literally repairing the structural damage caused by the Vagabonds using duct tape and baling wire.

Dave pulled the wire stitches tight, then added another layer of duct tape over the laced wire framework. Flicking the stub of a cigarette off into the distance he noticed the camera drone looking at him.

"What? A man can't get some work done without someone watching over his shoulder?" Dave threw the pair of pliers he'd been using to pull the wire tight at the camera drone. "Y'all want a show? I'll give you a show!" He shouted, then immediately turned and dropped his pants, mooning the camera. The video feed shifted to other members of the Atlanta pack, some shook their heads in embarrassment, and others laughed hysterically at the scene.

"And that folks is perfect timing for one of the event's primary sponsors."

"Uncle Al's, the Autoduellists pal…"

We'd pulled it over for repairs once we'd gotten out of what we thought was the range of those artillery pieces, jumping off of Highway 627, and heading eastbound on Interstate 64. It didn't take long before we found ourselves at another abandoned truck stop just outside of what was left of Owingsville, Kentucky. It wasn't much more than a pockmarked smear along the side of the road. Block walls of the main building still stood even though the roof had caved in some time ago. The station's pumps and awning probably hadn't seen servicing in well over a decade or more, not to mention the cracked and broken pavement around the truck stop looked more like a gravel parking lot from years of exposure to the sun and rain.

More than a few of the pack's vehicles had taken minor damage, but nothing compared to the total obliteration that team Inferno suffered. Deep down I hoped that both Chaz and Grace had their Gold Cross accounts paid up in full, but at the same time, I really wouldn't wish that experience on anyone after going through it myself.

"Are you stupid or something?" Vincent yelled at Dave. "That's the worst possible way to pick up a sponsor."

"I don't know," I said, chuckling. "With a view like that, we might manage to pick up a hemorrhoid cream or underwear sponsor."

Digger shook his head, pushing his sunglasses back up to the top of his nose. "Yeah… Sorry, no. Don't think that'll earn you any sponsors or bonus points as a fan favorite." He leaned back against the side of their luxury station wagon.

"More like scare them away," Freya added. She stared at Dave's posterior with a long, contemplative look before turning to me. "You know your friend is certifiable, don't you?"

I shook my head. "Certifiable? I don't understand what you mean."

"What senior Freya here means," Vincent interrupted, "is that he," he pointed toward Dave, "is a certifiable nut job." I guessed that I'd lost all chances at having a poker face since the reboot because Vincent must have been reading the confusion I was feeling on my face. "You know, whack job, schitzo, total bat shit crazy looney toon."

I really wasn't sure how to take that. Dave just zipped up his suit, smiled, and nodded proudly at the cameras. "Stick around and I might show you even more for the after-hours special." He waggled an eyebrow and blew a kiss toward the drone before strutting back to his toolbox.

Stepping closer to the commotion, Ruth Lezz loudly cleared her throat. "So what are we doing? If everyone has finished whatever repairs and reloads they're going to do, might I suggest we get back on the road?"

"But what direction are we going?" I asked. "I don't know about any of you, but Lexington is completely off my list for right now. I'd rather not be in the middle of a city siege."

"Any of the secondary county or state roads should be counted out," Vincent suggested. "Those roads aren't generally maintained by anyone unless the people living along it try to maintain it somewhat."

"Geeze, do I have to think of everything?" Dave packed up his toolbox and dropped it into Sally's trunk then reached through the passenger window, fishing around in the center console. He laid the GPS display on the hood and tapped at the screen. "Ada, please display the fastest route to Toledo, Ohio from our current location." The display flashed, GPS signal lost.

Sam stepped closer to get a better look at the screen. "That's not good."

"No, it isn't," Dave continued. "I'd heard from more than a few convoy truckers I know that out here in the wastes the triangulation towers for GPS are sometimes out of commission, killing that section of the location grid. But luckily, I came prepared." Dave produced a leatherbound case the thickness of a small novel from the cargo pocket on his right leg. Unwrapping the leather thongs that bound it, he unfolded a yellowed and coffee-stained map that covered most of the hood.

Vincent let out a long whistle. "Where did you get that from?"

"I found it in an old rig Henry had picked up for cheap a few years ago. We cannibalized it for parts before selling what we could of the chassis for scrap metal. Damned if it wasn't worth the work we put into it. Most of it was plastic and fiberglass that took me three days to strip away from the good stuff."

"So how exactly does this old ratty map help us out?" Freya asked.

"It'll have most routes already listed depending on the age of it," I said, scanning down to the key in the lower right corner to look for the publication date. Sure enough, there it was in big bold letters just under the distance scales and listing of line designations was the copyright date. American Autoduel Association North American Map, Copyright 2053.

"2053," I announced to the rest.

"How is a nearly twenty-year-old map going to be of any help? Repairs are one thing, but we're sitting ducks here. We need to get moving before someone or something catches up to us."

Jane from the Booze Reapers gasped. "That twenty-year-old map will have nearly every road listed. There haven't been any new road-building projects in the last twenty to thirty years at least. Most road crews are only worried about clearing and maintaining the roads we already have."

"She's probably right," Vincent said. "I don't know for sure, but I honestly don't remember ever seeing any new roads going in anywhere I've ever been."

"So then where should we go, mister genius?" Digger asked.

Everyone gathered, circling around Dave and the front of Sally as he studied the map. "If we keep heading east on I-64 we can pick up I-77 in Charleston, West Virginia, and then head north all the way into Ohio."

"That's if the roads are clear," someone muttered.

"We can either ride that all the way into Cleveland before cutting west on I-90 to Toledo or we can cut west toward Columbus on I-70 and pick up I-75 north in Dayton, but that'll be a long out-of-the-way route. If we need to do it like that, it's one thing. But we'll be better off in the long run if we can avoid that route all together at this point.

Jane, standing at the back of the crowd, looked up toward the east. I looked in the same direction to see what had caught their attention. I could hear the hypnotic hum of tires on the pavement approaching from that direction. The amount of noise from an electric drive system at full power surprised me, especially at this distance.

Surrounded by six smaller vehicles and several motorcycles, three squat, armored tractor-trailers appeared on the interstate heading west. They were all painted white with a royal blue stripe down either side, all the way down to the motorcyclists riding suits and helmets.

"Well, now I think I've seen everything." I said. "Does anyone have any idea of who they might be?"

No one answered, they only shook their heads as they watched the coordinated unit approaching.

"They really don't want to be going that way," Dave said.

"Think they know about the siege?" Ruth Lezz asked.

"Doubtful," I said. "We're too far out in the boonies for a good signal to travel very far."

Dave reached into Sally for the radio and keyed the mic. "Break break one nine. Anyone out there got their ears on? This is the JunkYard Dawgs. Y'all in your pretty little pack heading west on I-64 better listen up. You don't want to go that way. Lexington was under siege from the south when we came through off of I-75."

"We've got you loud and clear JunkYard Dawgs," a pretty-sounding voice said from the radio. "And we know about the siege, that's why we're heading for Lexington."

Dave looked at me with a twisted, what the hell kinda stupid is this look he'd given me on occasion when we'd see some kid trying something obviously and utterly stupid.

Dave started to key the mic and say something then shook off the thought with a giggle to himself before keying the mic. "Sister, I'm sorry to tell you this, but have you recently hit your head against something hard and are in need of medical treatment? You did just say that you're heading for Lexington because they were under siege?"

"Yes," the pretty voice answered. "I know, it's hard to believe, but we were called up to help deal with the issue."

"That happens up here?" I asked, blurting out the words before I realized what I had even said. Dave shrugged, keyed the mic, and repeated my question.

"It sure does. For the better part of twenty years now."

"Usually caravans are on their own down in Georgia," Dave said, getting into the relaxed beat of a normal conversation.

She laughed. "Well, we operate just a little differently up here."

"Who are you guys?"

"Ever heard of the Midville Organization for Neighborhood Defensive Ordinance? MONDOs for short."

"Who hasn't heard of them," Dave shouted into the mic. "They're only some of the most badass militia any town could get. I think I've seen all of the old episodes of Crash City at least a dozen times over."

"Well, we're an offshoot of the MONDOs, known around these parts as the Midville Regulators. Whenever some gang leader or warlord decides to get brave on one of our trade routes, we get called in to…um… tidy up the situation."

"Well, the best of luck to you on that mission. Fair warning, they have armor-piercing rounds and mobile artillery."

"Thanks, Dawgs. Good luck to you too."

"Hey," I jumped in. "Since they are coming from the east, ask them if the roads are clear that way."

"See," Vincent started, "that's what I like to see. Forward-thinking."

Dave keyed the mic again. "While I've got you on the horn, any idea what routes are clear that will take us north?"

"You could always jump onto US Route 23 just outside of Huntington, but that road hasn't been maintained in maybe the last decade. If you keep heading east into Charleston, you'll hit I-77, take that north and you'll find it nearly clear sailing all the way into Akron. We patrol those roads regularly to keep the trade caravans safe. When we came through they were clear, but that can change as quickly as the winds shift in these parts."

"Sounds like a plan. Much appreciated."

"You're very welcome."

"Oh, and whom do I have the pleasure to be speaking with?

"Skye Piper, leader of this little rag-tag band of misfits."

"Pleasure to meet you, Skye," Dave replied in his smoothest voice. "You can either call me David or call me yours. Whichever suits your fancy."

Skye laughed over the airwaves and paused for a moment. "David will do fine, for now."

Whoops and cat calls from the other pack members followed Skye's last transmission.

"But I tell you what, David. If you stop in Midville, stop in at Joe's Oil Pump. It's the best bar and grill in town and tell Joe I sent ya. He'll give you the lowdown on where to find everything in town."

"Sounds like a deal. Next time we meet, drinks are on me."

"That's a deal, good buddy. Regulators out."

Dave turned back to the rest of us with what had to be the smuggest look I'd ever seen cross his face.

"Don't none of you look at me like that. You know you're just jealous of my suave moves." He licked the tip of his pinky and forefingers then smoothed out his eyebrows. Buster barked and grumbled. Dave turned to look at the bug-eyed terrier. "You know what I'm talking about, don't ya?" Excited, Buster started licking Dave's face, grumbling with each stroke because Dave started licking him back.

I turned awkwardly to the others. "And with that, it's probably time we got back on the road and put some miles behind us." Everyone nodded in agreement and quickly headed back to their own vehicles.

Chapter 14

"Tell me, Devon, in all of your travels, have you ever seen a section of the countryside so devoid of traffic or population?"

The veteran racer scratched at the back of his head, momentarily contemplating the question. "In all honesty," he began, "I believe the most desolate area I have ever raced in would have been between two events. The first one being the Death Valley Ralleycross, and the second, the Andros Arctic Crossing. Both were desolate and devoid of anything we'd recognize or consider to be living. Either to the extreme of hot and cold, neither pleasant nor enjoyable, but we completed them nonetheless."

"That is something, isn't it Chuck?"

"It is Alex. And maybe that's something that has been lost in the sport of Autoduelling. Arena battles are one thing, but the sport has almost exclusively shifted over to that format. No longer are there the long-distance road rallies of yesteryear."

"The Deadman's Run may just be the turning point of that, Chuck. The ratings and viewership numbers across the board have skyrocketed since the beginning of the race."

"If that's the case, gentlemen," Devon glanced at both of the announcers on either side of him before looking dead forward into the camera. "May the gods of racers and racing have mercy on your souls."

Chuck Spigel and Alex Diaz both forced out nervous chuckles before Devon's holographic image blinked out of existence between the two of them.

"Speaking of traffic, Chuck, our forward scout drone for the Atalanta pack is picking up some activity just across the Kanawha River near what used to be Saint Albans West Virginia."

"Could our drought of action finally be over, Alex?"

"I sure hope so, Chuck. If we don't see some action soon, the viewers might end up tuning into the Combat Crocheting tournaments over on UDN channel five."

"Good god, that would be too horrible to even contemplate, Alex."

"Let's hope this activity pans out. It looks like we have a small pack of amateur…. No, wait, Chuck. I'm not sure that they are even amateur Autoduellists."

"But their cars look to be heavily modified from stock, Alex."

"Maybe so, but some of those weapons look as fake as a clown's nose to me. My god," Alex exclaimed, leaning forward to get a better look at the monitor. "Did they make those rocket pods out of cardboard?"

"It'll be an interesting and short-lived match if they did, Alex.

Chuck focused on his screen, trying to make out what he was seeing. "Can you tell what they're doing?"

"Not really, Chuck. They seem to be spreading something out across the bridge's roadway on the eastern side of the Kanawha River. Can we get in any closer to see what's going on?"

The camera view suddenly shifted to another mobile drone hovering no more than twenty feet away from the bridge. The drone rose up slowly, peeking over the top edge of the bridge's concrete side barrier. Three filthy and rough-looking men shook out jack-like objects made of metal across the roadway from duffel bags as they walked backward, slowly retreating to the eastern end of the bridge.

"What is it that they're spreading on the roadway?"

"They honestly look like large jacks to me, Chuck."

"But they're sharpened."

Alex pressed his earpiece tighter into place and listened intently for a moment. " I think I've got it, Chuck. I'm being told that in this part of the country, those are a form of deterrence. They were once used by striking miners to block vehicle traffic from crossing picket lines when union workers would strike for better wages or working conditions. Similar to the caltrops used in ancient warfare, jackrocks as they are called are considered an area denial weapon. And as with the caltrops of ancient times, which deterred elephants, camels, horses, and footmen alike, these jackrocks can easily deter vehicles from passing through an area without receiving extensive damage to their tires or more."

"Let's go to the in-car cameras to see if our racers have picked up on the threat ahead."

Debris on the roadway had started to get pretty heavy. It was bad enough that our speed had been slowed considerably to the point we had to maneuver around wrecked cars and other miscellaneous bits of junk lying scattered across the interstate, and the rain storm that had rolled into the area over the last hour wasn't helping anything either. Visibility had been cut down to maybe fifty yards in the dreary underdark of the storm.

We'd been running in a single file line for at least the last thirty miles because of the road conditions. There really hadn't been a good section to even get up to speed for a while, especially with all of the abandoned and burned-out vehicles taking up space on the roadway.

The Born Destroyers had burned up over half of their fuel supply just catching up to us after they'd gotten separated during the fight and subsequent flight from Lexington.

The lack of recent action and the hypnotic hum of the tires on the pavement was really starting to get to me. That combined with Dave and Buster's incessant snoring just made me want to go lay down someplace warm, curl up, and take a long overdue nap.

Chatter on the radio had been almost nonexistent for the last hour and the Clutch stream chat feed had died down to Henry and two other users, ShellBackBeau5918 and

Dwarfdave3672, who were arguing about which was the better method of fishing for bass, artificial lures or live bait. And man was there a lot of flashing red text up on that screen. Apparently, when Henry was passionate about something, it didn't matter if he was in person or on a chat feed. I could almost picture him hovering over the keyboard, hunting and pecking the keys with his index fingers to string together his responses.

The things that people focused on sometimes baffled me. I've never been a die-hard fan of anything; never been the true definition of a fanatic about anything. Well, with the exception of driving, but that was something more of a passion in my opinion and something I did, not followed.

"I have no idea, FishKiller2000, and no, I can't tell them what's right, because I've never even been fishing."

You're about as worthless as a tow hitch on a motorcycle.

"Hey, now. That's not nice, FishKiller," I argued against the flashing red string of words on the screen. "Remember, I can always perma-ban you from the chat stream if you get too rowdy on there."

A new username appeared on the Clutch feed and immediately started attacking Henry and the others. The new user went on about distracting me from driving and how unsafe it was to take my eyes off the road.

JFPosthumus3008 took off on a tirade like a rabid overprotective helicopter parent that couldn't let their devil spawn out of their sight for more than a few moments. I'd known some kids like that growing up. Their parents would have an aneurism if they got out of sight because the world might hurt their precious little darling. It was hard to keep up with the feed at the rate JFPosthumus3008 was spamming questions and the answers to their own questions. They weren't giving anyone else a chance to reply before the next string of text flooded the feed.

I couldn't help myself and nearly choked trying to hold it back. I laughed out loud at the newcomer. Henry might have finally found his match as an argumentative and grumpy curmudgeon. It almost seemed like a match made in heaven.

The roadway ahead suddenly erupted. Smoke and flame roiled upward into the sky, resembling a small mushroom cloud.

"Cold and free is the way I roll," Dave groggily slurred, snorting as he woke up. I slammed the brakes just in time to keep from rear-ending the Booze Reapers Venom racer. The Burning Foxes drag special soared high over the roadway. It spun on its long axis, sending smoldering pieces of debris flying in all directions as it soared sideways over the side of the bridge.

"Ambush!" someone shouted over the radio.

The Rust Brothers sedan shot out from the pack, passing the Queentastics combat camper.

Automatic gunfire erupted ahead from a ramshackle tower built along the side of the roadway.

The Rust Brothers barked tires and launched forward, followed by the Booze Reapers who raced away like we were standing still, leaving us in the dust and a cloud of white smoke in their wake.

Something nudged us from behind followed by an incessant honking of a horn.

"Come on," Trip shouted over the radio. "How about you get out of the way already!" The Grim Aces nudged us again with their armored push bar.

Machine gun fire peppered the pack from our left. Glancing in that direction while trying not to wreck, I found the source. Hidden behind piles of wrecked cars in the median to the left side of the roadway was an old tank whose main turret jockeyed about, making minute adjustments as they aimed the massive barrel. I could see two men sticking up from the top of the turret, one of which manned the top-mounted machine gun.

"Did no one else notice that there's a tank behind that wall of wrecks?" I asked over the radio waves.

The tank recoiled, its front end engulfed in flames and the concussion wave from the massive round leaving its rifled barrel at supersonic speed. The world exploded behind us. A quick glance in the rearview mirror revealed the unfortunate recipients of that round. What was left of the Born Destroyers pickup soared high into the air, tumbling nose over end as it returned unceremoniously to earth and exploded.

"Oh, yeah?" Dave shouted. "We've got guns too! Frack you!" Dave chuckled like a madman as fire spewed from our upper turret, tracer rounds peppering the tank emplacement.

The Rust Brothers veered off the road to the left, drifting sideways through the grassy median and the Booze Reapers launched ahead, jinking their way through the barriers and wreckage littering the roadway.

More rounds rained down from the makeshift tower and bandits on foot further down the highway.

Queentastic's combat camper braked hard, skidding sideways into a wrecked truck that lay half on its side in the right-hand lane, its nose propped up on the bridge railing. They ricocheted off of the wreck, tail sliding in the opposite direction. Over-correcting their skid they slid into the median side of the bridge, blocking the roadway ahead of us.

"Whoa whoa whoa," Dave shouted. I saw him flinch and grab for anything he could use as a brace.

Tapping the brakes, I cut the wheel hard to the right, steering into the skid I downshifted and feathered the throttle, directing us between the wrecked work truck and an overturned ambulance.

"Don't get your panties in a wad. I've got this all under control!"

I might have said that a little too quickly because that move turned out to be a big mistake. Yeah, I managed to steer us clear of the wreckage and not t-boning Queentastic's combat camper was an even better idea, but just as soon as we dipped out through the opening between the wrecked trucks I saw the triangular metal spikes littering our path. Popping both front tires, the steering fought against me, but the run-flat wheels kept us trucking, even if unsteady and a little slower.

A strange electrical discharge, like the sound of an exploding transformer, reverberated from our left. Sparks showered the area around behind the tank's position. Electrical arcs licked the sky, reaching out for anything close enough to form a solid ground connection.

"What the hell is that?"

I saw Dave look up from his station, craning his neck to see around me. "Looks like someone had a charged railgun tucked away for a rainy day.

The tank fired again, striking somewhere behind us along the interstate bridge.

Headlights flared to life to the east, heading in our direction. It was hard to make out any details about them through the rain.

"We've got trouble coming," I said over my shoulder. "Can you get a fix on them?"

Electric drive motors whirred as Dave adjusted the turret to get a lock on the new targets. "Not yet, they're still out of range."

Rounds from the tower peppered us, giving us a *Hey, how you doing neighbor? Great weather we're having,* reminders of their existence. I cut the wheel as hard as I dared to change our range and speed, making it harder for the bandits in the tower to score a hit on us.

Rockets soared in our direction from the new vehicles. Cutting the wheel as hard to the left as I dared, I changed our direction again, trying not to break the bead on the already flattened tires.

The sky lit up once more with a cacophony of electrical arcs, coloring the stormy gray sky with purples and blues of fiery electrical discharges.

I spotted the Booze Reapers racing across the grassy median toward the westbound lane of the interstate away from the position.

Rockets soared in from the north, impacting around the gunner's tower. Tracer rounds from the tower painted the sky in front of us, the impacts now doing enough damage to be a serious concern. Rounds from the first bandit vehicle cut a line across our driver's side fender.

Turning the wheel back, I brought the nose to aim for the oncoming enemy. Sally's forward-firing heavy machine guns came to life at the squeeze of the steering wheel-mounted triggers.

Dave didn't waste any time either, adding the firepower of our roof-mounted machine gun turret to the pummeling. "Oh, yeah, baby. You like that, don't you? Take it all!"

"Do you two need to get a room?" I shouted over my shoulder.

"Naw, I'm gonna frack them up good right here and now!"

The enemy vehicle continued toward us. It bobbed and weaved, trying to elude our concentration of fire.

Lightning arced once again followed by a massive fireball from the direction of the tank emplacement, but was quickly overshadowed by the roaring napalm flames unleashed by Queentastics combat camper on another of the mobile enemy units. The small buggy-like vehicle became a rolling fireball that crashed into the roof of the overturned ambulance.

Firing our right-side rockets at the first vehicle to charge toward us, I cut the wheel left, adjusting our course ever so slightly to keep Sally under control. The tires may have been shot, but the run flats were keeping us in the game. Aiming our primary forward weapons, I concentrated the machine gun fire on the second vehicle.

Dave shredded what was left of the first enemy after our rockets impacted, doing some serious damage.

The sky lit up like a fireworks show. Loud booms and bright white flashes that could have easily been something out of a war movie dominated the area, followed by secondary explosions erupting from the direction of the tank.

The Grim Aces must have shot through the same space we had, because they were suddenly off to our left, firing rockets at the first tower emplacement. One of the three unguided rockets found its target, and the other two passed through the stick-built legs, impacting somewhere within the treeline off in the distance behind the tower.

Dave shifted his target, tracer rounds now tracking a second vehicle racing at us from further down the highway near a second gunners tower. No sooner had he changed targets than the Grim Aces plowed through the fiery wreckage we'd left behind of the first enemy vehicle.

I activated our missile targeting, aiming for the second tower that'd started firing on us, but not doing much but peppering us at this range. Gunfire showed up on the green backlighting of the targeting screen as quick white flashes of light.

"There you are, you dirty son of a bitch." I locked my target on the gunner and waited for the automated confirmation.

Dave and the Grim Aces joined forces, concentrating their fire on the second vehicle. I was really wondering how these guys were still moving with the pounding they were taking. They had to have some insane armor on that thing, or just completely stupid luck.

Flipping the switch, I armed one of the missiles Dave had salvaged, then depressed the trigger releasing the missile.

"Missile away!"

"Missile away," Dave repeated.

It flew straight and true, skimming the bottom of the tower house, passing through the legs as harmlessly as the rockets.

"I had a target lock! How the hell does that happen?"

Dave chuckled. "Go figure, you've got some stupid dumb luck, and it isn't the good kind."

The second enemy vehicle raced by, engulfed in flames, exploding just as it passed my field of vision.

The Grim Aces buffalo gun chugged away, changing targets they pounded the tower with armor-piercing rounds that absolutely obliterated the structure. It seemed like a little more overkill than a missile in my opinion, but it sure as hell did the job.

It wasn't anything to run down the remaining bandits. The few remaining were on foot, scattered, and outnumbered, which quickly fueled a cat-and-mouse game of chase. As the pack reformed, pulling our resources together to mop up the competition, the last remnants of the bandit force were wiped out, with little more than the peep of a rifle.

Chapter 15

"Most of our viewers really don't know what it's like out there in the world, Chuck…."

"No, they really don't, Alex. The depravity and desperation of those living out there in the wastes between cities boggles the mind. What I don't get is why anyone would want to live anywhere but within the safety of a corporate-sponsored city."

"That is especially true when you don't have access to all of the things we take for granted every day. Freshly processed foodstuff, clean filtered water, and generally any entertainment known to man at your fingertips twenty-four hours a day, seven days a week. Why anyone would live out their lives in the ruins of an abandoned city, where the services of society aren't available, or to live where death, rape, and theft are a way of life is beyond me, Chuck."

"Life is cheap to that sort, Alex."

No doubt. Life is cheap, indeed."

It's funny how something that is supposed to represent the complete failure of a society could be so beautiful and serene as well. The enchanting silence of nature replaced the discordant chaos of the city. From where I sat on Sally's hood, overlooking the crumbling remains of what was once Parkersburg, West Virginia, it was almost heaven.

I had never seen anything like it before in my life. It was the total opposite of what I'd grown up with in Atlanta. Decaying factories, deteriorated skyscrapers, and the rotting ruins of homes had all been overtaken and returned at least partially to nature.

It made me wonder why we ever decided to build and pave over it at all. Here, an invigorating wind blew through that smelled fresh and sweet instead of the acrid smell of asphalt and stale air that I was used to in Atlanta. Even though we were on the verge of winter, songbirds chirped and warbled their calls as they sang and flew about through the carcasses of ruined buildings. I could have sat here forever, watching them dive and soar across my view.

It was barely afternoon, and we'd already had one hell of a day.

Three teams lost.

Three teams we'd had breakfast with, even if it was a rushed breakfast, before hauling ass out of Knoxville this morning before daybreak.

While Dave and others jumped on repairs or salvaged what they could of gear and ammo, a few of us checked on the downed teams.

Bingo and Bash were already long gone when we got to the remains of the Born Destroyers combat pickup. The scorched and still-burning shell of a truck was anything but salvageable after a direct hit from the tank's High Explosive Incendiary round.

The Burning Foxes, Ibis, and Rose Bud didn't stand a chance against the anti-tank mine they'd come across on the highway. Their drag special was covered in ablative plastic armor and geared to repel energy weapon strikes more than kinetic rounds. Their unarmored undercarriage turned out to be about as effective as tissue paper against the mine they'd manage to find. What was left of their racer had flipped and rolled its way over the edge of the bridge, landing in the swollen waters of the Kanawha River. We couldn't find it to recover anyone or anything. It had either sank below the muddy surface to be covered in layer after layer of silt, or it had been dragged away out of sight downstream.

Digger and Blaze of the Rust Brothers must have been the final recipient of the tank's concussive blasts. Their Tequila Slammer battle wagon looked like the round had penetrated the nose of the car and detonated somewhere near the rear of the cab interior. The entire rear end of the station wagon was a shredded and mangled mess. If we didn't know what model it was to begin with, we wouldn't have had any chance of identifying the vehicle from the chewed-up remains.

We'd decided to stop for a break after nearly another hundred miles or so. Some snacked, others napped, but we were all in agreement that after the morning we'd had so far, we needed a small respite before continuing with the rally.

I swatted at one of the many camera drones that had been trailing us since the beginning of the race then took another sip of my water.

Gravel crunched underfoot nearby. I spotted Freya Domme of team Queentastic climbing out of the combat camper. She was tall, well over six foot tall, heavily muscled, and built like a linebacker in a skin-tight hot pink bodysuit.

She stretched, grunting as she reached for the sky. Her heavy blonde extensions wriggled like the arms of an octopus as she twisted and turned, working out the kinks.

Seeing me sitting on top of Sally's hood she reached back into the camper and then proceeded to stroll in my direction, a small bundle wrapped in white cloth in her right hand.

"You handle yourself pretty good out there, kid. For being the rookie of the pack, you sure do know what you're doing behind the wheel."

I shrugged and took another sip of my water. "Just doing my job, man."

"Well," Freya started, "I appreciate you taking the time to steer away from us in that last fight. I saw you barreling down at us after we came to a stop and stalled out, blocking the road. You could have easily plowed through us to save your own skin, but you didn't."

She handed me the small wrapped bundle.

"What's this?" I asked.

"Just a little something to show my appreciation," she said, nervously shuffling her feet. "It isn't much, but it's at least something."

"Beautiful, isn't it?" She turned and smiled, admiring the view as she slowly strolled back towards the camper. Unwrapping the bundle, I stopped as soon as I peeled back the cloth. Even though they were cold, the smoked goodness of the barbequed ribs overwhelmed my sense of smell. For a moment I was confused. Where had she gotten real meat ribs from? Yeah, team Queentastic were veterans of the arena, so they had money, but still… You don't just give away real, honest-to-God meat. That's when I remembered the dinner party in Knoxville. She must have gathered them together into a napkin and pocketed them before we departed the restaurant.

I looked up in Freya's direction and caught a glimpse of her glancing back at me from around the edge of the camper, a wide smile painted her face. Lifting one of the three ribs from the bundle I held it up in salute to her and nodded before heartily digging in. Even though the ribs were over a day old by this point, they were still moist, savory, and delicious.

For her to share something as rare as real meat, it had to be a really big deal to her. Even if all I was trying to do was to keep from killing myself. I gnawed on the rib bone again, ripping off most of the meat in one bite. A light, almost whisper of a whimper drew my attention to the ground beside me.

Sitting there on his haunches, patiently hoping for a bite was Buster, steady streams of drool trickled from either side of his mouth. His big bug eyes were locked onto the rib in my hand and looked as if they had doubled in size at the sight of the bone. Digging a fresh rib out of the bundle, I had barely handed it down to him before he greedily snatched it from my hand. I dropped the bone onto the ground next to him, then turned to look into the cab. Dave had propped his feet up across the center console, arms crossed, chin on his chest, and hat pulled down over his face. I could hear the faint sound of snoring over the chirping of birds, and Buster's gnawing.

"Not going to let it go to waste," I said, before ripping another juicy piece of meat from the bone. It was a good break from an already bad morning.

Chapter 16

"I want to say, Chuck, that most of our viewers out there have at least heard about, if they are not intimately familiar with the award-winning and longest-running reality series in televised history. At its inception, Crash City fueled the fires of hometown vigilantes and freedom fighters against the rabid gangs of thieves and highway bandits who plagued this great country in the years following the grain blight."

"From trend-setting series to influential civil model, Midville and its defense force, the MONDOs, (Midville Organization for Neighborhood Defensive Ordinance), have been the standard that so many small towns across America have held themselves to," Alex added.

"That's right, Chuck. From the moment that Black Jessie's Crusaders set foot in town, Midville, Ohio has been at the forefront of small-town civil defense, and proof that communities coming together for a common cause have power over the forces of evil."

"It's almost fateful that one of the packs has ended up passing through this historic section of small-town middle America. Some of the most well-known Autoduel veterans got their start in Midville, back before they cleaned up the roadways, bringing an end to one of the most well-known and beloved series ever broadcast on network television."

Turning off the interstate and onto the streets of Midville where I had grown up watching them on the streams was such a strange and surreal feeling. I knew every corner, every street, and nearly every building because I'd seen all of the reruns of Crash City so many times that I could quote each episode word for word. I wouldn't be surprised if most people couldn't. The vid show was almost a prerequisite to being in the arena, almost like it was a training manual on what to do or what *not* to do to keep the viewers happy.

Midville could have easily fooled anyone not in the know. On its surface, it looked like any other mid-sized town in middle America. Park benches on the sidewalk, manicured flower beds outside of town hall, and that welcoming vibe that you'd never get in a big city like Atlanta.

We cruised along, creeping our way through town, partially starstruck to being on the set of our favorite vid show. We passed Sam's Grocery, the Acapulco Club, Banduch's Auto and Gun, and UBN studios, just taking in the iconic locations.

"Hey," Dave said, leaning forward. "I could seriously go for a burger and beer right about now. If I don't get something more than algae chips, I'm going to go ape on someone."

I keyed the team frequency. "I'm getting a little concerned for my life right now. Dave is getting a bit hangry. Anyone else up for a stop?"

Most of the team responded back in agreement, needing to stretch their legs and get out of their cars for a while. All the standard chain restaurants were in town, along with a few local joints, but in the end, I decided to pull into the nationally acclaimed, Joe's Oil Pump.

Joe's was an Autoduel-themed, pro-duelist bar and grill like no other in the country. The original building had burned to the ground after a mysterious and undisclosed *incident*, back in the 2030s.

The parking lot wasn't packed, but it was starting to get there by the time we pulled in. Family vans, sedans, and motorcycles sat parked next to all manner of vehicles owned by Autoduellists. From the obvious posers, with their duct tape and cardboard rocket pods to the pro-duelists, who had nothing but the latest in gear straight out of Uncle Al's fall collection catalog.

Chromed diamond plate wall panels and neon lights decorated the outside of the building. Two hostesses, in the latest Autoduel chic worn unzipped down to their belly buttons, welcomed us in.

If there was a square inch of wall space spared for the sake of hanging and displaying memorabilia, it would have been a miracle. Photos, race suits, helmets, sections of race cars, and even more race paraphernalia decorated the place. Several broken and damaged car bodies hung upside down from the steel trusses supporting the building's ceilings.

Vid screens were everywhere you looked. There was more action than one person could keep up with. Dozens of Autoduel events played across the array of displays suspended high on the walls.

"How many," the bubbly blond hostess asked, then her demeanor changed when she noticed Buster carried in the crook of Dave's arm. "I'm sorry, sir. No pets allowed."

"Oh, he is," Dave replied. "He's my emotional support dog, aren't you, you little shit?" Buster grumbled when Dave grabbed his paw to wave at the hostess. "Say hello to the nice lady," he said to Buster then turned his attention back to the hostess. "He doesn't eat much. I can pay for him separately if I need to, no worries," he told her, blowing it off as resolved before he turned and started counting heads, making sure to include Sam and Freya who'd gone ahead to find the restrooms.

"Follow me please," the blond begrudgingly announced then led the way. We were followed by the second hostess whose arms were full of napkin wrapped silverware and menus, a cute curly-haired brunette that couldn't be more than five foot even, they seated us at a long elevated table near the bar before taking our drink orders.

The chatter across the table ranged from matter-of-fact stats about matches and professional teams to the annoying minutia of everyday life. Freya's mom had been sick recently and Trip's uncle had passed away last week and was buried the day before we left.

"Hold the questions, no autographs, please. Joey, pour me a shot!"

At least, that was the chatter until one hell of a Booster walked in the front door. She strutted from the front door to the bar like she was the cock of the walk. All of the pack members watched her cross the room with rapt attention.

The locals just shook their heads and turned back to their previous conversations.

She was tall and lanky, dressed in a recycled race suit. It had been pieced together from at least a half dozen other suits and Frankenstein stitched with a heavy neon green twine, with an excessive amount of repurposed pockets and random patches sewn in for good measure. Her pants, mostly made from what was once a black fire-resistant material that was now a washed-out grey, were at least four sizes too large, cinched tightly about the waist with a wide studded leather belt.

Her race jacket was just as chaotic, pieced together from numerous others and stitched together at odd sections with the same neon green twine used on the pants. Team patches, buttons, and other randomness decorated it. Machine screws protruded from the shoulders and elbows where they had been screwed through the material and somehow secured in place.

All of this she managed to round out with fingerless gloves, steel toes, and a choppy chaotic mess of hair, cut short but at varying lengths like she strived to be the center of attention no matter what room she walked into.

She stopped at the end of our table on her way from the bar, slid her highly polished aviator shades down her nose, and turned toward us. That's when I noticed a heavy vertical scar running down her left eye, and several fresh cuts that had been sewn up with the same heavy green twine that was used on her jacket. She let out a nasal huff of a laugh, then chin nodded at us with a knowing smile before taking a seat at the bar.

"Joey! Where's my drink?" She slapped her hand flat against the bar top.

"You promise there won't be any trouble this time?" The bartender grumbled as he slowly waddled his way along behind the bar.

"What trouble?" she asked, defensively shrugging. "I didn't start anything. They were just sore that they lost to me in arm wrestling and had to buy my drinks the rest of the night."

He shook a thick sausage finger in her direction. "No trouble this time, Stitches. Promise me."

I watched her reach back, placing both hands on her lower back to stretch but then crossing the fingers on both hands behind her back.

"What do you take me for, Joey? And what exactly makes you think that *I* would ever go looking for trouble?" She grinned.

He stood there nonplused. His stare could have easily glared a hole through her. "Stitches?"

"Alright, alright," she relented. "I promise. I won't start any trouble."

He grunted then dropped a shot glass on the bartop, poured a long shot of what could have been a dark whiskey, then set a bottle of algae beer next to the shot glass. The bottle let out a fizzy hiss when he popped the bottle cap.

The big man patted the bar top. "Fifteen even."

She slammed back the shot and then picked up the bottle. "Just put it on my tab."

"You know I can't do that, Stitches."

"Come on, Joey." She took a gulp of beer and belched. "You know I'm good for it."

He closed his eyes and shook his head. "That doesn't matter, Stitches. You've walked out on too many tabs already. The owners don't mind you coming in here as long as you don't start nothing, and you pay for what you order."

"Fine."

Setting the beer down, she pulled a chained wallet out of her back pocket and fiddled around, sorting through receipts and other bits she'd stuffed into the wallet.

Dave got up, pulled a roll of bills from his pocket, and dropped a twenty on the counter. He said, "Keep the change," before returning to his seat across from me at our table and resituating Buster on his lap.

The bill disappeared in Joey's big hand. "Appreciate it," he said, then wandered away, back down toward the other end of the bar.

Stitches turned toward Dave and smiled wide, a confused look playing out across her face. "*Thank you.*"

He said, "Don't worry about it." before saluting her with his bottle over his shoulder without even looking back.

Three of the news crew drones had followed us into the bar, and all three were now focusing on Stitches.

She took another long gulp from her beer, finishing it before cracking her knuckles and heading in our direction. "Listen, I'm a little short on cash tonight, but you got to let me at least earn the drinks."

The octopus hat's tentacles shook back and forth when Dave shook his head. "Don't worry about it. Been there plenty of times myself. That round is on me."

"Come on," she pleaded. Buster grumbled and nipped at her shirt as she slid in close to Dave. Removing her jacket, she squeezed in between Dave and Jane from the Booze Reapers who she turned to and waggled her eyebrows at. "You're cute. How about we get together later if you don't have any pressing plans." Stitches propped her elbow onto the table and waited for Dave to take the challenge.

Dave smiled at her and shook his head. "Naw, I'm good." She looked absolutely dumbfounded.

"Come on, I'll make it worth your while." She held out left her arm for all to see, flexing the muscles in her forearm then held it out for Jane. "I'm not just some soft rag doll to toss around. See, feel that," she said, poking at the muscles with her opposite index finger.

Jane squeezed and looked surprised. "Oh, my."

Stitches smiled and nodded slowly. "Yeah, you like it, don't you?" She pounded both of her fists into her chest and flexed, tightening all of the muscles in her upper torso. "Firm, fit, and trim, babe."

Dave let out a chuckle under his breath. "Bless your heart."

Stitches turned her attention back to Dave and placed her elbow down on the tabletop with her hand upright, ready to arm wrestle. "Come on, let's do this."

Buster jumped for her but stopped short when Dave pulled him back, forcing him to sit on his lap instead of standing.

"Nope," he chuckled, then turned up his beer, finishing it.

"Why not?" She stepped back, the hurt to her pride was plastered across her face.

"Cause I cheat and you're too cute. I don't want to hurt you."

"I'd put money on me taking you," she said, giving Dave a gentle nudge to the back of his shoulder.

Buster's tone shifted. His grumble went from annoyed to seriously pissed off in a split second.

"Um… I wouldn't do that if I were you," I suggested.

Dave grabbed his sidearm and placed it on the table in front of him. "He's right," he said, before grabbing my beer. "You might not want to do that." Chuckling to himself, he turned up the bottle and finished my beer. "Didn't I just mention to you that I cheat? You've been fairly warned. Not my problem if you don't listen." Dave snapped his fingers toward Joey and held up the two empty beer bottles.

Rage flashing across her face, Stitches turned and paced for a few laps along the length of the bar before squeezing between Dave and Jane again. Pounding her fist against the table, she propped her elbow up once more in challenge.

"Let's fracking do this!"

Dave shook his head and laughed. "Nooope," he replied, slowly drawing out the word.

She pounded her fist on the table and pushed herself upright. "Can any of you believe this?" She paced the table for another quick moment, gathering her thoughts then smiled, snapping her fingers. "This outsider has refused a challenge!"

Silverware clanked against plates all around the restaurant as patrons dropped their utensils in surprise and turned their attention toward our table. Most, if not all looked offended at least, and downright pissed at the worst. The word MONDOs quietly slipped past the lips of a few of them that were dining near our table.

I gently leaned over in Dave's direction, trying not to draw too much attention to myself. "Maybe you should just arm wrestle her and get it over with, Dave."

He leaned in a little closer in my direction. "Are you fracking serious? Did you not see the cut six-pack she's sporting? She'd kick my ass. Nope, not going to happen."

Stitches climbed onto the bar and whistled loud enough that my ears felt like they were about to start bleeding.

"I declare a formal challenge against this outsider," she shouted, pointing down at Dave.

Joey hurriedly waddled over to the end of the bar and grabbed the string tied to the clacker of a large brass bell mounted to the end of the shelving. He rang the bell, furiously, then cupping his hands around his mouth announced. "A formal challenge has been declared. All present are hereby witness to the challenge and subsequent outcome."

Two uniformed MONDOs who had just walked through the front door returned their helmets to their heads and drew their sidearms, taking up positions at the main entrance. Three others scattered throughout the restaurant stood from their tables and did the same, taking up positions at the different exits around the building.

"Fracking hell," I heard Vincent mumble a few seats down. He rubbed his face, then pulled out his phone and quietly whispered into the receiver.

The looks from our pack were a mixture of amusement to annoyance. Dave looked anxious and worried. One of his nervous ticks must have been a bouncing knee, because the table started to vibrate, shaking Buster, drinks, and silverware alike.

Retrieving a tablet from beneath the bar, Joey made his way around the bar and toward our table. He tapped at the screen, which seemed to control *all* of the displays in the place because at that moment, every screen displayed the Midville Challenge Generator. It looked like a large pie chart that had been sectioned into hundreds of colorful slices.

Panting, Joey stopped just behind Dave, punching details into the device. Stitches appeared in big bold letters on the screens beneath the title *Challenge Initiator*. Then he tapped Dave on the back of his shoulder. "What's your name, sir?"

"Um…Mud?"

Joey gave him one of those annoyed, side-eyed glares. "Is that your legal name or callsign?"

Dave let out a tired sigh. "No, it's Dave."

"Dave what?"

"Just Dave," he said, shaking his head. He picked up our empty bottles and handed them to Joey. "Can I get two more while you're up?"

Most of us chuckled at that, but Joey gave Dave that perturbed glare again, then went back to punching the information into the device. Dave's name appeared beneath the title of *Challenger* on the screens.

"As per the Midville Organization for Neighborhood Ordinance rules of peaceful resolution, section five, subsection nine, paragraph two. Any publicly and formally declared challenge shall be acknowledged and administered by the nearest AADA-certified administrator, who will then register the combatants by entering them into the system, and by random chance, the challenge will be selected."

He leaned down to look at Dave who was trying his best to ignore the bartender. "Are you ready for selection?"

Dave glanced around the room, counting the helmeted heads of the MONDOs. "Nope." He removed his knitted octopus hat and scratched furiously at his head. "But I guess I don't really have a choice now, do I?"

"Well, there is another choice."

"What's the choice?"

"Public execution by firing squad."

"I think I'll take my chances with the challenge."

Joey spun on his heel and turned to Stitches. "Are you ready for selection?"

"I am," she said with an energetic nod.

"Both contestants are prepared for selection!"

The place erupted in clapping, cheers, and shouted taunts. At the sound of an electronic chime from every display in the place, the crowd went dead silent and turned to gaze toward the nearest screen.

Two gorgeous gun bunnies in camo bikinis and ammunition belts appeared on the screen. They clapped and bounced, cheering while the wheel started to spin. You could have heard a pin drop in the place. I glanced around and saw that everyone, including the MONDOs were focused on the vid screens and the spinning wheel. At the top of the screen between the names of the challengers, the stylized name of the challenge cycled as the wheel ticked along, passing each of the selections.

It became easier to read as the spin of the wheel slowed. I saw names like Killer Karts, High Stepping, and Dirty

Dip's flash by, ticking along like a rapidly advancing countdown to Dave's demise.

Gasps of anticipation from the crowd were loud and nearly overwhelming within the silence, until the wheel came to a complete stop, hung up on the clacker between challenges. Anxious winces and whispered prayers hung in the vacuum of the moment.

Then the wheel wobbled, shifting back and forth, both of the gun bunnies clapping and cheering, coaxing it to fall in their direction.

Then it shifted left, falling into a red-colored slice of the pie. The title flashed on the screen like a strobing red devil. All around the screens, Uncle Al's approved challenge logos scrolled and flashed with the title.

"Ladies and gentlemen," Joey announced in his best ringmaster's voice. "By the power vested in me, I declare the challenge to be…" He let the words hang in the air for a long moment before taking in a deep breath.

"Tag!"

The crowd went wild, cheering, clapping, and whistling.

"Yes," Stitches shouted with an excited fist pump.

Joey held up his hands and shouted, trying to get everyone calmed down and their attention back onto him.

"Tag is designated to be for at least four to six teams of two, driver and gunner." He looked down at his tablet, then continued. "Being that this is an Uncle Al's approved event, vehicles will be supplied to the arena for tonight's challenge and a pot of $5,000 will go to the winner. The winner will also receive two shred weapons of their choice and a thousand rounds of ammo for the new weapons, free of charge from our local Uncle Al's outlet mart. Second and third place will receive $1,000 and $500 respectively, as well as bragging rights against Stitches, our current local Tag champion. We need at least two more teams to proceed. Do we have any volunteers?"

The two MONDOs who'd walked through the front door at the beginning of this fiasco raised their hands to get Joey's attention. "We volunteer for the event."

"Alright, that's one. Any others?" Joey asked.

I leaned over the table toward Dave. "What in the hell have you gotten us into?"

Dave shrugged. He pursed his lips in one of those oh crap guilty looks while shaking his head. "In my defense, I had no idea we were walking into a town full of wacko cultists."

I couldn't help but agree with him. This wasn't anything like anything I'd ever seen on the vids, but some of those episodes were also recorded over thirty years ago. "I don't think any of us did, man," I replied.

Two more patrons toward the back stood, waving toward Joey. "We volunteer!" In moments two more teams volunteered, filling in the empty challenge slots. Joey waved each of the teams over toward the bar then turned back to Dave, "Do you have a partner? I'll need to register their information."

Dave and Buster both looked up at me with those pleading, sad, puppy dog eyes.

I rubbed at my temples. No way I could in good conscience let him go off and get himself killed. If that happened, then I'd be out another gunner. I'm not sure that my reputation could take another hit like that. I looked up at Joey and waved to get his attention.

"Ricky *The Ripper* Turner."

Chapter 17

"Well, this is an unexpected turn of events, Chuck. Not only did the Atlanta pack deviate a long way off from the expected course to reach their checkpoint, but Ricky 'The Ripper' Turner and his gunner have apparently gotten themselves into pretty hot water."

"You can say that again, Alex. And for those of you just tuning in, the Atlanta pack has found itself in the heart of corn country in Midville, Ohio. Or better known by some of you by its televised network name, Crash City."

"And our rookie home team has apparently stirred up quite a bit of trouble, being challenged to a duel by a local who is an amateur league champion of several named challenges and goes by the name of Stitches."

"We have some information that our network researchers were able to dig up, Chuck. Stitches, as she calls herself is a transplant to the area as of last year, who quickly began working her way through the amateur leagues, landing invites into the entry-class pro-duelist competitions in and around the Midville area. Anything before that about her is a complete enigma."

"Well, that surely makes things interesting, doesn't it? What can you tell us about this challenge, Alex?"

"Tag is just as simple as the game that we all loved and played during our childhood. At the start, the vehicle that is *it* will be randomly selected by the arena's main computer. That team can now fire upon all other teams in the match. While all other teams may only fire on the individual who is *it*. This match has been designated as a Last man standing event, and the last functional vehicle in this match will be declared the winner. If on the odd chance that the last two remaining vehicles disable each other, the tie will be broken by accumulated points scored by each successful hit and complex maneuvers completed."

"That seems simple and straightforward. And how does one become *it*, Alex?"

"By tagging, or ramming another team's vehicle."

"So tonight's match is going to be more of a contact sport, is that what you're saying?" Chuck interrupted.

"Too right, Chuck."

"And because of that, Uncle Al's, the top sponsor for tonight's special event has supplied our teams with brand new two-seater Hammer coupes from the Fnord motor corporation."

"And Uncle Al has spared no expense on tonight's load-outs, either."

"No, he hasn't, Alex."

"What kind of action can we look forward to tonight, Chuck?"

"Besides the standard armor plating, safety cage, and ramplate included with the AADA-approved Hammer chassis, Uncle Al's has equipped these deadly vehicles with the latest in linked shotgun technology mounted to either side covering the side firing arcs. To max out the shred capability on this load out, they have included the latest generation autocannon from Shredder Technologies Inc., with a much improved cyclic rate and jam-free construction."

"With this impressive amount of shredding capability, how will our teams be able to maintain the integrity of their tires during this match?"

"Uncle Al's has been kind enough to install improved wheel skirts around each of the wheels in order to extend the amount of action and the overall potential length of the event."

"I wouldn't expect any less from a sponsor like Uncle Al's."

Our cars had been spaced out evenly around the outer perimeter of the deathball-sized arena. It was probably close to one hundred meters long and seventy meters wide and paved from one end to the other. Each of the teams were loaded onto a small shuttle bus and dropped off at our respective vehicles.

On the way out to our assigned cars, I'd made sure to take note of the numerous wrecks and obstacles littering the combat area. Nothing really caught my attention as troubling, but this was a new arena. Every arena in the Atlanta area I'd driven in had its own tricks and personal favorites they'd throw into the mix to keep things interesting.

They dropped us off at a baby blue Hammer with rose red racing stripes and the number sixty-three painted inside of white circles on both of the doors. Even though the paint gleamed and shimmered in the bright stadium lights, it really didn't help the look of the already ugly car. It was boxy and simple, no flash about it, and the massive steel ramplate mounted to the front bumper didn't help the aesthetics in the slightest.

Dave let out a long whistle when he opened the passenger side door and started inspecting the door frame of our assigned Hammer.

"I don't think I've seen anything this heavily armored besides a tank."

"That isn't necessarily a bad thing," I replied and opened the driver's side door.

"It might actually be a bad thing," he said. "If she's as heavy as she looks, that's going to have a major effect on the handling."

"I'll just have to get a feel for her quickly, then." I slid into the driver's seat and took in the layout and location of all of the controls. It smelt like fresh leather and plastic that had been heated in the noonday sun a few times too many.

It was a good thing we'd left Buster behind with Bullseye, the gunner from the Booze Reapers. There wasn't an ounce of space wasted inside the cab of the Hammer. Buster would have been sitting in one of our laps or on the dashboard if he'd come along for the ride. Bullseye didn't even hesitate when I brought up Buster to Dave, who wanted to bring him along. He was a dog guy and was apparently missing his own pups pretty badly.

Dave's excuse for bringing Buster along was how else was he going to learn how to be a wingman if he didn't get any practical experience. I'd given him that slight bit of logic in his statement but argued against it because I didn't want the distraction in this competition.

We stood a chance to earn a decent bonus that could go a long way in reloading before we hit the road again, not to mention any points scored in the arena also counted against our Dead Man's Run total, which could easily put us ahead of the other teams no matter what the outcome of the match was as long as neither of us bit the big one.

The inside of the Hammer nearly felt what I imagined the inside of a closed coffin would feel like once we pulled the doors closed. Light streamed in through narrow slits cut into the armor plating that replaced the windshield and door glass.

I secured my five-point harness and then slid on the new helmet supplied by Uncle Al's for the match. Dave had struggled for a while before the match trying to fit his knitted octopus hat over the new helmet. I tried to talk some sense into him since we were only doing this one match, then it was back to the rally. He could do one match without it. He insisted he had to have it because it was his good luck charm, so I gave up and let him continue to struggle. He managed to solve the problem with the tried and true method of duct tape. It didn't look pretty, but it did the job without question.

When I powered up the Hammer Dave let out another long whistle as the heads-up display system within the helmets activated, lighting up the interior of the cab.

"No, kidding," I said, taking in the three-dimensional wireframe of the arena from our perspective. More information started to flash within my view as the helmets connected with our car and Ada's voice came over the built-in speakers of the helmet.

"Welcome to Dynatec Industries combat management system version 7.0. Damage control, fire suppression, power plant, drive systems, weapons management, hull integrity, all register active and online."

And just like that, the status of every system registered within the HUD along the right-hand side of my view. Besides a three-dimensional wireframe of the arena and the systems status, the HUD displayed a targeting reticle with elevation in the center of the view and designated what the currently active weapon was within that particular firing arc. It jumped, showing Dave's direction of view with a separate colored crosshair. Weapons shifted between us depending on who was pressing the trigger down to the first detent, locking in control of that particular weapon. The current speed which showed zero at the moment was in the lower left corner, current compass heading was at the very top of the view with ammo counts listed in the top right corner. A circular radar-type readout overlaid across everything, registering the other five vehicles within fifty meters of us according to their location.

Dave leaned down, doubling himself over to the point of putting his head on the floorboard. "Well, this makes things interesting."

"How so?"

"Even if I turn my head sideways, it keeps everything in perspective in the HUD overlay. The horizon line stays exactly where it should be. So if we get flipped on our side or top, we'll still be seeing things the way that they are."

"But what happens if the HUDs fail?"

Dave shrugged. "Use your best guess?"

"You're a lot of help, you know that?"

A start warning chimed over the helmet speakers, and a countdown from five flashed across the HUD.

The orange number ninety-seven car flashed then the label *'It'* appeared over its icon. Since we were dropped off in teams at our cars, I had no idea which car Stitches would be in, and it would be a complete crap shoot to figure it out.

"Hold on one Fracking minute already!" Dave fumbled with his harness, getting it buckled just as I floored the accelerator. The electric drive motors clicked loudly and then hummed from the sudden flood of power passing through to them from the Variable Frequency Controllers.

Gunfire quickly erupted ahead from the orange number 97 car. Their autocannon rapped off two rounds before they leapt forward, accelerating hard toward the red number 13 car.

I lined up the targeting reticle with the number 97, leading the target ever so slightly when the reticle jumped, turning over control to Dave. "How the hell is this going to work if we keep taking the target from each other?

"You just have to look at whatever I ain't," Dave said then fired our first shot. The autocannon barked, scoring hits to the front driver's fender of the number 97 car. "You got this one or you gonna let me go after it?"

"I got it," he said. "You pay attention to these other socket heads so they don't get the jump on us. I'm the one that got us into this. Let me do my job."

The field ahead of us erupted in a flash of fire and light. Flames and smoke roiled upward, slowly boiling and tumbling into the sky.

The HUD system now designated number 13 as the *it* car. As the smoke started to clear I could make out what had just gone down. The number 97 had rammed into the number 13 and pushed them into one of the barrels scattered around the arena.

"Hey, Dave."

"Yeah."

"Don't let me forget, not to hit any of those barrels."

"Hey, Ricky."

"Yeah."

"Don't hit any of those barrels. Barrels bad. Barrels bad."

Asshole.

"Ha, ha…"

Dave adjusted his aim toward the number 13 car, laying down a constant pounding of autocannon rounds.

The damage was overly apparent as we got closer. The number 13 car had been blown back and its front passenger fender and wheel were all but gone. The number 97 had been deflected after the collision and redirected from the strike and was now on a collision course with us.

I adjusted our course, but the number 97 car matched us.

"Was there anything in the rules about ramming anyone that wasn't *it?*"

"Hell, if I know," Dave said. "You expected me to read the rules? I just blow things up!"

Before I could answer, our back end slid out from under us, the impact kicking our tail to the right. That's when the number 97 car struck our front right side, spinning us out of control. Shotgun rounds peppered us as we spun.

Braking hard, I cut the wheel and then floored the accelerator, pulling us out of the spin.

"Can you see them?"

"See who?" Dave shouted.

"The car that's *it!* The HUD still has number 13 as the *it* car."

Heavy rounds pounded our rear.

He turned and twisted in his seat trying to look behind us. "I don't see a fracking thing, man."

"Those rounds aren't just coming out of thin air."

Car number 97 was off to our right racing away at a good pace, while number 28 had continued hauling away to our left.

Another volley of rounds struck our rear armor. Damage warnings flashed within the HUD, indicating the right rear drive motor had taken damage.

Dave reached across and punched me in the shoulder. "Come on already, Ricky!" Get us turned around so I can shoot back!"

I popped the brake, cut the wheel hard, and floored it, steering into the turn. Two blasts of buckshot peppered our driver's side. Number 13 was suddenly on our left and barreling down on us.

"Dave!"

"Frack!"

He fired our driver's side shotgun at number 13. The buckshot didn't do anything other than remove paint from the massive ramplate. They followed up with a double tap to our driver's side with a double tap from their autocannon.

New damage registered on my HUD view, the driver's side shotgun was destroyed. The nearly point-blank hits from the autocannon also carried enough force behind the rounds to damage the armor plating on that side. The armor plating wasn't going to hold up to another hit like that without letting the rounds penetrate and spiral around inside the cab doing ten times as much damage to us versus the car. A dead crew was still a disabled vehicle.

"Come on, man! Get us turned so I can get a shot off at them."

"What do you think I'm trying to do?" I shouted in reply.

I cut the wheel hard left, keeping the accelerator to the floor trying to drift my way out of danger and around the number 13 car, but it was too late. They had to be maxed out on speed to have crossed that amount of distance that quickly. When they hit, it felt like we'd been t-boned by a freight train, pinning us against a pile of burned-out wrecks. The sudden and abrupt stop jerked us hard enough that my five-point harness broke loose from the two connecting points on the left and Dave's helmet bounced off of the armored door with a loud plastic crack. He hung limp in his harness.

The HUD pinged, designating us as the vehicle that was *it*. New warnings flashed showing total damage to the driver's side shotgun and armor. The rear driver's side drive motor flashed intermittently like it had a bad connector on a sensor or the main power bus. To top it all off, three of our power packs were offline and overheating with core temps climbing toward critical.

"Dave!"

I smacked him across the chest with the back of my hand. "Dave! Wake up!"

Our drive motors hummed with power when I floored the accelerator, but we didn't so much as budge. I shifted us into reverse and floored it again with the same results. Reaching across I smacked him again. We had to get free and get the hell out of there before one of the other competitors finished us off. We were complete and utter sitting ducks right at that moment.

Sparks flew from the passenger side of the number 13 car. Autocannon rounds pummeled their side armor and the number 97 car suddenly appeared beside us, shoving the number 13 car free from our side.

I floored it again, rocking us forward and back, trying to break free from the pileup. Number 13's autocannon fired once more. Their rounds just missed us, skimming across the nose of our ramplate and, impacting the burned-out wreck we were pinned against just as I rocked us in reverse.

I spotted the lime green number 52 charging in our direction. Autocannon rounds that were most likely intended for us pounded the rear of the number 13 car before slamming into them, driving them into our nose and ahead of us. I slid sideways, slightly out of my seat where the harness had broken loose. Dave flopped like a rag doll in his seat. The impact twisted us, pivoting our nose against the wreck and breaking our rear free, simultaneously shoving the number 97 car sideways.

"Dave!" He was still out cold, and I didn't want to waste the shot. I fired our autocannon point-blank into the front end of the number 13 car, which immediately began to smoke. Flames erupted from beneath their hood.

Shifting back to reverse, I floored it, pulling us away from the pileup. I fired again into the side of the number 13 car and they exploded. The last thing I ever expected was to see a power plant explode from a kinetic round. Maybe I'd managed to hit one of the main burst capacitors that held energy in reserve for those immediate demands for speed or as a charge bank for energy-based weapons.

The force of the explosion knocked both the number 97 and number 52 cars back, dislodging them from each other. Off in the distance, the yellow number 3 car was heading our way, followed close behind by the purple number 28 car.

Turning left, I aimed and fired into the rear of the number 97 with our autocannon then shifted into drive, firing off a round from our passenger-side shotgun. I was surprised that it was still functioning after being crunched so badly by the number 13 car. But I'd take what I could get for wins at this point.

I did a quick systems check. Our power plant was still online, and sixty percent of our power packs were in good shape, even though two of them were flashing with overheating warnings. That autocannon was hanging in there as well as the passenger-side shotgun. The rear and driver's side armor plating were gone at this point, and our only real advantage was that we were still mobile. If we were to lose that we'd be toast in minutes. It would be suicide if we bailed out and made a run for the exits. Kills were kills, points were points, and pedestrians were easy pickings.

Dave jerked awake when I fired the shotgun into the rear driver's side of number 97 as when we cruised by.

"Welcome back to the world of the living," I said.

"Where…"

"At our three o'clock. Fire again!"

He must have come to enough, because the passenger side shotgun fired into number 97's side again, shredding the paint and the thin outer layers of armor sheeting covering the wheels.

Secondary explosions sparked and flamed from car number 13. The fire must have breached the ammo canisters, igniting the ammo inside. Dave fired the shotgun into the side of number 97 once more before it too ignited, flames leaping over from number 13, feeding on all nearby combustibles.

"Get us out of this before we light off," Dave shouted. He grabbed his helmet with both hands like it was the morning after a pub crawl binger, wishing he hadn't yelled.

Before we were out of range of the pile-up, Dave slammed another shotgun round into number 97 for good measure while the number 3 car greeted us with an autocannon round for our trouble. The shot struck our rear passenger quarter but didn't feel like it had done much more than ricochet off the back corner and scratch the paint.

Number 3 had barely gotten off their shot when the purple number 28 car slammed into their right rear corner, spinning them out of control in a pit maneuver.

Cutting the wheel hard to the right, we broke traction, and I turned into the skid. Sliding across the pavement we just missed the now out-of-control number 3 car that passed by us in reverse. They attempted to correct, but their wheels caught as they attempted a sliding turn that sent them tumbling sideways across the pavement.

Turning slightly more to the right, I aimed ahead of the number 28 car, putting us on a collision course. Dave carved two of our autocannon rounds into the side of number 28 before we made contact. Connecting with the rear corner of their passenger side we sent them spinning tail-first into the burning remains of number 52.

"Look out," Dave said, smacking my shoulder to get my attention before pointing off to our left. "Don't hit the fracking barrel!"

That was the last thing I'd want to do out here in this arena. That last barrel had one hell of a punch and I didn't want to find myself the direct recipient of that sort of blast. Dave managed to fire off one last shot with the passenger shotgun before number 28 was out of range.

We trudged ahead as fast as I could get our Hammer to go. It wasn't its best possible speed, but it wasn't horrible either. It wasn't like I could expect too much out of it since we were racing along with two damaged drive motors.

Rounding the burning pile of wreckage, we spotted number 28, circling the number 3 car like a ravenous shark. The number 3 car had come to a stop, landing on its top, and its crew had climbed out, abandoning what protection the disabled car provided, and sprinted north.

I checked our six then brought us around, bringing our nose to bear on number 28. They smoked all four wheels, drifting their way around another of the red explosive barrels placed within the arena.

"Are they in range of the Autocannon?"

Dave shrugged. "They should be."

"Then why aren't you firing?"

"Do you really want me to hit the guys hiding behind the barrel? I mean, I can without a problem…"

"Wait, what?" I looked closer and there behind the barrel were two figures crouched down, side-stepping around the barrel staying opposite from car number 28. "Hold fire."

"Yeah…," Dave said. "I figured that's what you'd say. I've still got a solid bead on them though."

"Let's see if we can't draw number 28 away…"

No sooner had the words come out of my mouth than the figures sprinted in opposite directions. One sprinted north while the other sprinted south in our direction, drawing in number 28 for the kill.

"Frack me!"

"I've got them in my sights."

"Take the shot!" I ordered. "I don't care if you do any damage. At least try to distract them."

Dave took the shot. The autocannon round sparked off of the front passenger roof support, leaving behind one hell of a crater in the armor plating. He fired again, impacting their passenger-side shotgun, again leaving another crater in the side armor.

It wasn't enough to stop them or even dissuade them from their course. I wasn't sure who the individual was that had been in the number 3 car, but they never stood a chance against the rolling death machine that didn't so much as consider them a speed bump in the grand scheme of things.

Car number 28 needed to be stopped before they could run down the other team member from car number 3.

A screaming rage roared in my ears, drowning out the heavy pounding of blood that had previously been there. Someone, somewhere, roared with the power of loss and hate.

That someone was me.

Dave unleashed another volley from our autocannon, scoring a hit and punching a hole through their side, penetrating the added armor plating.

I stood on the accelerator and prayed for an excess of speed.

"Ricky!"

"Hang on to something or kiss your ass goodbye!"

For no reason at all, I let out a gut wrenching laugh. I laughed harder than I had probably ever laughed in my life, and it felt fracking good.

Then we made contact.

We plowed into the side of number 28. Steel crunched and crumpled under the impact of our ramplate. I slid forward, slipping out of the half-attached harness, smashing my helmet against the driver's side roof pillar and dash.

Then the world exploded around us.

Our impact with the other car was enough to nudge them into the explosive barrel that the two crewmen of car number 3 had been hiding behind.

We bounced back from the force of the explosion.

Shaking off the encounter, Dave squeezed off one more round with the autocannon before I could throw the Hammer into reverse, backing us out of the already spreading flames. The impact tore through the upper rear corner of the cab, leaving ragged torn metal in its wake.

"Are they out?" Dave asked.

The HUD readout still had them designated at it, even though it looked as if they were dead in the water.

"The computer says they are still in."

"Then why aren't they moving?"

"How the hell should I know? Maybe they stopped for afternoon tea and biscuits."

By some miracle, the number 28 car's passenger side shotgun was still functioning and fired in our direction. The load of buckshot pinged off the ramplate, but it didn't even register anything of significance in the damage control systems.

Adjusting our position, I aimed our nose toward the rear of their car. "Put a round through that rear drive motor."

And Dave did just that. He centered the targeting reticle over the wheel skirt, estimating where the center of the wheel should have been, and fired.

"Huh," I grunted and laughed. "They still aren't dead."

"Maybe the blast knocked them out?" Dave offered. So I adjusted our position again, aiming this time for the front passenger wheel. Again, Dave fired into what looked like the center of the wheel, but they were still listed as *it*.

"Why don't we just put a round through the cab?" Dave argued. "There are already a few holes that we could easily open up a bit more. Or get a round clean through one of those holes so it sprawls around, ricocheting around the inside of the cab. It's a guaranteed kill if I can hit the hole."

I shifted back to drive and brought us around to face the driver's side of the car. "How about we don't and say we did."

"Don't you want to win this thing?"

"Yeah, of course, I do."

"Then let's end it, quick and simple like."

I lined us up on the rear driver's side wheel. "How about we win this by not killing a defenseless crew."

"Bet they'd do it to us if they had the chance."

I lined up the shot and pulled the trigger, firing the autocannon round through the rear driver's side wheel. I started to think to myself, these guys should be renamed team cockroach, because they just wouldn't die. The HUD still had them listed as active and *it*. I shifted into reverse, readjusting to aim for the remaining wheel when the driver's door opened, and the driver slumped out, falling to the ground. They grabbed the side of the car and pulled on the door frame, forcing themselves upright.

Through the open driver's door, I could see the gunner still strapped into their harness slumped over in the passenger seat, their head hung at an odd angle

Dave took aim at the final wheel drive and fired. The HUD flashed, declaring us the winner of the match. Slowly, the driver removed their helmet, revealing blood along the back and side of their neck.

Stitches stood there looking vulnerable and the worse for wear. She must have mustered every ounce of strength she had left because she stumbled and fell when she threw her helmet at us. It bounced off the windshield armor and slid harmlessly off the hood to the ground.

I backed up, adjusted our angle, and started back toward the pits. A loud crack resonated through the otherwise quiet arena and a single round struck the rear of our car.

I floored it, sliding our tail and bringing us around to aim our autocannon at the open driver's door just behind her and I fired. The door slammed shut behind her, sporting a brand new crater where the shotgun had been mounted. I stood on the brake with my left foot and the accelerator with my right. The Hammer's rear rose up like an angry cat, the front wheels locked. Billowing white smoke roiled from the rear wheels that squealed, breaking traction. Stitches' eyes went wide, her face awash with fear.

She ran.

Or at least she tried to run. There was something about the sight of her limping away that nagged at me to give chase. Something that urged me forward, that promised the blood would be so much sweeter after a good chase. It was something primal at the back of my mind that begged me to go.

I could almost taste the kill…

"Ricky!" Dave punched me. "Don't do it!"

"She fracking deserves it!"

I let off the brake.

"You won't be able to live with yourself if you do!"

"She didn't have to run down that other crewmember."

"And neither do you!"

"Frack her and her cocky ass!"

Dave released his harness and grabbed for the wheel, jerking it to the right, missing her in the nick of time. I shoved him back into his seat, regaining control, and spun us around to aim at her for another pass.

"You didn't want to kill them in cold blood just a few minutes ago. What's the difference between then and now, Ricky?"

"Now she has a chance to get away if she's fast or smart enough, and she can feel what that other team member felt before she ran them down. She'll know the fear and desperation that they felt!"

"Who the frack made you judge, jury, and executioner, Ricky? Who? Be smart. Don't pull the same sort of dumb shit I would because you're pissed."

"She did!"

"Do you really want to be that guy, Ricky? Do you want to keep the title Ricky *The Ripper*? This is how you do that! This is how you forever lock in that name because no one will forget the guy who ran down a nearly defenseless driver in the arena when the match was already over."

She was right in front of us, each of her steps an exhausted, desperate stride. The Hammer ate up the distance like it wasn't anything.

"Ricky!"

Just one more drop of blood for the arena gods. One more drop for the defenseless.

"Ricky!"

I veered to the right and opened the driver's door as we skirted past her, knocking her aside. She tumbled, sprawling across the ground.

Bracing myself, I adjusted the harness and then stood on the brakes. We skidded, sliding sideways to a complete stop.

She lay there, moving one limb, then another like she was slowly regaining control of her extremities.

"Come on, Ricky," Dave said, almost whining. "What are you doing? We've got cold beer waiting on us back at the pits."

I watched her for a long moment as she struggled to get her knees up under her. A swarm of drones had all but surrounded her. The shimmer of light gave away the movement of camera lenses, panning from her to a shot of us off in the distance behind her. The networks were going to milk this moment for all it was worth.

I released my harness and opened the door. I hadn't taken two steps away from the car before there were so many drones and a thick cloud of dust settling all around me.

She rocked back, half sitting on her heels, half about to collapse to the ground as I walked up to her. When I stopped maybe ten feet away, she smiled that same cocky, challenging smile she'd had back at the Oil Pump and gave me a chin nod.

"Damn fine match. Where'd you learn to drive like that?"

"Driving taxi routes in Atlanta."

"Yeah," she said, pursing her lips. She nodded. "Big city like that, I can see how you'd learn to bob and weave like you did." She sat back on her rear, pulling her knees up to her chest, she wrapped her arms around them. "So, now what?"

I looked up at the hypnotic humming cloud that surrounded us. Drones jockeyed for the best position to record the scene for their viewers. "That depends," I said, then loosened the leather thong that held my revolver securely in the holster.

"Depends on what?"

I drew my revolver, cocked the hammer, and aimed it at her head. "Why did you run down the driver of that other car? There was no need in going to that extreme. They were already out of the match."

Stitches chewed on her lower lip. I knew she was carefully considering her answer with the way she kept glancing my way. She let out a nasally huff and shrugged. A smug smile crossed her face. "Because it's all part of the game. It was fun." She leaned forward and started to crawl toward me. "Didn't you feel the same rush when you were running me down? It's the age-old game of cat and mouse, the weak versus the strong, predator and prey."

"And how did that work out for you?"

"I was stronger than they were." She halted in mid-crawl when I pulled the trigger, placing a round into the pavement next to her left hand.

"Why don't you just get it over with and put me out of my misery?"

"Naw…" I shook my head furiously. "You'll suffer longer if I let you live." I pointed at the swarm of flying cameras surrounding us. "And they'll make sure of it for me."

As fickle as the viewership was, half of them would be angry because they didn't get to see me blow her brains out. And they'd consider what had just happened to be fair since I interrupted her plans, while others would be cheering to burn her at the stake, calling her out for the witch that she was.

I holstered my revolver and turned on my heel, heading back to the car.

"Try to have a nice day," I said back over my shoulder.

Chapter 18

"It is quite rare to see an established toll road within a city's limits, these days, Alex. Most municipalities stopped using them for the simple fact that people would just go the long way around in order to save their hard-earned cash. The concept was one that had its time and place, but these days municipalities are generally better off when they don't upset their populous."

"I completely agree. But how is it Chuck, that the Atlanta pack left out from Midville this morning, riding high on the title of heroes and champions with that amazing impromptu win by Ricky the Ripper and his gunner, but now there are warrants out for their arrest? And they are being pursued by no less than twelve Akron municipal defensive force vehicles for having blown through a municipal toll point."

"I'm honestly surprised that they have that many vehicles manning a toll road in the first place."

"Perhaps today was an exceptionally quiet day, Chuck?"

"Or it was a trap, Alex. What if they set out to catch a number of high-profile targets once they learned about the route that the Atlanta pack were planning to take."

"This is true, Chuck. The pack wasn't shy about letting the cameras know what route they planned to take when leaving Midville."

"Let's just hope they can get themselves out of this predicament. The pack has until 7 am tomorrow morning to reach the Toledo checkpoint and the goal for the first leg of the Dead Man's Run."

Dave reached up and grabbed the handset, keying the mic. "Why is it that we can't take you anywhere, Vinny? You're the reason we can't have nice things."

"It's Vincent you, moron. Call me Vinny one more time, I swear on my dear mother's grave that you'll end up on a nice long vacation that you won't ever come back from if you catch my meaning."

I took the handset out of Dave's hand. "How about maybe we stop and ask the next time there's any question if we should stop or not."

Something close behind us exploded. Our tail slid left, I tapped the brake, then feathering the accelerator I pulled Sally back under control. "Is there any way you can at least slow them down, Dave?'

"That all depends."

I glanced back over my shoulder at him. "Depends on what?"

We were running at the back of the pack, three abreast where we could so we could stay together. The Blackskulls were to our right and Disaster Force was to our left. This section of highway just happened to be surprisingly clear of wrecks since the cops started chasing us.

"If we get a warrant for us in Toledo does it transfer back to Atlanta?"

Rounds peppered our tail. Buster grumbled and let out a whimpering whine before he climbed down into the floorboard.

"I'm not sure that really matters right at this particular moment."

"Why do you say that?"

"Because it doesn't matter in the long run if we don't survive."

"You've got a point," Dave conceded. "Still, it would be nice to know why they're chasing us."

I jinked left as the next barrage of rounds peppered our rear and checked the mirrors. The pack of police cruisers were slowly gaining on us. They must have had some serious horsepower under their hoods to close the distance as fast as they were.

Out of the corner of my eye, I caught the flash of angry red letters on the chat feed.

"Ahhhh, well that explains it," Dave blurted out, pointing at the Clutch feed.

"Explains what?" I asked. I'd have looked over at the chat feed myself, but I was a little preoccupied with not getting us killed at that particular moment.

"Why they're chasing us."

"Well, are you going to spit it out or are you going to make me guess?"

I heard the door of the beer fridge clatter open.

"The hell are you doing?"

"Getting a beer," he said, then popped the top off the bottle and took a sip.

"For the love of all that is unholy, why?" I yelled.

Through the rearview mirror, I saw Dave defensively cuddling the bottle, nuzzling its frosty exterior. "I'm nervous."

"What the frack does that have to do with anything?"

"I drink when I'm nervous?"

"Is there a time that you won't drink?"

I saw him shrug again through the rearview then take another drink before letting out a gurgly wet burp. "No, not really."

If we didn't have a pack of pissed-off cops on our asses, I'd have pulled it over and kicked him to the curb. He was beyond frustrating sometimes, but right now I just wanted to wrap my hands around his neck and squeeze. A long walk in the wasteland would be a good character-building moment for him.

Another strafing burst of fire brought me back to the here and now instead of daydreaming. "So why are they chasing us?"

"Oh, yeah." Dave leaned up and studied the chat. "Apparently they are reporting that we are criminally trespassing because we blew through a toll point and didn't pay the access fee."

"Are you serious?"

The timing couldn't have been more perfect for the delivery of my words. No sooner had the word serious left my lips than something exploded on the highway to our right, between us and the Blackskulls' sedan.

That's when I saw another red flash on the screen. Henry had spelled out DUMBASS in all caps.

A hard chuckle escaped before I'd realized it. "Is that it, old man? I expected something a whole hell of a lot more angry and demeaning from you."

I must have gotten Henry pissed with that comment. A long series of expletives flashed up on the feed.

"Why, thank you for that FishKiller. We're glad that you're thinking about us in that way."

Dave grunted a laugh.

I grabbed the handset and keyed the mic. "Did anyone know that this was a toll road? Because apparently we blew through a toll point and that's why they're following us."

Freya keyed her mic and chimed in. "How the hell did you find that out?"

"Our clutch feed said that's what the networks are reporting."

"Frack me," Vincent said, breaking into the conversation. "Don't stop, just keep going. I've already made a call to an acquaintance I have up here. These socket-headed hotheads will be out for blood if they catch us, but I'm told that they usually give up pursuit once you get out of their jurisdiction. We just have to outrun them."

"What if we scatter?" Payne suggested. "We take different routes and scatter, then meet back up at a designated point outside of their jurisdiction afterward?"

"That's as good a plan as any," I replied. "Any suggestions on the rally point?"

Sam chimed in. "How about River Styx Park? If we jump off of I-77 onto 277, it'll take us to I-76. It's a little off the beaten path west of Akron, but I bet it'll be safe enough to meet up. From there we can jump onto I-71 to I-80, bypassing most of Cleveland."

Vincent chimed in with that nonchalant, uncaring tone to his voice. "Sounds good enough to me. Whatever we're going to do, let's just do it already."

I glanced back at Dave. "Can you keep them off our backs if we run?" He popped a snack cake in his mouth then finished the beer and began chewing loudly. Buster barked, begging for a bite.

"Yeah," Dave mumbled, crumbs tumbling out of his mouth. "I think I can manage that."

I keyed the mic. "We're jumping off at the next exit to throw them off. We'll see you at the River Styx."

I checked our six. "You ready, Dave?"

Dave switched between screens on the display, bringing up the GPS map. "Setting our destination waypoint to the River Styx Park," he said, then adjusted himself in his seat before tapping me on the back of the arm. "I'm as ready as I'll ever be."

"Then hang on." I hard braked Sally and her large tires barked in protest. We skidded along the pavement as the rest of the pack raced ahead, then I cut the wheel hard to the right, heading for the exit ramp.

Three of the pursuit cruisers broke off from the main pack following close behind us as we reached the end of the off-ramp and turned left onto South Arlington Road.

The unmistakable boom of a large caliber cannon pounded out behind us, the round missing by quite a bit. It impacted the side of a building ahead of us on our left followed by a rocket that flew wide, impacting the office of an abandoned used car lot.

These guys must not have cared about collateral damage on the outskirts of town. Granted, the area looked like it had been all but abandoned years ago, you'd think they would be a little more careful. At least the roads were clear of wrecks and debris.

"In about four thousand feet it's going to be a hard ninety-degree right turn onto East Turkeyfoot Lake Road," Dave called out. "And get ready to work your magic cuz here they come."

"Well, no shit Sherlock. What gave it away? The great big boom or the wild rocket?"

I downshifted, dropping it into third gear as we approached the intersection, and popped the brake, throwing us into a controlled skid around the corner. Regaining our traction I floored it again, pushing Sally for all she was worth.

Rounds ricochet off the hood and nose of the car. Instinctively I ducked, searching for the shooters.

"Dave!"

"What?" he shouted back, then fired the quad turret-mounted machine guns.

"Can you tell where those shots are coming from?"

"No! But I can tell you where they are about to come from."

There was barely enough time to check my mirrors before two of the pursuit cruisers expertly drifted through the intersection side by side in formation and the radar detector spiked. The detector warning buzzer screamed at us, picking up a target lock attempt by the cops.

"Go, go, go," Dave yelled. "Missile away!"

"Hang on!"

I jerked the wheel left, diving off of the paved road into an overgrown grassy field, heading for the back of a run-down church. Even with a decently aggressive tread for street tires, they still managed to slip and spin out on the damp grass. I downshifted, feathering the throttle causing us to slide.

The warning alarm became a solid symmetric tone and reached an ear-splitting crescendo.

"You know that missile pack we had installed last night?"

"Yeah…," Dave said.

"Fire her up."

I cut the wheel hard to the right, sliding around the back of the church across the slick grass, then downshifted, cutting the wheel left, and floored it. The back of the old church shattered in a blast of fire and shrapnel.

We cut a wide path around the edge of the blast zone, heading back the way we'd come. Our own target tone sounded out in the cab as I locked in the cruiser on the right as our target and fired.

The fire-and-forget missile shot ahead at an insane rate of speed. Dave opened fire on the cruiser to the left with all of our forward-firing machine guns, laying down an insanely beautiful line of destruction ahead of us. White hot phosphorus glowed as tracer rounds ricocheted across the front of the cruiser, skipping off in all directions.

Attempting to dodge the incoming missile, the cruiser on the right cut hard to their left, only presenting a larger target picture. The missile smashed into the side of the cruiser, striking low on the door. The explosion leveraged enough force to lift the side of the cruiser, rolling it over in mid-air.

"Ho…ly hell," Dave muttered in awe. "I love these missiles!"

The other cruiser fired its main gun again, striking somewhere on the driver's rear quarter, sending our rear end fishtailing. Warnings erupted across the dash. The left rear armor had been blown away, and one of the fuel cells flashed catastrophic damage. I watched in horror as the fuel gauge ticked downward, putting us at twenty-five gallons left.

In fighting to regain control, I diverted our course just enough to rake the driver's side edge of our ramplate down their side, shearing away the receiver section of their main gun and driver's side mirror in the process.

I fired off our driver's side mini rockets and Dave continued hammering home the pain, tracking the target as we blew by, making a bee-line for the pavement.

Sally lurched oddly, lumbering into the turn almost once we hit the blacktop. The steering suddenly felt sloppy, but it wasn't anything I couldn't work with. It was really more of an annoyance than anything.

Dave shifted, adjusting himself in the seat as he peered through the turret sights. "I think we lost them."

There wasn't a cruiser in sight when I checked the rearview mirror. Maybe he was right and we had gotten away.

"Could it really have been that easy to get away from two hot rod police cruisers?"

I saw Dave do his little shrug again through the rearview mirror. "Maybe they just look badass, but they are really piles of crap? You can make anything look pretty, but if it's made with cheap parts, it'll show in the end."

Maybe he was right. It felt nice to have a bit of good luck for a change.

Chapter 19

"Are you's guys going to be done any time soon?" Vincent impatiently shouted from across the parking lot. "Cause if not, I'm tempted to get back on the road to Toledo and just leave you here. The rest of us are ready to go."

"And the rest of you have had sponsors that give a shit," Dave rebutted a little less tactfully than I would have before I could open my mouth. The winnings and the new gear we'd picked up in Midville were damn nice to have, but they didn't help to repair damage in the field.

I installed the final self-sealing rivet into the patch of armor plating I'd been working on then dropped the rivet gun into the tool bag Dave had placed on the ground next to Sally. The patch wasn't pretty, but it would do as a field repair to cover the hole that those cannon rounds had put into Sally's quarter panel.

Dave kicked the rear bumper. "Come the frack on, already!" he reached into the trunk and started jerking at something, then fell backward when that something broke loose. He picked himself up off the ground and stared at the damaged fuel cell. The lower half dangled by a ragged strip of metal. Apparently, that last cannon hit had removed the missing material and carried it out through the hole it had created in the rear plating. Dave spun in place and chucked the cell off into the woods with an angry roar.

"You mean you can't fix that?"

Dave just glared at me with that defeated, don't frack with me look that mechanics sometimes get, then he took a deep breath. "There is a point, where parts do become irreparable, especially when you're lacking a shop or tools in order to carry out those repairs. That's when replacement becomes your only option." He angrily waggled an index finger at me, closed his eyes, and took in another slow, calming breath.

Buster barked in the distance. When I looked up I found him barking and chasing a grubby little girl and her mother who approached the parking lot of the park. She spun, danced, and giggled at the ugly, bug-eyed dog. The two happily played, circling around the mother as she continued toward us.

I'd met them earlier after I spotted the little girl spying on us from a distance. She'd been peeking out of her family's makeshift home, built from pieces of tarp, plywood, and what seemed like anything that could be stacked, taped, or nailed into place over a massive abandoned playground set that had incorporated the ten or so feet to the park's old restroom building, adding it to the structure.

When I saw how she stared at any of us who'd broken out anything at all to eat, even rations, I figured she was hungry and took over a few things we had that we could easily spare. It wouldn't hurt us in the least since we'd be in Toledo before the day was out and we would be able to restock there. And, besides, it wasn't like we hadn't eaten well on this trip, anyways.

When they reached us I gave Buster a treat. Then I handed the little girl the last of the small mint candies I'd snagged from the dinner in Knoxville. The mom couldn't have been much older than I was, but she proudly wore the lines of worry and a hard life. She looked like a bundle of nerves, beside herself with worry, and about to hurl chunks at any moment. She carried a small bundle, wrapped in a dingy grey cloth that she handed to me with a stiff curtsey and not another sound otherwise.

Slowly I peeled back the layers of cloth, revealing two small…, pastries, I guess would be the best description for it, both of which were still warm to the touch.

I turned and looked to Dave who shrugged, then turned back to the mother. "For us?"

She nodded with nervous anticipation, so I handed one of the small pastries to Dave and kept one for myself, handing the aged cloth back to the middle-aged woman. Breaking it open, I found it filled with a sticky brown and chunky mixture. It didn't look out of the ordinary compared to any other dessert I'd ever had that was similar, but the smell struck my senses so drastically to be nearly overwhelming. It had a sweet, tart, and oddly familiar underlying scent that I just couldn't put my finger on.

Dave sucked down his pastry in one bite, washing it down with a beer, and went right back to work, thanking her with a grunt and a nod that she returned in kind.

She watched me with rapt anticipation, anxiously waiting for my response, so I took a bite of the small morsel.

The explosion of flavors wrapped my senses in a warm and cozy combination of euphoric bliss that soothed my senses into submission as I slowly chewed. It tasted sweeter than it smelled, blended perfectly with the tart, tangy, and earthy flavor that she'd managed to pack into the tiny package.

The woman smiled.

"My husband and I agreed it were only fair to share in the spoils of what you'd provided us and make something special for the two of you. I'd been saving a few of the ingredients for a special occasion, and this seemed to be special enough to me. It isn't often at all that we get visitors. Let alone ones willing to share what little they have. So I told him, this is what it was going to be, and he dropped the argument."

She flashed another smile. Taking another bite I chewed slowly, letting it mingle on my tongue. None of the key flavors were individually overpowering, they were easily complimentary, creating a beautiful culinary concoction. I savored every bite of the small morsel.

"What is in this? It is heavenly, but I can't say that I know any of these flavors." The woman glowed at the sound of my words. She turned, covering her mouth and shying away like a nervous girl out on her first date. Color slowly crept up her neck as she flushed.

"I made it from dried Granny Smith apples we'd picked this year. James found a few trees growing wild back that way in the forest," she said, pointing off to the west. "There are also wild strawberries I'd collected this season, honey from a wild hive we were lucky enough to find, and dried sassafras root that I'd been saving back for a while."

I blinked, confused if I'd heard her right or not. I took another bite and chewed slowly, letting the flavors disperse evenly across my tastebuds. I tried to pick out each of the individual flavors from the constituted mixture so I wouldn't forget them, but they mixed together so well. I'd never had anything like this before in my life.

I swallowed and asked, "Did I hear you correctly? You used real fruit, that you'd picked?"

She smiled and excitedly nodded. "Yes, fresh picked this season too. Well, except for the sassafras root. The fruit was fresh this year and dried for keeping."

I'd had nothing but algae and algae-based products my entire life, and now multiple times during the course of this race I'd managed to be given real food. I could so easily get used to being spoiled by eating the real thing, not some reconstituted and chemically flavored algae product. Even though they filled up my stomach the same, there was something much more satisfying about the real thing. Maybe it was something about the flavor of the food itself, or maybe it was just the perceived difference, I really wasn't sure.

"I don't think I have ever had anything that tasted this wonderful in my life. Thank you."

She smiled, nodding again before she shied away and called for the little girl. Buster followed behind, barking and chasing the dirty, giggling ball of energy. The mother picked up the little girl and hurried back toward their shack once she noticed Vincent heading our way.

"Now that you're done schmoozing with the locals, can we get back on the fracking road?" He nervously shifted, adjusting the rings he wore on each finger like he was anxious about something. "Because I've got no problem leaving you's guys here. We still have about one hundred and twenty miles to go and a deadline to keep."

Dave slammed the trunk lid closed. "What's wrong, Vinny? Afraid you're going to miss a hot date or something? Trust me, she ain't missing out on much."

"Oh…" Vincent laughed. He spread his open palms out to either side. "I see how it is." He chuckled and looked around at the other pack members whose attention was now focused on him. "This *dog* apparently didn't get the hint before."

The camera drones were circling again, gathering as close as possible to catch the action and drama of the moment. Ruth Lezz, Trip, Payne, and a few others had started to amble their way closer to us.

Dave had stepped over next to me and leaned up against Sally's front fender. He pulled a small knife from his pocket and started cleaning under his nails with the tip of the blade. "You apparently missed the part where I really don't give a frack, didn't you, Vinny."

He lowered his head and charged toward Dave. I stepped in, intercepting him. Shoulder checking him, I wrapped my arms around his torso, the full force of his bull charge spinning us so that I slammed him against Sally's driver's side door. In one swift motion, I grabbed him by the collar and started lifting him off the ground.

"If you've got a problem with my gunner, then you've got a problem with me," I said. The seething anger that had all of a sudden crept into my voice surprised even me. "I don't have much to lose; I've already died. Did you want to join the club?"

"Hey," Ruth Lezz shouted. "You children need to be done with your pissing contest because we've got company." She pointed high into the sky at two larger drones that were about as big as a regular-sized family sedan, each carrying a bundle that dangled from a cable beneath them.

I turned my attention back to Vincent and growled before shoving him away. He started to reach for his side piece, but as soon as I noticed the indecision on his face, I'd already removed the securing thong and had a firm grip on my own weapon. He thought better of it and huffed off back to his own car.

"You know we'll need to really watch our backs here on out," Dave warned.

I had already been calculating the risk in the back of my head of what had just happened and what could happen in the near future. I didn't like the odds, but it was all part of the gig. And to rule the airwaves, it was all about the ratings, drama being the next best ratings draw to action and destruction.

"Yeah." I sighed. "I know." I turned to Dave. "As much as I hate playing politics, it's just all part of the game." He nodded in agreement and we both turned our attention to the large drone that had begun its descent just above us. The second drone had descended next to the family's makeshift shack, dropped its cargo, and had begun ascending by the time the first one had made it over to us.

Our drone set its cargo down gently about twenty feet away, detached the cable, and quickly ascended, heading off in the direction its wingman had taken toward the east.

Dave had made it over to the package ahead of me and began removing the tarp wrapped around a cardboard box that was about the size of a coffee table. He tore away an envelope that had been taped to the top and handed it to me, then cut open the top of the box with his pocket knife.

"It's packed full of foodstuff. Protein bars, supplemental nutrition boosters, energy drinks," he said, digging through the box. He popped the top of one of the energy drinks and took two good chugs from the can. "Hell, yeah. I could get used to this."

"Does it have any markings on it anywhere?"

He rocked the box back and forth, looking at all sides including the bottom, and shook his head. "Nothing that I can see." He nodded at the envelope in my hand. What's that say?"

A drone swooped in close, trying to get a closer peek of the envelope over my shoulder. I grabbed it by its undercarriage and pulled it in close, staring into the camera. The blades whirred, trying to pull itself away, but I had a good grip on the framework.

"You know, it's kinda rude to try and read over someone else's shoulder." I reared back and flung the drone into the air, giving it a good spin as I did. Frantically the controller had righted the drone and regained control a few feet short of the ground. I glanced around at the other drones surrounding me. "Anyone else want to try that?" The buzzing mechanical swarm seemed to take a step back in response to my question, so I turned my attention back to the envelope.

Opening it, I found a letter and a cred chip.

From the offices of Lifoods, Limited Inc.
Attention: Team JunkYard Dawgs

Thank you for using several of the Lifoods family of products in your recent act of kindness shown to those in a situation less fortunate than your own. Please accept this small gift as a token of our gratitude for your continued support and use of the Lifoods family of products.

Also, you will find a credit chip with a $5,000 limit enclosed. Please consider this initial stipend our pledge to you as an active supporting team sponsor that you can count on. Feel free to use these funds at your discretion.

Good luck in your endeavors
Gina Howe CEO Lifoods, Limited Inc.

Never in my wildest dreams would I have expected anything like this for sharing what I had with anyone else.

I always had what I needed. My dad made damn sure of that. But we never had a lot of extra. At least not a lot of extra that would have been considered an extravagance. We made do with what we had, and if someone in our building needed something, there were more than a few of the other tenants who were willing and made sure that those in need had what they needed. Even if it happened to be anonymously delivered to their doorstep when there were conveniently no witnesses around.

It was just the way it was. And it never fails to amaze me when people find that as something special.

Chapter 20

"It looks to me like our teams are going to be in for a world of hurt very soon, Alex."

"Why would you say something like that, Chuck?"

"Well, for starters, rumor has it that there are scores of unknown and amateur Autoduellists who are fired up over the Dead Man's Run. Even though they didn't qualify for the event, they are bound and determined to make a name for themselves out there on the open road."

"Sounds like there might be a number of jealous and spiteful Autoduellists out there with a chip on their shoulders."

"Indeed, there are, Chuck. The thought is, that if they can take out one of our teams, they'll get the attention that they deserve."

"Does the AADA have protocols in place should there be irrefutable evidence of unsolicited tampering with a sanctioned event?"

"There are, and the penalties are aggressively severe in comparison to even a federal felony charge."

"I'm sure that only time will tell what level of stupid rears its head during the course of this event."

"No doubt, Chuck. I'm sure that it will turn out to be a case of frack around and find out to the extreme."

Liquid fire poured across Sally's hood scorching the paint and windshield. Smoke rolled into the cab where the napalm melted through the windshield seals.

It was a good thing we were in the middle of a downpour because that was probably the only thing keeping us alive at that moment. Otherwise, I would have expected the glass to melt under the intense heat of the fire and fill the cab, baking us inside with it. The ones on motorcycles must have been either desperate or stupid to be putting up a fight in this kinda weather because the odds were seriously stacked against them.

They had boxed us in while the rest of the pack scattered and ran ahead. A car on either side slammed into us, pinning us in place while another brought up the rear, pushing us along whether we wanted to go or not. The motorcycle ahead of us had swung into position and began spewing the naphtha mixture across our nose in an attempt to cook us out.

Dave wasted the guys on the bike, unloading our quad turret-mounted machine guns into them. The gunner and his flame thrower fell backward, bouncing on the pavement before abruptly meeting our reinforced steel ramplate. The driverless chopper swerved to the left, bounced off of the guardrail, cut sharply back to the right, and crossed our path before colliding with the car on our right.

Pinky the minivan on the left braked hard in an attempt to avoid the out-of-control bike, anticipating the collision. I stomped on the brake pedal, locking up all four wheels. The tires barked and screamed at the sudden lack of rotation.

While brake-checking tailgaters was generally a bad idea, this was one time that it was acceptable. The socket head behind us must not have been paying attention, because it felt like he'd hit us at full speed from behind, lifting our rear wheels off the ground.

Accessing the rear targeting camera I powered on the flaming oil jet and fired, coating the car behind us. Shifting Sally's differential into four-wheel drive, I floored it, pulling us ahead and off of the nose of the trailing vehicle. Jinking left, we broke away from the blockade, streaming a trail of fiery oil behind us.

I grabbed the handset and keyed the mic. "It would be really nice if someone were back here giving us a hand. It's kinda hard to work as a pack when the pack keeps running away."

I was seriously starting to think that more of our pack mates besides Vincent didn't actually like us and were only putting up with us while they had to.

"Do we really need them?" Dave asked, then fired off another volley from the upper machine guns.

Three more bikes soared across the opposite lanes, landing in the overgrown grassy median of the highway before racing up the steep shoulder and leaping into our path.

I didn't waste any time and pulled both triggers for our forward-firing machine guns. The first tracer rounds penetrated the rider and ricocheted off of the first bike to hit the pavement. The rider fell to the side, dragging the bike with him and the pair skidded out of control, spinning as they slid across the asphalt.

"What's with these idiots?" Dave shouted. "You'd think they'd be smart enough to come at us in something with a bit more armor to it."

"Your guess is as good as mine."

Amateurs

Flashed in angry red letters across the Clutch feed.

"No, really FishKiller? I don't know what would ever give you the idea that these guys were amateurs"

"Sorry guys," came a softly cute voice over the radio. It was Jane from the Booze Reapers. "It's survival of the fittest. If they are focused on you, then we can all get away to finish the rally."

She wasn't wrong, but that didn't make me any less pissed off.

"Frack 'em," Dave shouted, then fired off one of the passenger side rockets at a truck that raced down the on-ramp. "Who needs them anyways!"

"Mayday," another call came over the radios. "Razor is down, I repeat, Razor is down." It was Payne from Disaster Force. She sounded panicked. But that wasn't much of a surprise considering the pummeling her car was taking that we could easily hear over the transmission.

We rounded the next corner amid a spray of gunfire being poured into Disaster Force's low-rider luxury sedan. Two pickups took turns bumping their tail end, causing them to skid slightly out of control. In the distance I spotted the rest of the pack, their taillights marking their location on the highway ahead through the storm.

"Someone, H…," she'd started to beg, almost screaming when the transmission was suddenly cut off in time to three rockets hammering home into the driver's side of Disaster Force's car. Both trucks rammed the car from behind, sending it spiraling out of control into the median where it slammed into a stand of trees. From what I could tell, it looked like the impact had crumpled the front end so badly that the power plant was now sitting partially in the cab.

Then it exploded.

The world went blindingly bright in the flash of an instant. I could have sworn I felt the heat coming off the ball of flames that roiled out from what remained of the once gorgeous dark blue sedan.

I hoped she died in either the instant that the rockets hit or when she'd slammed into the trees. Because seeing the flames lick out from the inside of the cab like they were, brought up an entire mess of feelings. The pit of my stomach ached at the thought of ever being trapped again in a vehicle, burning alive.

Chapter 21

The word had to be getting out because it seemed like anyone with a chip on their shoulder trying to make a name for themselves had come out of the woodwork. Mile after excruciating mile turned up more and more amateurs or bandits just trying to make a fast buck that turned out to be as harmless as a swarm of lovebugs, and we were still on the outskirts of what remained of Cleveland, Ohio.

Then there were the hastily assembled roadblocks that seemed to be getting more and more elaborate the further along we went.

People were opportunistic, and they'd take advantage of any opportunity that would allow them a quick win, even if there was a chance that their lives would be forfeited in the end.

Maybe the draw for a piece of any pie was just too much for them to resist. Or maybe it was a matter of what they loved, their passion, where they could have their cake and eat it too.

Either way, for the moment, we were sitting ducks.

This most recent roadblock had been slapped together using several heavy construction vehicles parked perpendicular to the interstate blocking off an underpass. Dozens of junk cars and shipping containers were stacked around, creating layers upon layers that needed to be cleared somehow, topped with what seemed like anything else they could get their hands on to roll out onto the highway and drop onto the pile.

While Vincent, Sam, and Trip argued about the best way to clear the debris, I took the opportunity to give back a little to our growing number of viewers. Even though I personally despised doing it, I kicked back in the driver's seat with the door open and my feet propped through the open window while sipping on the last beer in the fridge and interacting with our viewers.

There were all sorts of questions coming from other amateur drivers, old-school fans and just Autoduelling enthusiasts in general. The ones that I wasn't sure how to take were a couple of rabid fan girls in the chat that wanted my devoted attention and had started arguing amongst themselves. At the point that they started sending direct messages aside from the chat feed, I started to get a little creeped out. They were stating things like they wanted to have my babies and they'd be my *good little girls* if I'd be their *daddy.*

Yeah… I'm sure that if I'd said yes, I would have had an experience that I'd never forget, but I just wasn't into that sorta thing. But to each their own, ya know.

That's when I started banning them from the chat and managed to figure out how to give ShellBackBeau5918 and Dwarfdave3672 admin rights within the server so they could help me to corral the craziness.

The other major upside to the wait was that Dave had time to scrounge around to see what he could scavenge from the barricade and the raiders' vehicles. He'd managed to stock us up pretty well on personal rounds, but the icing on the cake was the two serviceable Jackhammers he'd found. There were big and heavy slug throwers, with a slow cyclic firing rate. But the kicker was that the projectile they fired was quite a bit larger than say a 40mm grenade. And the rounds could be made of a number of base metals or alloys including depleted uranium rounds.

And we just happened to be in luck…

Because Dave turned into a giddy schoolgirl at the prospect of mounting those weapons onto his car. Using scrap from the barricade to build a frame, Dave mounted one of the Jackhammers to the top of the front passenger fender, then mounted the other to the driver's rear quarter panel in order to balance the load so it wasn't horribly weighed down on one side or the other.

Besides rigging up the two new guns, he'd found quite a bit of spare ammo that he confiscated to replenish our supplies before passing out the rest of what he'd come across with the other teams. After that earlier comment from Jane, I'd seriously considered letting the spare ammo rot in the ditch before giving it away, but that just didn't feel right.

After a while, I got bored sitting there and basically doing nothing. So I said my goodbyes for the moment and started walking toward the barricade to see how things were going. On the way, I stopped and checked over some of the bandit's bodies. Emptying all of their pockets out onto the ground as I searched, looking for anything of use. I pocketed a lighter and a few random loose rounds of ammunition I'd come across. What I had really hoped to find was anything that would identify the individuals, even though I really didn't expect to find much of anything. If we could get an idea of who they were or if they were part of a specific gang, then we might be able to get a better idea of how to deal with them.

Pulling the last bandit free of the vehicle he'd been driving, I repeated what I'd done almost a dozen times already to this point and emptied the guy's pockets out on the ground.

Random detritus, a folded sheet of paper tucked into a cargo pocket, two loose shotgun shells that I pocketed myself, and a decent-looking boot knife with a sheath that I removed and strapped onto my own leg and tucked under the pant leg of my racing suit.

The folded sheet of paper was black in spots from dried spatters of blood. It looked like it had been hastily folded and tucked away in the pocket with little care. For all that I knew they could just be the guy's grocery list if bandits and raiders made grocery lists, but I unfolded it anyway, just in case they contained anything useful.

I froze. It was a call-to-arms type bounty sheet like you'd see in one of those old western vids. Nothing fancy, no graphics even. Just a cut-and-dry statement and payout.

$2,000 reward!
per confirmed kill of rally racers
participating in the
Dead Man's Run road rally.

I stood up and yelled at the others. "We might have a slight problem!"

That's when the body suddenly let out a coughing groan and shifted, attempting to roll over onto his side. He blinked and winced in pain when I pushed him back and tapped him on the chest. The side of his head was caked with dried blood, nearly matting his eye shut.

"Hey, man, hold still." I pulled a cloth from the car he was in and dabbed at the blood, trying to clear his eye. "You with me, man?"

He nodded, and weakly whispered, "Yeah."

"Do you know where you are?"

He opened his good eye, forcing the bloody and swollen eye open, and glanced about, then he locked in on me. His eyes went wide with surprise.

"I'll take that as a yes," I said, then held up the sheet of paper so he could see it. "Who hired out a hit on us?"

He shook his head and pursed his lips.

"You've got a better chance of living if you talk.

He shook his head again and whispered, "I don't know nothing, man."

"Naw, I think this was something," I said, pointing at the paper again.

Vincent suddenly rounded the rear of the guy's car and stepped over beside where I knelt next to him. "What pain in the ass are you causing me now? Do you want to get out of here before another batch of asshats with an agenda shows up?"

"We've got a major problem," I said, nearly growling at Vincent.

"We've got a hundred different problems right now, so what's your point."

"I'd be willing to be that this is a bit bigger than the rest of them put together."

"So then spit it out already and make it quick, what's the problem?"

I just held the paper up in his direction, handing it back over my shoulder.

He unfolded the paper, then smacked it with the back of his hand. "The frack is this shit? And who the frack are you?" he shouted then buried the tip of his shoe into the guy's unprotected side.

The guy let out a cry of pain and curled up into a ball. I stood and shoved Vincent back then stood between the two of them. "The guy is already beaten up enough. He can't tell us anything if you kill him."

By now, Dave and a few others had gathered to see what was going on. I turned my back on Vincent and knelt back down next to the guy.

"Hey man, you got family?"

He nodded slowly. Worry, or maybe it was the realization of what his situation was showed on his tear-streaked and blood-crusted face.

"You got a Gold Cross membership?"

Slowly he shook his head from side to side and the tears flowed even more heavily.

"Then you need to help us to help yourself," I said as calmly as I could. "Who sent out this bounty?"

"Who do report to in order to be paid?" Vincent shouted over my shoulder.

The guy dryly swallowed, trying to get his breath before he whispered, "Owligation."

Vincent shoved me to the side and kicked the guy again. "You're lying!"

It took me half a moment to be back up on my feet and shoulder-checking Vincent. We tumbled against the side of the guy's car, my momentum carrying us along and spinning us along the length of the car. Vincent brought his knee up into my groin at the same time he brought down both of his fists onto my back. I felt more than heard a sickening crack when the blow connected, knocking the wind clean out of me. I collapsed to my knees at Vincent's feet.

I started to pull myself back up when the crack of a gunshot halted everyone in their tracks.

We turned, looking in the direction of the shot, and found Dave, wisps of smoke rolling from the barrel of his drawn weapon. Vincent quickly checked himself, then noticed the small concealed gun in the bandit's hand.

We looked back to Dave who shrugged, then holstered his gun. Vincent screamed and then kicked the body. "What the hell are you doing?"

"I could have just let him shoot you in the back."

Vincent stormed off, rushing back toward his car. "Sam! We've got ourselves a major problem! Get the boss on the horn!"

Chapter 22

After quite a bit of more or less begging, Vincent finally let us in on the little secret as to why he started to lose his shit when the bandit had mentioned the name Owligation.

After a little digging around on the net, Bullseye from the Booze Reapers was able to find out that Owligation was owned by the Groller family, and controlled a large portion of territory in the southeast, which happened to be primarily Atlanta, Georgia to Charleston, South Carolina, to Raleigh, North Carolina, to Knoxville, Tennessee.

And the Groller's just happened to be the quote, unquote *family* that Vincent and Sam worked for.

That wasn't good.

That wasn't good for any of us. If our own sponsors were putting out bounties on our heads, that turned this into a whole other ballgame. It wasn't just a matter of finishing the rally anymore. It was a matter of literal life or death at this point.

Not to say that it wasn't in the first place, but when there's a chance that someone could be gunning for you, even off the track or outside of the arena, that completely changes the rules of engagement for the event.

And I had no doubt that even if someone decided to quit, completely walk away from the rally, and never look back that their head would still count as a bounty payout.

The thing that unnerved me the most was how many more bounties were out there? How many more sponsors, corporations, or even rich as frack viewers out there that wanted to do nothing more than sow chaos and up the ratings had hired out hits on all of us working stiffs that were just trying to earn a living?

Only time would tell at this point.

After clearing a large enough hole in the barricade for all of us to get through, it wasn't long before we found ourselves heading west on I-80 and finally making good time.

That was before this hot little brunette in a leather top, daisy dukes, and fishnets happened to be standing in the middle of the interstate where the roadway leveled out as we crested a rise. She was a bit on the grubby side, dirt or rust maybe caked the side of her leg like she'd fallen. She also wasn't starved or plump, so she'd been at least eating on a semi-regular basis.

"Anyone else got a bad feeling about this?" Ruth Lezz said across the radios.

I grabbed the handset and keyed the mic. "Oh," I said, laughing, "you mean after finding out that Vincent and Sam's people have hits out on us? Nope," I said, accentuating the P with an extra hard pop. "Are you kidding?" I said sarcastically. "I don't get any creepy feelings whatsoever about some hot little number standing in the middle of the highway in fishnets trying to hitchhike from the middle of nowhere. How about the rest of you?"

More chatter came across the frequency, but nothing that helped in any way.

So, I slowed, coming to a stop maybe twenty feet away from where she stood, then I unlatched my harness and got out.

"Are you stupid or something?" Dave shouted after me, and Buster grumbled at his uneasiness.

"Just need to stretch my legs is all."

The other pack members had pulled up next to us and were all looking at me like they were questioning my sanity.

Ruth Lezz rolled down the driver's window of the combat camper and stared at me with that look like she'd slap me upside the head if I were closer. "Did you hit your head or something? Or maybe you've got exhaust fumes leaking into the cab of that junk heap of yours?"

"Naw," I said, shaking my head slowly. "Just wanted to stretch my legs is all."

"Thank you," the woman said and took a step toward us. I think I may have heard the click of her heel on the pavement before my brain even registered the motion from her step.

I realized that I was really going to need a vacation of some kind to wind down after this because, in that split second of motion, my revolver was in my hand, hammer back, and aimed between the woman's eyes.

The look on her face told me that she was as confused as my pack mates had been about my impromptu stop.

I opened the face of my helmet and nodded at her with a slight salute. "No offense, ma'am, but I'd be much more comfortable if you stayed right where you are. Now… Do you care to explain to us what you're doing standing in the middle of the highway?"

"They have my family, my kids for fracks sake. There's a bunch of others down there that they've taken prisoner too." She threw her hands out to the side, pleading, and took another step forward.

"I wouldn't do that," I warned and re-centered my sights on the center of her forehead. "I told you to say where you are."

Cringing, she put her hands up and started to cry, begging for help through heavy sobs and a shower of tears. "It's the Sleepless."

"The Sleepless," I asked. "Never heard of them before."

"They're a new biker gang to the area that has taken over an old truck stop just off of the turnpike in the heart of Elyria and turned it into a roadhouse."

"And exactly why is that supposed to be our problem?"

"They've got our kids." Her face scrunched and twisted as she fought off another agonizing bout of sobbing.

"That still doesn't have anything to do with us", Ruth Lezz stated plainly.

"And we are limited on time to make it to Toledo," Vincent added. "Not to mention, we now have bounties out on our heads. I for one am continuing on," he said then rolled up his window and drove away, giving the woman a wide berth as he drove past.

"Sorry, guys," Ruth apologized. "I've got to agree with Vincent. This isn't our problem. But maybe once we make it to Toledo we can send someone with authority back here to deal with the problem." She pulled away trailing behind the Blackskulls followed by The Booze Reapers and the Grim Aces.

I leaned down and looked back toward Dave. "What do you think?"

"Something tells me that she's telling the truth. They need help. Just got this good gut feeling about it."

I looked down at Buster who was propped up on the dashboard, keeping an eye on the woman. "What do you think?" He grumbled and shook like an anxious chihuahua.

I holstered my gun and turned back to the woman. "Alright, so come on and get in. Tell us more about what we're up against.

We continued down the highway for a few more miles before she directed us to pull off and head behind an old shopping plaza where the truck stop was located.

According to the woman, Clarita, The Sleepless had been terrorizing small towns up and down I-80 all summer and had only recently set up shop in the truck stop as their new home base. I parked a good distance away behind some defunct and abandoned fast-food restaurant and we hoofed it over from there to get a better idea of what we were dealing with.

Dave wanted to go in guns blazing and waste the lot of them, but that wouldn't help us in the least when it came to rescuing the hostages. We surveyed the area, and found lines of bikes parked out front of the roadhouse. Hidden just around the side of the building Dave managed to spot two tractor-trailers that had been built out as rolling battle wagons. We could barely make them out from this angle, but we could see the fronts of each rig as well as the top of what looked like forward and aft gun tower positions built onto the tops of both rigs.

Dave put away his binoculars. "The element of surprise is our only advantage."

"Why don't we just drive down there so you can talk to them and show them you mean business," Clarita urged.

I scratched at the days worth of growth on my chin and slapped Dave across the arm with the back of my hand. "How many points do you think it would be worth if we could take out both of the gang's battle wagons?"

Dave chewed on his lower lip for a moment while he thought it over. "Few hundred at least I would expect.:

"I wonder if we'd get bonus points for taking out the clubhouse too?"

He looked at me with a wide, shit-eating grin that crossed his face. "Now you're talking my kinda chaos. We could burn it down."

Clarita let out a frustrated huff and turned, stepping away from us. Buster grumbled, but Dave covered his snout before he could bark and give us away. Then she suddenly turned back around, gun in hand, and leveled right between my eyes. I could see the built-in laser sight of the easily concealable Saturday night special dancing across my nose, temporarily flashing into each of my eyes.

"I'm so tired of you two's back and forth. Yako wanted meat; I found him meat. Now, walk," she said, motioning with the pistol.

I swallowed hard and asked her probably the last question that I really wanted an answer to. "What do you mean, meat?"

"You, you're meat. And the club works so much better after they've had meat in their bellies. Walk.".

I turned and looked back at Dave. "I really hate you right now."

He shrugged his noncommital shrug. "I never said my gut ever made sense."

"But look at where we are now." I shoved Dave then he dropped Buster before returning the shove, pushing me backward into her.

Buster locked onto her left ankle and she swatted at him with the barrel of the gun. I turned, slamming my elbow into the side of her head while Dave wrestled the gun from her grip.

"I normally have a rule against hitting a woman," I said as I turned back to face her and hit her with my very best right cross. "But you've earned an exception to that rule."

After tying her up with what we could find nearby, we left her behind one of the buildings and hot-footed it back to Sally.

"With it starting to get dark and these guys are already drinking, it'll be a cakewalk to score extra points and rack up before the gang even knew what hit them."

"Is your gut telling you that too?" I chided.

"Oh, haha, fracking ha," Dave said laughing then suddenly froze. A gleaming smile crept slowly across his face. I knew that mischievous look in his eyes. And any time he'd gotten that look, it didn't end well for the other party. "I've got an idea." He dove into the back seat and rummaged around, stuffing things into his pockets. "You and Buster sit tight and wait for my signal, then come in blazing. Take out anything that looks like a biker," he said then sprinted off into the growing darkness.

I wasn't sure if I wanted to wait around while he did something epically sketchy compared to his normal sort of questionable actions, but I didn't want to just up and leave him here on his own either. Henry would kill me if I did.

I switched back to the Clutch feed at that thought and guessed that Henry was probably pretty pissed off at this point. Angry red letters flashed across the screen, filling up the chat feed without giving anyone the chance to get a word in edgewise. I could almost hear Henry half pleading half angry yelling at me with the final message in the feed.

Don't let him go off on his own!

I shrugged and looked straight into the camera. "He's a grown man who can take care of himself. Not much I can do when he gets a wild hair up his ass. You know that."

Two bright red flares shot high into the sky, followed by a massive explosion from behind the roadhouse.

Buster barked and growled at the pyrotechnics.

"Yeah, I bet you're right. That's probably the signal." I shifted into first and floored it, weapons hot.

Cutting around the shopping plaza, I cut the wheel hard, heading into the old truck stop parking lot. The bikers had made their pride and joy way too tempting of a target by lining up the two dozen or so bikes side by side in front of the building.

I circled around to the far end of the parking lot to get a good angle at the run and floored it. Metal twisted and glass shattered as bikes flew to the left and the right, bouncing off the cattleguard-style ramplate that Dave had installed on Sally's nose.

Bikers poured out of the building into the parking lot and unloaded everything they had in my direction, pounding Sally's rear end so hard it sounded like the hailstorm of the apocalypse.

I rounded a burned-out wreck left in the parking lot and floored it again, breaking traction and skidding sideways. Even after adding the new weapons, Sally was a little bit slower but still handled nearly as well as she did to start with. Steering into the skid, I brought our forward machine guns to bear on the gathered bikers and unleashed a fiery hell upon them. They scattered in all directions. Some ducked back inside while others ran around the edge of the building or dove behind anything that afforded some touch of cover.

The entire area lit up. Flood lights mounted high on the front of the building flashed to life, turning the darkened parking lot into a bright-as-day shooting gallery.

As I made another pass at the far end of the parking lot an ancient-looking SWAT team transport rounded the end of the building. It had been heavily modified and added to at some point in its history. Pieces of raw steel sheet metal from stripped cars and what looked like chain link fencing had been added to the outer shell of the transport for some reason.

The transports turret aimed in our direction and fired. Heavy caliber rounds pounded our ramplate, chewing away at it so heavily that chunks near the edges flew away, giving it a serrated look along the top and right edges of the plate. I cut it hard to the right, swerving behind a demolished truck, trying to flank the transport. Then I popped the parking brake and floored it, drifting to the left around the wreck and steering into the skid.

"It would really be nice to have some help, Dave," I shouted out of frustration.

More of the high-caliber rounds from the transport pounded the driver's side, penetrating the door. One of the rounds penetrated the bulletproof glass of the passenger door, grazing my forehead just above my right eyebrow. Another clipped the lower left side of my back. Any further to the left and it would have easily removed my left kidney.

I jerked, yanking the wheel to the right which caused us to spin out of control. We slid sideways through the wreckage of motorcycles and came skidding to a sudden stop against the side of the building. Sally's engine sputtered and clacked to a halt.

I cycled the switches and pressed the start button. A low, chugging whirr followed slowly by another answered the call and then stopped.

"Dammit, Dave," I shouted, slamming my fists into the steering wheel. "Where the hell are you!"

I held down the ignition this time, hoping it would make a difference, but it didn't.

The transport reappeared and fired, tearing two holes through the passenger side door that impacted the beer fridge, causing the pressurized keg Dave had picked up in Midville to explode, spewing beer throughout the cab.

If I couldn't get this thing moving I was going to be toast. I pressed the ignition again and tapped at the gas pedal, but nothing happened.

Then the transport slammed headlong into me, pushing Sally backward like she was a plastic kids' toy. When I tried the brakes, the wheels only locked and skidded across the crumbling concrete of the sidewalk.

Then I shifted, throwing the shifter into reverse before popping the clutch. Sally lurched to life, and I floored the accelerator. Cutting the wheel, I spun her one hundred and eighty degrees, shifting to first and dumping the clutch as soon as I'd slammed the shifter into gear.

My head slammed back against the headrest. The transport had caught up and crushed in our rear. Before I could pull away the transport slammed into Sally's rear again, spinning me out of control.

I smacked the steering wheel again. "The hell is wrong with me? This is easy driving!" Rubbing my face, I sucked in a deep breath and pulled it together. There was no way we were going to take down this roadhouse with that transport running loose. I had to take it out, but with what? Then I remembered the large caliber Jackhammers that Dave had installed.

They were both online and ready to fire, so I floored it again in pursuit of the transport. It hadn't gotten too far and was rounding the pile of junk cars near the end of the building when I centered my reticle on it and fired. The Jackhammer sequentially double-tapped two rounds out in under a second, sending shock waves through Sally's beaten and broken frame.

The depleted uranium rounds penetrated the forward armor like it was nothing more than tissue paper.

I fired again and Sally groaned, pulling to the right under the strain of the recoil. Smoke rolled from multiple points across the transport's armor. If those rounds hadn't disabled the thing or killed the crew, at least it would smoke them out.

Cutting right and then swerving left around more abandoned vehicles I managed to get behind the transport and get a missile lock on the rear hatch. I fired the

Jackhammer once more just to soften up the rear armor then depressed the trigger, launching two missiles from their racks.

Both missiles flew true, impacting the rear of the transport just as something large and black plowed into the side of it. One of the tractor-trailer battle wagons we'd spotted earlier had flanked and t-boned the transport. The transport's wheels violently caught on the pavement causing it to buck, lifting the front end of the tractor-trailer off the ground. The transport landed on its side with the truck mounted like some wild mating of mechanical beasts. A shower of sparks poured from under the transport as the pair skidded across the pavement to a halt.

I pulled alongside to find Dave climbing down from the driver's seat of the truck. He bounced when he dropped to the ground and rubbed at his right shoulder. He was smiling his big mischievous shit-eating grin at me.

"About damned time you showed up!"

"Awwww, I didn't know you cared. You really did miss me, didn't you?"

"Not at all. You can go ahead and stop fooling yourself if that's what you were thinking. I was out here having the time of my life without you."

"Well, it isn't my fault, anyways. The wiring on that thing is tangled worse than a bowl of spaghetti. Took me forever to figure out how these idiots had rewired it."

The handle of the top hatch on the transport started to wiggle. Dave smiled and held up a finger, motioning for me to be quiet then stepped toward the hatch. Producing a grenade from his pocket, he pulled the pin, jerked the hatch open, and tossed it in before dogging the hatch shut.

Dave paused, patiently staring at the hatch. There was a muffled whump from inside the transport. He let out a low chuckle, then turned, heading back toward me.

"Maybe I should be worried that you're enjoying yourself a little too much."

He shook his head and opened the passenger door. "Naw, you don't have to worry about that none. There are a few things I enjoy more."

"Then why are you smiling?"

"Because those fuel tanks on those trucks are almost full and I might be able to make a few upgrades before we take off again."

"You okay?" I nodded to where he was holding his shoulder.

"Yeah, I'll be fine. Just banged up a bit from running the truck into that tin can." He flashed a smile and then started to climb in, but suddenly stopped.

"What the frack happened to my beer fridge?"

I looked back at the devastation the APC's rounds had caused, and it was a mess. Shoving the half-opened door back into place, he let out a quiet whimper.

"Those guys," I said, pointing at the transport.

Dave unholstered his sidearm and fired two rounds into the rear armor of the transport before he slid into his beer-soaked seat and checked his systems. Buster climbed into his lap and started licking his face.

"Why'd you waste the ammo?"

He shrugged. "Felt good."

"Let's get this wrapped up and see what we can do to help the prisoners."

"Sounds like a plan to me."

Chapter 23

"You know Chuck, even though the rest of the pack is a few hours ahead, the JunkYard Dawgs have managed to rack up an impressive amount of points in a short period of time with that stop to rescue the damsel in distress.

Not only did they completely eliminate The Sleepless, but they also destroyed thirty-two combat-capable motorcycles, two tractor-trailer battle wagons, the gang's clubhouse, and took out an APC of all things completely on their own."

"And who can forget this heartwarming scene, Alex." The view shifted to a replay of a little girl handing Dave a flower and of him being very uncomfortable, then he gave her a fist bump.

"Not to mention saving the townspeople."

"Too right, Chuck."

"And to be in their position with that stockpile of weapons, ammunition, and supplies that The Sleepless had accumulated over the last few months must be overwhelming for them."

"It's like being a kid in a candy store, I'm sure, Chuck."

"Or a big kid in a gun store," Alex said then laughed.

"Right you are Chuck," Alex said, chuckling. "How right you are."

You'd think that something resembling authority would make a concerted effort to remove threats like The Sleepless had been.

We managed to release thirty-two souls from enslavement by the gang. They were mostly recent captures that the gang had picked up from Elyria and the surrounding area.

And the worst part was what we found out after the fact. Once anyone had become useless, no matter if they had been captured or were part of the gang, they were immediately placed on the menu.

The locals helped us to knock out several repairs and fill our tanks with anything that would work as fuel, as well as several jerry cans that we slung to the side with cargo netting.

Dave had been ready to set the roadhouse on fire once we'd finished going room to room clearing it of all the bikers, but I made him wait. There were too many supplies and too much valuable gear there to just burn it. The locals loaded up a few vehicles and the undamaged battle wagon with what they could before we placed the bodies inside, and had all gathered out front of the building.

At that point, we watched with rapt anticipation as Dave ignited the building. And it wasn't a simple matter of lighting the trail of gas and running. He'd taken the time to carefully run trails throughout every room, then by combining the fuel with styrofoam, turning it into a gel-like substance that he painted across the front of the building.

When he did light the single point he'd trailed all the others together for ignition, the flames chased the line of fuel into the building. As the warm, orange glow grew from inside, the trail of fire raced back out the door and ignited the words that Dave had painted across the front of the building.

Here The Sleepless rest, for the longest sleep of their lives, burned with odd greenish-blue flames.

Everyone stood around, watching the fire grow higher until the building was completely consumed in flames.

"I can't thank you enough for what you've done for us," an older man with what looked like an old school grenade launcher and a bandoleer of 40mm grenades said as he approached where we'd parked Sally in the parking lot out front of the building. "Many of us wouldn't have lasted much longer if you two hadn't come along."

"It was our pleasure." I took his offered hand and shook.

"The name is Dirk, Dirk Deal. And believe it or not, I was once the mayor around these parts."

"Pleasure to meet you Dirk, I'm Ricky and that's Dave," I said, thumbing back over my shoulder toward my gunner.

Removing the bandoleer from over his shoulder he held it and the launcher out to me. "I'd like you to have these as a token of our appreciation. They were my grandfather's, and I think he'd approve of what you've done here."

The man's eyes glistened as he patiently waited for me to take the gift.

"Don't you need them?"

"Yes," he said questioningly. "but there are plenty of other weapons we've acquired from the gang that I can pick from."

I took the launcher from him and admired the classic rugged design. It was an older military design with a six-round drum that nobody had been able to improve on over the years.

"I promise I'll take good care of it for you." He smiled at that and turned to walk away when a middle-aged woman was the next person who wanted to thank us and handed me a sack of apples.

Other members of the community stepped up offering small gifts and trinkets in thanks. One older gentleman even offered his daughter's hand in marriage. While she was beyond cute and more likely fell into the category of a true-to-life baby doll with those big blue doe eyes of hers, I had to refuse. I explained to him that a road rally was no place for a young bride, not to mention we didn't have any room in the car for her. He thought for a moment, kicking at the dirt then mentioned that he had a young son who was also available if that happened to be the case.

It was sometime well after midnight by the time we got on the road heading west for Toledo. After the flood of gifts, we inquired about the route ahead, then double-checked our gear once more before heading out and putting the miles behind us as fast as we could.

Chapter 24

I'd expected to roll into Toledo amid fanfare and scores of Autoduel fans welcoming us into the city.

What we got was the furthest possible thing from it that would qualify as the exact and total opposite. We rolled into Toledo just before daybreak, minutes from the deadline to reach the checkpoint for the first leg of the race, and it was an absolute ghost town.

We were directed to the pits, where we were assigned a garage stall that was stocked with a full assortment of Kern-Tools that were at our disposal. After a tour of the shop and services that was more lengthy than we really cared about given by our checkpoint liaison, we were escorted to the green room and one hell of a breakfast buffet. Even though it looked good and smelled amazing, I was sure that it wouldn't come close to holding a candle to the real food we'd already had along the way over the last few days..

Ruth and Freya from team Queentastic, Vincent and Sam from the Blackskulls, as well as The Booze Reapers, Jane and Bullseye, and The Grim Aces, were seated at a long table.

Two drones followed us into the room and swung wide in opposite directions, getting a wide-angle shot of the entire room.

"Long time no see, fellas," Vincent shouted in our direction. Buster growled and fought against Dave to be set down. When Dave set him down on the ground, he grumbled and barked, but otherwise stayed right next to Dave, more or less hiding from the others by keeping Dave's legs between him and Vincent.

"Vincent," I said, nodding in acknowledgment toward him. Dave ignored the lot of them, heading straight for the stack of clean plates at the end of the buffet.

"I heard that you two seriously racked up on points with that stop. At least that's the chatter coming from our viewers on the feed."

"Oh, they didn't tell you?"

"No one here will tell us anything," Sam added "Every one of them are as tight-lipped as a new fish in the yard."

"It's good to see you boys again," Ruth Lezz added. "The most that we've gotten out of anyone so far is that the main event will be held this evening at an undisclosed location."

"Then you will have all morning for any repairs we or our crews need to make," interrupted an eye-blindingly bright-dressed woman with an overly annoying nasal voice. She approached the table and continued. "There will be interviews this afternoon that you are all contractually obligated to attend, then when the time comes, you will all be transported by limo to the main event site."

"And you are?" I asked, turning to face the newcomer.

"Sandra Von Kamph, project coordinator for the Atlanta pack during this rally," she replied. After years of driving a cab, she was one of the stranger-looking network types I'd ever met. She wore a bright yellow wide-collared jumpsuit with fluffy tuxedo cravat, white knee-high pleather boots all topped off with a neon yellow bouffant hairdo that had to have stood at least six inches high from the top of her head. "It's a pleasure to finally meet all of you."

Dave raised his hand above his head.

"Yes," she asked, enthusiastically calling on him like a teacher in the classroom.

Dave lowered his hand. "If you're supposed to be our liaison, then why haven't we met you before now?"

With a derisive smirk, she waved off his question and continued toward us, taking a small piece of something resembling meat from Jane's plate. Tasting the morsel by dabbing it against the tip of her tongue, she shrugged and then nibbled lightly on the tidbit. Rounding the end of the table she half sat on the corner, turning to face in our direction.

"It really would have been counterproductive," she continued. "By getting to know each and every one of you before the race had started would have only amounted to the majority of that work going to waste, my boy." She winked and waggled her eyebrows at Dave while suggestively nibbling on the morsel.

"What do you mean a waste of time," Jane asked.

Sandra let out a long sigh as if the explanation was painfully inconvenient for her. "I mean, my dear girl, that it would have been a waste of my time to have gotten to know the twelve teams that left Atlanta, because only five teams made it to the checkpoint. In the grander scheme of things, it's much easier to work with the living," she giggle snorted. "Don't you think?"

"Geeze," Trip grumbled under his breath, going back to poking at the food on his plate, stabbing this or that with the tines of his fork.

"I going to have to agree with Trip's sentiment," I mentioned, breaking into the conversation. "Exactly what is it that you do?"

She pushed herself upright off the table and paced around where I was standing. Then, looking down her nose at me she took a deep breath and began her explanation. "I will be your personal liaison to the networks, to the AADA, and to the world. Should you manage to complete the next challenge, I will advise you on how to best benefit and profit from your success. I will help you to manage your fame in such a way, that in the end, everyone *will* know your name."

She flashed a shark-like smile then turned and strutted away to the other end of the room where she began mixing herself a cocktail with one of those tiny beach umbrellas.

Dave laughed. "And you thought I was bad for having a shower beer, Ricky. She's going after the hard stuff before breakfast."

She snubbed her nose at Dave and then huffed. "There is never an inappropriate time for a well-mixed cocktail or to look absolutely fabulous. It's just all part of the gig, darling."

I grabbed a biscuit from the table and took a bite. "Then let's stop screwing off and get to work. We didn't drive all this way just to look pretty."

And that's where I should have kept my mouth shut, because to my surprise, looking good was exactly what we were supposed to be doing. As part of what they had planned out for the pregame show, we were to all look our finest for team interviews broadcast over most networks. Dave refused to get gussied up and paraded around like some prize purebred, so instead he adamantly insisted on staying behind to work on Sally's repairs.

According to Sandra, the viewers adored Buster in his cute little racing suit, and she insisted that I bring him along for the interview. So with Buster under my arm, we were each escorted to our own trailers where a team of makeup and wardrobe experts took on the challenge of each team.

Taking mine and Dave's regular occupation into account, they decided to dress me up in jeans and a black button-down shirt with an embroidered name tag that said Ricky over the pocket. On the back, they'd printed a large Henry's Garage logo that took up most of the space, and sponsor patches decorated the sleeves. I knew about Lifoods, because of the letter we'd received with the supply drop, but my shirt had two patches on each sleeve. Lifoods and Beedle tools had been sewn to the left while Ravencoms and Iron Mountain Brewing were on the right. I'd have to check out the clutch feed and the AADA messaging service. I was sure there would be a notification in there somewhere. Or maybe the official notification was sent to my apartment, or to Henry's garage?"

That was something that could be figured out easily enough later on, but curiosity was really starting to get the better of me.

Even with his bulging bug eyes, Buster looked cute. They'd bathed him, trimmed his nails, and had given him a full work over before dressing him in a much smaller, but an exact duplicate of my shirt with his own mini name tag and sponsor patches. I was without a doubt sure that someone out there would fall in love with the little shit and want a stuffed plushie or something after seeing him on the vids.

After makeup and wardrobe had finished with us, we were delivered via limos to the local Pinnacle Productions studio.

Based out of Chicago, they tended to produce a more urban-centric type of programming than anything else. Everything from cooking shows to dramas, family sitcoms, and live-action reality television, all based in Chicago. I hadn't seen a lot of shows produced by Pinnacle, but every now and then Peachmedia, our local Atlanta network would license a show from Pinnacle as reruns in our market. They turned out to be mostly investigative live-action cop shows or the Illegal Duelist, which was one of my favorites. It followed a group of underground Autoduellists through their day-to-day lives, dealing with competing gangs and groups for the coveted title of Chicago's biggest baddest Autoduellists.

As soon as we arrived, they ushered us inside and lined us up backstage. The pre-game show for tonight's event was already underway.

Ruth Lezz and Freya Domme of Queentastic were dressed to the nines in the latest and greatest drag queen fashions. Vincent and Sam of the Blackskulls looked like dapper gangsters or maybe even secret service agents in their pinstripe suits and sunglasses. Jane 'Thunder' Cooper & Bullseye of The Booze Reapers had been dressed up to resemble Bonnie and Clyde, or maybe like they'd just stepped out of a nineteen twenties speakeasy. Bullseye wore what amounted to an oversized zoot suit, while Jane looked extremely uncomfortable in a tassel-covered flappers dress. Then there were the Grim Aces, Trip and Holeshot, who they'd decked out in the latest of cyberduel ware, slacks, silk jackets, and wrap-around shades trimmed in micro neon strip lights that gave them the impression of glowing racing stripes.

Ruth and Freya were announced first and ushered onto the stage by backstage workers amid strobing lights, fireworks, and dancing lasers. They were met center stage by the hostess, Anushree Parekh, superstar of the stage, screen, and the runway, who introduced the team before escorting them to two billowy couches placed at an angle to each other, like a chevron with the point aimed toward the back of the stage.

Then Anushree announced the interviewer, who was none other than Devon Varady, the legendary TranceRacer himself who strutted out on stage, shook hands and fake hugged Anushree, then Ruth, then Freya with a mock kiss to either cheek before each of them took their seats. TranceRacer sat on the right-hand couch at the point of the chevron while Anushree sat on the opposite end. Ruth and Freya sat across from them on the opposite couch.

Discussing a number of topics, the guests and hosts laughed, cried, and brought light to some of the discrimination they'd faced and hardships they'd been through on their climb up the ladder of the Autoduelling world. The interview lasted around thirty minutes and seemed to leave most of the live audience empowered and contemplative about what really happens behind the scenes of the Autoduelling world. Next they called up the Grim Aces, followed by the Blackskulls, and The Booze Reapers, following a similar pattern to their line of questioning with each team.

Then it was my turn.

Buster had been squirming and grumbling the entire time we'd been waiting, so I just set him down and told him to go. Wouldn't you know it, the little attention whore pranced out on the stage, head high, tongue lolling out of one side of his mouth. He stopped dead in his tracks and looked out at the live audience when the entire studio erupted in a collective monophonic *awwwww*. He bounced and barked at the crowd, eliciting laughs and even more guffawing over his goofy ass.

After shaking hands with TranceRacer, I sat on the couch opposite of him and called Buster up by patting the seat next to me and calling his name. The little shit grumbled then hopped up and sat in my lap.

"I have to say," TranceRacer began, "that you, your gunner, and Buster have created quite a stir among the fans and viewers."

Without thinking, I laughed nervously. "You don't say, TranceRacer? I hope that it's for the positive and not the negative."

He put on a fake smile and laughed, then crossed his legs. "Please, call me Devon."

"Alright, Devon. If that's what you prefer."

He nodded then said, "I do," before drifting off into momentary thought. "You started off like many other Autoduellists, working your way up the ranks through the amateur leagues, building a name for yourself. Then you managed to earn the title of first, Reboot Ricky, followed by Ricky the Ripper, which had an entirely negative connotation in the beginning but has since pulled a one-hundred-and-eighty-degree turn, becoming a name that is now held in a positive light."

I shook my head, unsure of what he was talking about. "I'm not sure that I follow."

Devon chuckled again. "You mean you didn't know that you were the talk of the event?"

"Um…No. Not really. I mean, it's not like I've had a whole lot of time to watch the vids or anything the last few days."

"My boy…" Devon waved toward the off-stage crew. "Can we bring up the viewer ratings?"

The curtain covering the back wall of the stage opened, revealing three massive screens that displayed a splash screen with the Dead Man's Run logo spread across all three screens. Dramatically, it flashed, like the signal was being corrupted with gibberish transmissions mixed with static before the display shifted showing multiple bar graphs across the three screens. AADA special event ranking stood out in bold letters across the top of the screen and each of the graphs were labeled with the names of all twelve teams that started out in Atlanta, with only five of them illuminated. The others were dark and greyed out with Eliminated stamped diagonally across their graphs in bloody red letters.

"Now, if you take a look at the current standings of the JunkYard Dawgs against the other teams from Pack Atlanta, you'll see a marked difference in viewership, with many more heroic deeds, compassionate moments, and so on and so forth over your compatriots. And according to your AADA records report, there has been more than fifteen thousand dollars deposited by fans alone into your AADA account since the beginning of the event."

I'd turned and stared up blankly at the screen, unsure what to even say.

"The cut and dry of it is that the people love you, Ricky," Devon continued. "Even now, your numbers are climbing," he pointed out, then waved at someone off-stage again. "Bring up his Clutch feed, please."

The screens shifted once again to display the Clutch feed I'd gotten so used to seeing and most of the time dreaded interacting with. But it was all part of the gig, and I suppose what I had been doing was working. And there, prominent on the screen in flashing angry red letters was FishKiller2000

Roll Dawgs!
Shake the Ground!

Several other usernames popped off with the same phrase, and how much they loved team JunkYard Dawgs, but nothing compared to seeing those huge flashing red letters on the screen.

"And there," Devon said, pointing at the screen. "You just had another," squinting, he counted, "another fifty dollars just got donated to the cause."

I turned to look at the screen again, confused at what he was looking at. "How do you know that?"

"See those gold coins at the end of the message?"

"Yeah, I said, nodding."

"Each one of those is equal to ten dollars pledged and directly deposited into your AADA account. If you see an emoji that looks like a stack of bills, that's one hundred dollars pledged to the cause."

I thought back for a moment and realized there had been a lot of those at times, especially while Dave had been working on repairs and I'd be checking in on the feed, interacting with the viewers.

"Huh…"

Devon chuckled and smiled at the live audience. "Isn't it amazing how innocent he is, folks?"

"Before this week, I'd never spent any time on Clutch. It just never dawned on me that donating through the feed was some kind of a thing."

"Well, believe it, because even now, it's happening," Devon said, pointing up at the feed once again. I looked back to see a line of hearts, coins, and hearts from Gamermaid992.

"Thank you Gamermaid! The support is appreciated more than you could ever know."

"So," Devon started, "how have things been since you jumped back into the saddle?"

"What do you mean?"

"I can't speak from experience, but I've heard from several professional Autoduellists that I have known over the years that a Gold Cross reboot can be a life-changing experience. More than a few of those have hung up their hats afterward, never entering the arena again.

"It's… Strange," I started, thinking about what to really tell the world. "It's very confusing and disorienting at first. The most disconcerting part of it to me was the loss of time. That's nine weeks that I'll never get back, because I technically didn't exist during that time. I'd died, burned to ash. But then at the same time, I was still alive in a sense as a braintape that would eventually be uploaded into my clone."

I swallowed and thought for a moment. "It makes you wonder if it was all a dream, or how real anything before was, while fighting with the idea that they were technically someone else's memories."

"That's pretty heavy." Devon chuckled. "Is that why you did this?" He pointed toward the screen and nodded to the offstage crew.

The screen came to life with the dash cam view of The Miracle Mutant's cab, and Vision, their pink mohawked driver who was bloody and gasping for breath. I suddenly appeared in the view. Kneeling down beside her I took her left hand in mine then leaned in close and spoke softly. "Do you have Gold Cross?" Which just as before, she slowly nodded, wincing in pain at the motion.

That's when I removed the dash-mounted camera from its mounting and aimed it at myself.

"Someone out there, I don't care who, an announcer, a fan, someone from their family, make sure that they see *all* of the footage leading up to this moment. They need to know what happened. I happen to know that there is nothing fun about the cold emptiness left behind after a reboot."

Letting the camera drop loose, it flopped behind the steering wheel and hung there upside down, but still transmitting the feed.

Pulling my sidearm, I stood, cocked the hammer, and aimed the revolver between her eyes. The crack of a smile appeared at the edges of her mouth before she mouthed the words, *thank you*, tears streaming down her blood-caked cheeks.

What felt like an eternity when it was happening turned out to be only moments before Dave appeared behind me, his weapon drawn and firing, the video feed frozen at that moment.

Devon continued in a soft, caring tone, "What exactly was going through your mind at that moment when you hesitated?"

I thought back, but all I could see ahead was nothing. The dark coldness of the void engulfed me once again. I took a deep breath and turned back to Devon, wiping at the tears that threatened to escape. Then I told him plainly. "Nothing," I said. "Absolute cold, dark, nothing."

He nodded, satisfied with my answer, and turned back to the studio audience. "Now, to something a bit lighter." He motioned back toward the screens. "Roll the clip."

A montage of videos and still images of Buster raced across the screens to cheers and exhalations of joy and laughter from the studio audience, finishing up with a camera close-up of the bug-eyed little freak as he sat on my lap, tongue lolled out to the side. Members of the audience held up signs with *'We love buster'* and *'The real JunkYard Dawg'* for the roving camera drones.

"If I didn't know any better," he continued with another chuckle. "I'd say that Buster had just as many if not more fans than you do."

"I'm starting to wonder myself."

"So, what's the deal with this little guy and why on Earth did you think bringing a dog along for the event was a good idea?"

I shrugged. "There really isn't much to tell. He was the pet of my former gunner, Parker Hensley, who'd left Buster to me in his will. Since Dave was coming along with me on the event, I really didn't have anyone to watch him, and he didn't seem to like the idea of being left behind either." I scratched him on the back of the head. "So, we just brought him along with us. We figured it wouldn't hurt anything to have him along for the ride. It wasn't like he was going to eat a lot or really get in the way, so why not?"

"Fair enough," Devon agreed with a nod, then pointed back to the screens. "Now, what about your gunner, Dave? Why isn't he here to share in the limelight with the two of you?"

"He's never been much for unwarranted attention, so he stayed back in the pits to get as many repairs done as possible."

Devon laughed again. "Why is he doing the repairs? Where's your pit crew?"

"He is the pit crew."

"Oh…," Devon said in realization. "Now I see." He let out a long sigh and momentarily stared at the floor as if in contemplation. He nodded and laughed. "I remember those days all too well. We were our own pit crew as well in the early days of the Cosmic Eagles.

Still, images of Dave flashed across the screen spanning from his half-naked moment in the pits at the starting line while climbing into his race suit to Dave fist bumping a little girl just before we left Elyria, finishing on the image of him firing that first shot into Vision before the feed faded to black.

"I'm not sure what you want to know about him. He's just…," I stopped, struggling to come up with a good description of my gunner and cohort, "he's just Dave, man."

"I have to say, he is a man of almost complete obscurity. We have had trouble finding nearly any information on him with the exception of a driver's license and citizen registration with the city of Atlanta. Otherwise, he is a complete enigma."

I thought for a minute, trying to recall anything he might have told me about his past or anything beyond the day-to-day drudgery, and came up empty-handed. I shrugged, attempting to duplicate Dave's own nonplussed gesture. "Your guess is as good as mine. You probably know more about him than I do, honestly."

"Then let's take it to the pits and see what he has to say for himself." Devon motioned off stage and the video feed shifted to a view of the pits from the many camera drones roaming the area. Rounding a corner into a repair bay, Sally sat on the lift a few feet off the ground, all four wheels removed as well as other miscellaneous bits and pieces scattered about the shop area. Dave sat at the back of the bay on a stool, his coveralls unzipped and the arms tied around his waist. Nearly every inch of his white wife beater tank top was as stained and dirty as his arms and face were.

Dave perked up and stopped in mid-drink as he turned up a beer can, scrutinizing the drone that approached.

"The frack do you want? Can't you see I'm busy in here?" He turned up the beer and chugged.

"Mind if we ask you a question?" Devon shouted, startling Dave who spit out the mouth full of beer he'd just poured into his mouth.

"The frack?" Dave yelled, then threw the half-empty can of beer at the drone before reaching for a large wrench laying on the top of the tool bench. "You can fracking frack off before I really get fracking pissed and use this wrench for a proper attitude adjustment on your fracking scrap metal ass." Dave tapped the drone on the underside with the tip of the wrench before it could back out of range. "You'll leave now if you know what's good for you." He grabbed the drone with his free hand and walked it out of the bay, then flung it into the air before the drone controller could react.

"I told you, Dave is Dave."

"Apparently so," Devon replied. "I'd like to thank you for coming out today to talk with us and good luck with tonight's match. I've heard that it will be one hell of a challenge to complete." He turned back to face the studio audience and cameras. "Stay tuned for more action, as we broadcast live coverage of the Atlanta Pack's first checkpoint battle in, the Dead Man's Run!"

Chapter 25

"Can you believe it, Chuck? We are at the first checkpoint challenge of the Dead Man's Run! I haven't been this excited about an Autoduel match in a very long time."

"You and me both, Alex. I'd like to welcome all of our viewers to stay tuned to tonight's main event because you're sure to see some true carnage and mayhem. Tonight's landmark event at the Hensville Park Memorial Battle Arena marks the official end of the first leg of this three-leg rally. The teams remaining after the completion of tonight's match will have their points totaled in order to determine initial winnings and the bonuses to be awarded to the top three teams."

"And just to remind our viewers, Chuck, that any team unable to complete the match does not qualify for any bonuses, no matter what their point count is in the end."

"That's good to know, Alex. Now, what type of event can we all expect to see tonight?"

"Tonight's event is one part cat and mouse, three parts mayhem, Chuck. In this match of Buffalo Hunt, our teams will be working together to take down two SWAT-style combat vans equipped with oversized power plants, heavy armor, and spiked ram plates. They will be scored by any hits or damage sustained to the target vans caused by one of our teams. Secondly, any takedowns, i.e., disabling one of the combat vans will earn that team an additional one hundred points toward their final tally. The match is over when both battle vans have been disabled, or alternatively, our teams."

"The track is a classic three-tiered tower of power with connecting ramps at four points between levels. While the *Buffalo'* will be starting on the main oval at the base of the track, our teams will be starting at the top level of the course and must race down the tower to catch these overpowered beasts."

"That does sound like one intense challenge, Chuck. What can we expect our teams to have in the way of hardware for tonight's event?"

"The teams will use brand new factory-produced Joseph Specials, supplied by tonight's primary sponsor, Uncle Al, exactly as they rolled off the assembly line back in 2029.

"While the Joseph Special," Alex broke in, "was one of the earliest factory-ready dueling vehicles to roll off of any assembly line in 2029 to great fanfare of the customer base, it remained a solid seller for years. Despite the original Joseph Special's side plating being severely under-armored by current standards, many of the original models are still on the road today, with too many victories to their credit to count."

"For tonight's event," Chuck continued, "we will see the use of a modified Joseph Special B variant for load outs. Linked machine guns have been installed in the roof-mounted turrets with a single heavy rocket mounted in the rear and a single buffalo gun mounted to the hood to round things out. But the trickiest part of this match is that our teams only have three shots from their buffalo guns, so they had better make every shot count."

"No doubt, Chuck, but what are those machine guns going to do against the heavy plate armor on those battle vans?"

"Make it mad?" Alex chuckled. "In all seriousness, the machine guns may not be able to do much, but a skilled gunner might be able to get past the wheel skirting and take out a tire, but that's only if they happen to get really lucky, Chuck."

"Well, let's hope that they do because I have a feeling that our teams may be up against nearly impossible odds in the first checkpoint challenge of the Dead Man's Run! Stay tuned for the main event, right after a short word from our sponsors."

In no time flat, they had us back to the pits and out of our fancy getups. They supplied us with fresh race suits, sporting the new sponsor patches on either sleeve. When I held up Buster's jacket, he fussed until I got it over his head and fastened it in place. I was starting to think that the little shit was enjoying all of the extra attention he was getting.

When the transport picked us up from makeup and wardrobe with the rest of the teams, Dave was already on board, grumpy and dressed in his own new race suit.

En route, they'd given us the briefing of the match and rules, but when we entered the arena and spotted the *Buffalos*, my heart sank. Those battle vans were painted a deep shade of black as dark and bleak as our chances of us doing any damage to them. They were absolute beasts, even without any weapons aboard. With only three rounds in the buffalo gun and a single heavy rocket each, we would have to concentrate our fire and coordinate our attacks in order to disable both of them. Dave guessed that the best we'd be able to do with the machine guns was to piss them off, or potentially blind them with enough fire to the bulletproof window slits.

They dropped us off behind our line of vehicles, which were parked side by side on the top tier of the pyramid. Each car was painted in our primary sponsor's colors, sporting their logo across the hood and all other sponsor's logos were scattered and spread out across the vehicle's body panels.

The Joseph Special wasn't a bad-looking car. A larger sedan design with squarish but sleek lines, accented by the addition of weapons points.

Dave did a quick walk-around inspection; checking under the hood, in the trunk, and each of the weapons points for a once over before sliding into the passenger seat and activating the gunner's controls.

"This is going to be interesting," he said, nearly giddy.

"What's going to be interesting?"

I dropped Buster into the driver's seat and he immediately hopped into the back and walked in circles for a moment before settling down into his spot.

"The turret has the mark two auto-center option. Basically, I tap anywhere around on this diagram, and the turret will quickly center itself to aim in that direction." He tapped the screen, and the machine guns quickly turned, aiming in my direction.

I sidestepped the barrels and did my own quick walkaround. The car bristled with camera points installed inside and out, and a number of them tracked me as I slid into the driver's seat.

Dave froze and looked over at the moving cameras, then stared at the three cameras on the dash in front of him. "Well, that's just a bit creepy."

"Yeah…," I said, then slid my helmet into place.

He tried to go back to his controls but the cameras staring at him unnerved him badly enough that he reached up and popped the three mounted to the dash off of their mounts. Ripping the connected wiring away, he tossed the micro cameras out onto the ground, then closed the passenger door.

The ready warning warbled across the arena.

I smacked him across the chest with the back of my hand. "You ready?"

"Ready as I'll ever be," he responded and slid his own helmet into place.

I powered up the Joseph Special, and the scent of fresh ozone filled the cab. "Gotta love that new car smell."

Dave shrugged and mumbled a meh.

I activated the team comms. "JunkYard Dawgs, online." The others followed suit, chiming in as they powered up and prepared to go.

Then the boom of the start gun resounded across the arena.

"Let's shake the ground," I shouted, chanting our battle cry.

Dave turned his helmeted head toward me, and I could just imagine the glare behind his face shield. "Not in this thing we won't. Sally is not a Joseph Special."

"Fair enough," I said and shifted into drive. Flooring the accelerator I cut hard to the left, directing us toward the nearest of the four ramps leading off of this level.

Off to our right, I caught the Grim Aces running parallel with us and the Booze Reapers following in line just behind us.

"What in the hell kind of shady matches is this?" Vincent shouted over the comms.

I didn't even have to ask what he meant. As soon as we'd come to within twenty feet of the ramp, a pop-up turret appeared and started spewing liquid fire in our direction.

"That's going to make things a bit more interesting," Dave said, then opened fire on the flamethrower emplacement.

"You think?"

I jerked the wheel, cutting left and then cutting the wheel hard back to the right, trying to avoid the burning stream. No sooner had we reached the ramp that the turret exploded, showering liquid fire down on us and in at least a twenty-foot radius across the arena floor.

Before we'd even reached the bottom of the ramp, another turret nearly blocking the next ramp popped up from the arena floor.

"Dave, turret!"

"Already on it."

The machine guns spun, centering in the direction of the next threat, and began pounding away, quickly penetrating the turret's defenses. It exploded just as the previous one had, showering liquid fire across a wide area of the arena to include us. Luckily it was only a few flaming spatters that stuck, but otherwise, it wasn't anything serious to worry about.

Reaching the next and final ramp before reaching the main raceway activated yet another of the flaming turrets. Dave and Holeshot from the Grim Aces unloaded on the turret, detonating it like the others in three quick bursts.

We hit the ramp, or maybe I should say the lack of ramp, and the sickening lurch of zero-G kicked in momentarily as we soared over the edge from the second tier. One of the Buffalo vans raced by the ramp, continuing around the oval at what I guessed was their top speed. The Buffalo van barreled along at a speed greater than I expected them to be capable of considering their size, but they did say that the power plants had been upgraded.

Buster squeaked out a grumbling bark just before we touched down near the bottom of the ramp. "Yeah, yeah," I grumbled back at him. "I'd like to see you try and do any better."

Catching pavement, I cut the wheel hard to the right and floored it, attempting to keep as much of our forward momentum as possible while drifting the corner.

Even with the accelerator to the floor, we weren't making much progress, we were barely gaining on the hulk of a vehicle. I was starting to think they'd made this match overly difficult to complete. If we couldn't catch the target, we couldn't disable it.

I thought for a brief moment about turning it around and heading in the opposite direction to intercept them, but then I spotted the Grim Aces coming down the ramp from the second tier ahead. I thought they'd been following us down the ramps, but apparently, I was wrong.

The Grim Aces turret spun around, spitting fire back toward the battle van before firing their single heavy rocket that impacted the thick ramplate mounted to the front of the vehicle.

Then the battle van lurched ahead, fishtailing slightly as its rear tires billowed white smoke. It slammed into the back of the Grim Aces sedan, destroying its rear end.

"Trip! What the hell are you doing," I called over the team comm channel.

"Scoring some serious points, bro!"

"Dave, do you think you can hit their tires?"

"Trip or that battle van?"

"Dave!"

"Alright, alright. Dunno, but I can sure give it a try."

Tracers bounced off of the raceway and the back of the battle van, pockmarking the rear passenger wheel skirt.

I thought for a split second about cutting back up the ramp the Grim Aces had come down to reach the second level and bypass this lower and longer section of track, potentially cutting ahead unless the arena had some other surprise waiting for us that just hadn't been played out yet.

Then the buffalo lurched forward again in a blur of speed, colliding with the Grim Aces once again. They swerved, attempting to lose the van, but only managing to skid out of control, slamming sideways into the front of the battle van.

"Keep her steady," Dave said.

The tires of the Grim Aces sedan must have caught just right on the pavement because they started to roll. Over and over they tumbled like a barrel being bucked by a bull in the ring, flinging pieces and parts all over the roadway.

I cut the wheel hard to the right and aimed for the ramp.

"What the hell are you doing?" Dave shouted. "I was about to put a buffalo-sized hole in them!"

"Saving our asses."

No sooner had we detoured up the ramp than I saw what was left of the Grim Aces sedan soaring over the top of the battle van and come crashing down onto the pavement behind it. The car crumpled in such a way that I was sure the unibody frame had broken at multiple points.

I hoped that the Autoduel gods had taken pity on them and released their souls from their bodies the moment the van slammed into them, because I couldn't imagine what would have been going through their minds if they were still alive at the point that they went airborne.

Reaching the top of the ramp, two new turrets emerged on either side of the ramp from the arena floor. Before both autocannons opened fire, the report of our machine guns overhead barked, and empty brass rained down from above.

"Dave! Do something!"

"What the hell do you think I'm doing?"

I cut the wheel sharp, bobbing right then left, grazing the side of the autocannon on the left, then buzzed by another of the machine gun turrets that sprung up, skipping off it with our right side. Rounds peppered our rear as we continued past, fleeing the mechanical onslaught.

"At this rate, there won't be anything left for the buffalo to destroy." Dave chided.

"Think you're funny, don't you? While I'm trying to keep us from getting the car shot out from under us, you're cracking horrible jokes."

A boom drew my attention to the lower raceway on my left. The Booze Reapers trailed behind the buffalo van and fired their buffalo gun.

"Make 'em count," I mumbled more to myself than anyone else.. I watched the large lumbering vehicle as it started into the turn of the oval.

It leaned.

"What kind of damage do you think it would do to us if I rammed one of these bastards?"

"Suicide."

"Seriously. Look how it's leaning on the turn. If I can time it just right and tap its rear corner just as we're coming off the next ramp, maybe we can tip it over. I saw Dave's head turn in my direction and lean back in surprise.

"Cow tipping?"

"What?"

"You seriously want to go cow-tipping at a time like this?"

"Frack yes! If we can tip them, we can get to their unarmored underbelly."

"What makes you think the underside is unarmored?" Dave asked.

"Doesn't make sense to armor it when we don't have any mines or anything else to use against it."

"Not like mines would do any good against the skirting on those vans anyways if we had them."

"So, what about tapping them?"

"Don't go square on," he answered. "Hit them with a glancing blow on the back corner so it doesn't screw us up so bad, but it needs to be solid enough that it over centers them."

"Easy enough. I think."

I slowed us enough to get around the ramp to the upper level and floored it again. I'd gotten so used to driving Sally over the last few days that I missed the extra actions of clutch, shift, and gas. There was something comforting in dropping a gear and having additional power available that no electric vehicle could match.

Another boom from below echoed through the arena.

"Jane," I called over the pack frequency. Don't waste your shots."

"How else are we supposed to take out these things?"

"I have a plan."

"Oh, really? And what sort of brilliant plan is that?"

"Just trust me. Keep trying to pop their tires, but otherwise, we'll meet you at the bottom of the next ramp."

"Roger that. It better be a good one, 'cause we're out of ideas."

I watched the van and the Booze Reapers rounding the corner. I was going to have to time this just right. Hitting the ramp too early would put us hitting the van too far forward or square on in the side, and we'd most likely just bounce off and be dead in the water. Hitting the ramp too late just meant we'd miss our opportunity and be trailing behind again like before.

Nearing the ramp, I braked, avoiding the debris from a destroyed machine gun turret emplacement near the top of the ramp. I tried my best to avoid the mess scattered across the ground. The last thing we needed was a flat tire when that was about the only thing we had going for us.

"Jane, back it off. Don't want you to get caught in a pile-up if this plan goes south."

I watched the van near the target zone, pacing it as we dropped over the top of the ramp, flooring it when we started our downhill run.

The van lurched forward with a burst of speed. Its driver must have spotted us and guessed what we were about to do.

"Can you distract them a bit?"

"On it," Dave answered as if we were a well-oiled military team. Adjusting, I changed our angle of attack, timing our descent. The new course would drop us onto the main track, skimming the edge of the ramp.

We didn't have many other choices at that point. It was what it was. I had the accelerator smashed against the floor.

"Hang on!"

The buffalo van was even larger than I thought it would be up close. Racing by it was a massive black blur.

The world jerked sideways.

We connected, and the front right corner of our nose wrapped itself around the rear corner of the van.

I cut the wheel to the left, steering into the strike. The van shifted, the rear wheel lifting off from the ground.

Rubber barked against the pavement first from the sideways skid as we pushed their tail, second, from their sudden burst of power to pull away, which only pulled us around with them where our nose was still connected.

Dave belted out a cheerful whoop. "Frack me!"

Cutting the wheel hard to the right, I steered into the turn and they started to roll, lifting our nose skyward. There was nothing I could do to control our direction and just kept the pedal smashed down against the floor. We went for a ride. The moment the van over-centered and toppled, I felt our rear end leave the pavement before our nose broke free from the collision.

"Hot damn! You did it, Ricky," Jane shouted over the comms.

We bounced hard three times before the front regained traction, and I cut the wheel, bringing the skid back under control. Sparks rolled ahead of the van as it skidded across the pavement on its side. The distinctive booming report of a buffalo gun sounded off to our rear, and impacted the underside of the buffalo van.

The Booze Reapers raced ahead of us, firing their final shot into the belly of the van before I could get us aimed in the right direction.

Dave immediately unloaded our machine guns once he'd gotten his bearings and re-targeted the van. Tracers splintered off the underside of the downed vehicle and I cut the wheel hard right, bringing our rear to bear in a rearward slide, blindly firing the heavy rocket installed in our trunk.

Roiling red flames followed the impact. Adjusting our course, our nose swung around, sliding us sideways. Before I could regain control we slammed into the underside of the burning van and came to a sudden stop.

Buster yelped, colliding with the side panel in the back seat, then climbed into the front and hid in the floorboard between Dave's legs.

"You okay, little buddy?" He reached down and scratched the back of Buster's head.

I tapped the pack frequency. "First buffalo down. Anyone got a bead on the other one?"

"We're hot on its tail," Ruth reported, "with the Blackskulls right here next to us."

"How did you take it out?" Vincent asked, breaking into the conversation.

"Get up on them and pull a PIT maneuver if you can," I replied. "We hit them hard coming off a ramp and managed to roll them, but they were already lumbering from being in the turn."

"We can barely keep up with this one when it hits the boost." Ruth continued. "How did you get ahead of them?"

"We took a shortcut by cutting up to the second level and just managed to get ahead of them. The roadway is partially blocked on this end, so they'll have to slow it down. If you can cut across the top like we did there's a good chance you can get ahead too.."

"Well, that was a good idea while it lasted," Vincent interrupted.

"Why, what happened?"

"They just turned up the ramp to the second level," Ruth answered.

Vincent laughed. "Either these guys know what's up or it could have been a pre-planned route. They could easily be listening in to our comms channel."

"Either way, keep on them. Let me know which way they go, we're on our way up. Jane, Bullseye, did either of you catch all of that?"

"We copy," Jane replied.

"And be ready for autocannon turrets," I warned. "Two of them popped up on us when we went up the last ramp." All other teams chimed in that they copied the last transmission.

I rocked us back and forth till our side plating broke free from the underside of the downed buffalo van and floored it, heading for the ramp we'd originally descended.

"You weren't lying about the turrets," Vincent said. "These things are brutal."

"Just keep pounding at them with your machine gun while you're nearby," Dave said, breaking into the conversation. "I've already put a bunch of rounds into them. They have to have some sort of a weak spot and we're bound to find it the more we hit them."

And sure enough, nearing the top of the ramp, another pair of turrets appeared from the arena floor and began to turn, aiming in our direction.

The comms chimed. "We're coming up the north ramp to the second level," Jane announced. "Which way should we go?"

"This guy turned east when he hit the top of the ramp," Ruth replied.

"The Booze Reapers copy, heading your way."

We had enough momentum at the top of the ramp that we caught air coming over the rise. The tires barked, reconnecting with the pavement on landing and I cut the wheel sharp left, skidding into the turn. The autocannon turrets boomed behind us. I weaved our way across the course toward the ramp leading up to the top tier, not giving them even a second to get a bead on us. Rounding the end of the ramp I turned, heading back toward the top level. Two new autocannons sprung up at the top of the ramp ahead of us on the north side of the course and began firing.

I was relieved that it wasn't more rounds in our direction. I'd slowed us just enough to make the turn to take the ramp to the third level, and in the arena, speed was king. Speed could mean the difference between life and death. The faster you went, the harder it was for a gunner, especially a bad one to score a hit on you.

The Booze Reapers launched from the north ramp onto the second tier, turning left to head East in the direction of the Buffalo van. Jane dodged and swerved to avoid both the autocannons and the flamethrower turret that swung about, turning in their direction.

We crested the ramp onto the third level and liquid Flames shot out ahead of us. Striking our nose it flowed across our hood. The report of our machine guns answered my order faster than Dave could shout over the din. I swerved right, triggering the next closest flame thrower that immediately spewed liquid flames over the pavement ahead of us.

Vincent came across the comms. "They shot past the first ramp to the upper level. Almost to the second ramp on the east end of the arena."

"Roger that," I chimed in. "We're on the third level heading east."

"Think we can corner this guy and pin him down?" Jane asked.

"Are you kidding?" Freya interrupted. "What are you going to do? Tell it to sit and that it's been a bad boy?"

Dave snorted a laugh at that.

"Yeah…" I said. "The other one plowed through Trip and Holeshot like they were nothing and we nearly destroyed our car taking it down. You aren't going to easily corner this one."

Dave patiently fired burst after burst into the next flamethrower turret on the north side of the field, counting how many rounds it took him to find the fuel tank. Squeezing off three round bursts, this one blew at fifteen, spraying burning liquid across a thirty-foot diameter area from the explosion's epicenter.

"I see it," Jane shouted. "If I slow them down do you think you can spin them?"

"Sorry to tell you this, doll," Vincent said, "but I am absolutely certain that you'll end up as a hood ornament if you do try it."

I angled us closer to the edge of the top level and saw the massive black buffalo van round the corner at the far end of the second level. It lurched forward with a sudden burst of speed, heading directly for Jane and Bullseye.

The pedal was floored, and the drive motors on our car were wound out to their maximum by this point.

"Jane, get clear," I shouted, but it was too late. I could feel the impact, even at this distance. Jane had cut right then sharply back to the left. It looked like she tried to spin them from the front like a reverse PIT maneuver. She did at least get her last buffalo gun shot off before being eaten alive by a roving wild beast of a vehicle.

The Booze Reapers came off the ground and rotated in mid-air, lumbering to the side from the buffalo van's strike that had plowed through them, swatting them to the side like they were nothing more than a pesky gnat.

There was no way that the Blackskulls or Queentastic would catch this thing with the speed boost they occasionally seemed capable of. They'd always be perpetually two steps behind and there weren't any other better options that I could think of.

"Dave, hold onto Buster!"

"What?"

"Grab the fracking dog!"

I cut the wheel hard to the left. Our wheels broke free from the Earthly confines of the pavement. We soared over the edge of the field and flew in the direction of our target.

Dave screamed unintelligible jumbles of curses in time to the barking yelps from Buster.

The deep black darkness of the buffalo van raced closer and closer. I caught a peek at the bewildered expression the driver wore on his face through the narrow window slit on the driver's door. It was almost comical. If his eyes could have easily popped out of his head like a cartoon character, I was sure that they would have.

I fired the remaining shots from our buffalo gun in rapid-fire succession, each round striking the side of the target.

Then, we hit.

The nose of our Johnson Special crumpled. Then the world slowed. I watched in horror as the front end of our car collapsed in on itself, progressively getting closer and closer to the front end of the cab. And then the world spun around us, twisting in a sickeningly myriad of colors and blurred shapes. We struck, bounced, and spun again. Over and over for what had felt like an eternity before the warm, familiar darkness enveloped me once again.

Chapter 26

"Have you ever seen such a move of self-sacrifice in your life, Chuck?"

"Never, in all my years as an Autoduel announcer have I seen anything like this, Alex. It's insane!"

"I don't think anyone has ever to my knowledge called 'Ricky the Ripper', sane. And after that move, I don't think that anyone ever will."

My head pounded to the point that it was almost buzzing, and it felt like I'd been chewing on cotton balls all night long.

"Well, his sacrifice was just what the Atlanta pack needed."

"Ada, shut off the vid screen."

"Ricky, baby," Johnny B. said happily and let out a nervous laugh.

My eyes immediately opened, flying in the direction of Johnny's voice. Sure enough, there he stood in all of his bright sun-kissed orange zoot-suited glory.

I pushed myself up and found the last thing I ever wanted to find. The room was small, barely big enough for the hospital bed I was sitting on. And it looked odd. The room wasn't made of normal walls. Everything seemed to be made of brushed stainless steel plate.

Johnny sat himself down slowly at the end of the bed and patted my shin. On the wall behind him was a large golden cross inside of a golden circle, and beneath it written in a bold but soothing font was the slogan,

Out of darkness, we bring light.
Thank you for trusting Gold Cross with all of your rebirth needs.
Don't forget to ask an associate about our monthly premium renewal specials.

I scrambled backward, pushing myself further up on the bed against the wall. "Johnny, what the hell happened? Why am I in a Gold Cross room?"

Johnny put up both of his hands defensively. "It isn't what it looks like, Ricky. You just need to calm down, okay? Slow, deep breaths mi amigo."

Pulling the pillow from behind me I hurled it as hard as I could toward Johnny, ripping out the several IV's and monitor wires in the process.

Then I heard an all too familiar grumple as the door to the room opened. "Look! It's your buddy, Ricky," Dave excitedly shouted as he entered the room and dropped Buster on the end of the bed next to Johnny. They were both covered in cuts and scrapes. Dave sported one hell of a bruise on the side of his head that reached down to the cheekbone on the right side of his face. Buster rushed across the distance and plopped his rear down in my lap, tongue lolled out to the side and his little nub wagging so hard I thought it was going to fall off. I gave him a scritch behind both ears and his leg immediately thumped out a beat.

"What's the last thing that you remember?" Johnny asked.

I smiled with the biggest and widest smile I could put on before looking up at Dave with the sappiest look that I could muster. And in the softest, caring voice I said, "The day that we brought this little guy home from the hospital, when he took over our lives and our hearts."

Dave and Johnny both stared at me like I'd completely lost my mind.

"Nurse?" Dave mumbled, taking a step back.

"Now, are one of you two going to explain to me why I'm in a Gold Cross room again?"

Johnny started to stutter but I cut him off before he could manage to form a solid word.

"Did you have me reboot me again, Johnny?"

"No, no, nothing like that," he said defensively. "You were just a little banged up after the crash and they wanted to keep you under observation."

"Then why am I in a Gold Cross room?"

"Because Gold Cross sponsored the arena side medical services," Dave interrupted.

"So, I didn't die?"

"Nope," both of them answered, shaking their heads in sync.

I pushed Buster off of my lap and tossed off the thin white sheet as I turned to slide out of the bed, finding myself stripped down to my boxers.

"Hold up there, Ricky," Johnny said, putting a hand on my shoulder. "The nurses haven't released you yet. And before you step foot out of this room I need you to answer something for me."

"How about you answer something for me instead?"

"Alright, shoot."

"What happened? How did I end up here?"

"Well," Johnny said hesitantly. "What is the last thing you actually remember?"

"We were in the arena," I said as I thought back. "Chasing down the second buffalo van."

Johnny nodded slowly. "Okay, that's good," he said, patting my shoulder. "Well…"

"You drove us off the edge of the cliff," Dave finished.

"I what?"

Dave chuckled. "Yeah… It was pretty badass, man. We were racing along the top level of the pyramid and you drove us off the edge into the side of the buffalo van. Death from fracking above!"

"And that move, while devastating to your car, carried enough momentum to shove the van over the edge of the second level where it landed face down, leaving its underside exposed."

"The queens and skulls pounded a mudhole in that van for us," Dave said. "They didn't stand a chance once we pushed them off the edge.

"Then who won the match?"

"Sam and Vinny scored the kill, but the judges are still in deliberation on the final points for the match."

"Now, my question," Johnny said. "Considering how this leg of the race went, do you want to keep going?"

Dave slapped him across the back. "Why the hell wouldn't he want to keep going?"

Johnny gave Dave one of those head nod side shrugs. "I don't know. Considering some of the sponsors have put out bounties on the teams, I wouldn't blame either of you for stopping now."

There was a slight chill to the air in the room, but the way Johnny said that sent goosebumps running up my arms. Something wasn't right. I narrowed my eyes at him and he nervously looked between Dave and myself.

"Why all of a sudden would you want me to quit what I'd guess is one of the more lucrative matches I've been in?"

"Maybe someone is scared that we'll actually win," Dave suggested.

"No, nothing like that at all," Johnny defended.

"Then what is it?"

"Just concerned for both your physical and mental well being is all."

Dave snorted a laugh. "I call bullshit. You can't trust anything an ambulance chaser ever says. I don't care what he says in his ads."

"And what about the rest of the sponsors?" I asked.

"They don't care," Johnny answered. "It's all about the ratings. You've seen it."

"And if we aren't giving them a good enough show, then they'll replace us," Dave added.

"Exactly," Johnny said. "So, is it worth it to you in the end?" He let out one of those defensive, nervous laughs. "Like I said, I'm just trying to look out for you. You're not just a client, Ricky. I consider you a friend as well."

Dave laughed out a "Bullshit" under his breath before I could say it. I could have easily said I quit and go back to driving taxis for Henry without a problem. But driving a taxi wasn't anywhere near the same as driving in the arena. And continuing on that path didn't pay off the contract debt that Johnny still held over me. He could milk that contract for the rest of my life if I let him, or I could wipe it out in one shot. I thought a moment more before looking back at him.

"I've got fifteen million reasons to keep going, Johnny. It's a fresh start at a new life without any debt."

"Alright, then." Johnny sighed. He tapped out a nervous beat on his legs then hesitantly left the room. I slid off the bed to my feet and looked at Dave.

"We've got work to do."

"Damn skippy we do."

"How much time do we have?"

Dave looked at his watch and thought for a moment. "If we don't worry about sleep, a solid fourteen hours before we're supposed to be at the rally line."

"Then let's go get Sally ready. We've got a race to win."

The End

We hope that you enjoyed this title and look forward to many more to come in the Car Warriors: Autoduel Chronicles. Please, leave us a review! Reviews matter to all of our authors.

And don't forget to check out the latest edition of ***Car Wars***

http://www.sjgames.com/car-wars/

Or the other amazing titles from
Steve Jackson Games

http://www.sjgames.com

Take a look at some of our other award-winning series at https://threeravenspublishing.com/series-universes/

Visit us at https://www.threeravenspublishing.com and sign up for our newsletter for the latest and greatest news on upcoming titles and events.

Other series and titles you might enjoy.

DECLAN FINN
DECLAN FINN
DECLAN FINN DECLAN FINN
Demons are Forever
LOVE AT FIRST BITE TWO
Honor at Stake
LOVE AT FIRST BITE ONE
Live & Let Bite
LOVE AT FIRST BITE THREE
Good to the Last Drop
LOVE AT FIRST BITE FOUR
The Dragon Award Nominated Series
FREE on Kindle Unlimited!

AVAILABLE ON
AMAZON
JOINT TASK FORCE 13
HOLDING THE LINE
BETWEEN HEAVEN AND HELL
13

MYSTERY,
MAGIC &
MAYHEM
WITH A TWIST
OF ROMANCE
J.F. POSTHUMUS
ON AMAZON
FIND ME

B.E.N.T.
BIOLOGIC   ENHANCED   NASCENT   TALENT

THE RAVEN
AND
THE CROW
MICHAEL K. FALCIANI
FIND ME
ON AMAZON

STARFLIGHT
IT CAME FROM THE
TRAILER PARK

3R
Three Ravens Publishing
Are you looking for fun, new fiction?
The FEATHER and the LAMP
LEGENDS
DARK STORM RISING
CROSSWAYS THE WAYMAN CHRONICLES
MICHAEL J ALLEN
STAFF OF CHAOS
The Written Word Will Never Be The Same…
https://www.threeravenspublishing.com
Veteran Owned and Operated

You can also keep up to date with our latest release announcements on <u>Scifi.radio</u> and get some of the best fandom programing on the planet.

Scifi for your Wifi

Spare Parts Emporium
and Towing
EST. Henry's Garage ™
For all of your Rare
& Spare Parts Needs

SILLY LADY
PEPPER
COMPANY

FELLHAVEN
Restaurant & Tavern